JOURNEY TOWARDS HIMSELF

Books by Roy Holland

Insights and Outsights: Poems by Roy Holland
Cape Town: David Philip. ISBN: 0864861214

Just A Bit Touched: Tales of Perspective
Writers Club Press.   ISBN: 0-595-15874-9

Flakes of Dark and Light: Tales from Southern Africa and Elsewhere
Writers Club Press.   ISBN: 0-595-17423-X

Pivot of Violence: Tales of the New South Africa
Writers Club Press.   ISBN: 0-595-15821-8

News From Parched Mountain: Tales from the Karoo in the new South Africa
Writers Club Press. ISBN: 0-595-14612-0

The Waking & Making of Paul Gauguin –
Conversations with Himself: A Play for Voices
Diadem Books, 2008   ISBN: 978-0-9559741-3-7

Alan Paton Speaking: The Lintrose Conversations
Edited by Charles Muller. Diadem Books, 2008.

The Jonathan Three (published by Diadem Books):

The Nowhere Man   978-0-9559741-0-6

Journey Towards Himself   ISBN: 978-0-9559741-1-3

Now Lead Me Home ISBN: 978-0-9559741-2-0

JOURNEY TOWARDS HIMSELF

THE JONATHAN THREE: VOLUME 2

Roy Holland

DB

DIADEM BOOKS

Published by Diadem Books

For information, please contact:

Diadem Books
Ocean Surf
CLASHNESSIE
IV27 4JF
Scotland UK

www.diadembooks.com

**This is a work of fiction. Characters and situations are
entirely a result of the author's imagination.**

ISBN: 978-0-9559741-1-3

1

Jonty, on his boneshaker, his gown flying out behind him, came round the corner of Mill Road into Dust Road like a circus acrobat.

By leaning acutely, so that the rims nearly scraped the tarmac, he had discovered he could get round without turning his handlebars. He didn't understand the mechanics or dynamics of it, and it had worried him at first. But soon after coming up to Cambridge, he had stopped thinking about all the why-ies of it and started wondering if he was getting better or worse at it.

On the whole, he considered he was improving.

Even so, it was a fairly hazardous operation between twelve and one. Dr Lovingood held his surgery at that time. Jonty had to watch out for expectant mothers, carpet-slippered old dears, chronic arthritics and, sometimes, the doctor himself leaving for lunch.

Of course, if there had been accidents, the surgery was handily placed for everybody but the doctor.

However, the single advantage of proximity was impaired by a group of disadvantages, the most serious of which were (a) the doctor didn't like students on principle, (b) he was a big man with a grandiose moustache, and (c) played second row forward for the local rugby club.

Another group of disadvantages was tied up with the fact that whenever he saw Jonty go into 1, Dust Road, the house next to his, he prescribed a scowl for himself that managed to bring his eyebrows into one solid band of hair across his medical forehead.

Jonty resolved never to consult him on even the most minor of complaints.

Furthermore, the scowl seemed to deepen and bring his moustache into line with his eyebrows whenever he saw Jonty stopping his bike by jamming a shoe between the rim of the wheel and the front fork.

Why the doctor reacted like that was a puzzle: surely he realized it was the only alternative to getting it fixed, and that fixing cost money?

But Jonty had come to understand, in time, that Dr Lovingood had four main reasons for reacting as he did. (1). Dust Road had funny people living in it. (2). They were funny in ways the doctor didn't find funny. (3). His surgery was on the corner of Dust Road. (4). Jonty lived at 1, Dust Road. *Ergo...*

Yes! They seemed to cover the situation all right.

At that point in his review, Jonty tripped on a loose black-and-white tile in the middle of the path that was composed entirely of loose black-and-white tiles.

Its uniquely dangerous position on the highest point of the camber had been carefully selected by Mrs Cough, the landlady, in one of her frequent inspections of her property.

He had kept intending to throw it away on a dark night, and now felt sorry he had not done so.

Perhaps a fifth reason should be added to Jonty's list? The appearance of 1, Dust Road was unendurably funny in itself!

"You do see what I mean, don't you?" he said to the tile.

Without waiting for an answer, he lifted his bicycle off the path and leaned it against the privet hedge, which, Mrs Cough had had planted right under the front windows of what was intended to be a lounge: THAT necessitated the hedge being kept short. It was currently made up of a set of thick robust stems with pruned tops that were entirely nude of leaves.

Between the hedge and the tiled path was a pyramid of twenty or so empty milk-bottles built round a detergent packet, which gave its heart a touch of welcome colour. Some broken grey bricks, the hue of the local clay, were piled in the corner nearest to Dr Lovingood's surgery.

Where, asked Jonty, could they be more appropriately placed?

He regarded the garden with satisfaction: it looked lived in, nobody could deny that!

Sofia kept asking him to remove the bricks, but he refused because they seemed to be fully emblematic of the way life happened.

"Another bit of your private arcana, that's all!" said Sofia, disparagingly.

"No, it isn't!"

"Because you don't want the trouble of doing it," she added.

"Less trouble to shift 'em than listen to your lament! It's based on experience. Don't you remember?"

"Could I forget?"

One day, Jonty and Twaggin, his friend from Jesus College, had been discussing strategies for avoiding the Proctors' bulldogs when Twaggin, after putting what Twaggin supposed was an unanswerable argument to some point Jonty made, had casually leaned on Mrs Cough's front garden wall.

Now, there was a pile of bricks in the garden.

What explanation could be simpler, more elegant, more emblematic, more historic than that?

One day Cromwell came, and now we've got all these ruins. One day Twaggin came, and now we've got all these bricks. Beautiful.

It somehow took the accidental out of life and made it sound inevitable; and, at the same time, took the inevitable out of life and made it sound accidental. The reciprocal ambiguity appealed to Jonty.

Apart from which, as long as the bricks were there, they provided a steady reproach to taunt Twaggin with, whose clumsiness was already legendary in Cambridge – besides serving as a fairly unobtrusive reminder to Sofia that she would never be successful in her quiet but unremitting efforts to dominate him.

"Stand still, Monster!" said Jonty, pulling and struggling to pick up his bicycle for the third time.

Mrs Cough's privet seemed to be related to those plants that wanted to eat things like flies and bees.

It had somehow induced Monster to turn his front wheel to dislocation point, had begun to ingest his handlebars into its thick tangle of stems, and rock Monster backwards and forwards until it settled the machine almost parallel with the ground.

Finally, it locked Monster's brake rods into sappy lengths of growth and gripped them like frenzied gorillas, ready for total absorption. But this time, Jonty managed to get a substantial, woody limb jammed under the saddle and the bicycle remained upright at last.

"Okay, Monster, don't move till I get back!"

As he straightened, he found himself once again looking directly into the notice that had been stuck to the inside of the lounge windows by a previous occupant of Mrs Cough's establishment. No-one had bothered to remove it. He knew exactly what it said.

It announced that a Brahms Concert by the University Players was to be given free for spinsters on Sunday 26 November. It was rumoured that many of them still turned up at the Hall, three years later, saying: "But this IS the twenty sixth, isn't it? The notice says..."

Sofia had wanted to pull that down, too, but Twaggin wouldn't let her.

Jonty had wondered vaguely how many of the town's spinsters were musical.

Twaggin maintained that, for those with eyes to see, it announced, albeit enigmatically, what 1 Dust Road stood for; namely, 'Relevance to life'.

"Relevance to Life is what Boynton Kingmaker has been, and will be, pointing out in his lectures, isn't it?" asked Twaggin.

"But this is a relevance Kingmaker wouldn't appreciate! NEVERTHELESS – "

As Jonty climbed the stairs to their first floor flat, he reminded himself that he must get a good squint at Dr Lovingood's pinna, sometime. Then, he'd really know what to think of him.

He swung deftly round the newel post at the top and onto the landing in one smooth movement, noticing, as he did so, that their sitting-room door today looked more than usually blistered and under the weather.

He opened it. Inside was worse.

"What in the name of Jesus College is going on?" asked Jonty.

"I lost the coal scuttle," said Sofia.

Sofia sat at an easel in the middle of the cleared floor, painting something which resembled one of the fifty-seven varieties that had just been shaken from its can.

She had her paint spaced out on a square of hardboard with two finger-holes in it and two fingers in them.

She was wearing long hair, a pair of mules and a skimpy T-shirt. Little else.

That wasn't unusual in itself, but the appearance of the rest of the room was.

Three prized items of Mrs Cough's inventory were piled up in a corner: the armchairs on top of the sofa. The carpet, which suffered from alopecia and dandruff, had been rolled back to reveal a patternless lino, the hue of burnt toast. Other odds and ends had been herded into pens elsewhere. The sideboard's legs were bowed under a large lopsided basket of washing, an enormous folder of Sofia's drawings and the kitchen chairs.

Jonty felt sorry that the sofa was being maltreated and said so.

"Don't make me laugh," said Sofia.

"Mrs Cough has lavished care and attention on that item."

Mrs Cough had covered up the sunken seats with some hugely floral material she called loose-covers.

Loose, they certainly were, even downright immoral; but they had enabled Sofia to stuff some dropsical cushions into the glades and hollows and now they were very comfortable.

Sofia laughed.

Jonty regarded her.

She was utterly at ease amid the chaos, wearing next to nothing, dabbing at her easel. The way her hair lay on her head and the way her neck came out of her shoulders and the way those sloped down to her loins and the way her doopers were marvellous (in the way they had of being marvellous) made him feel all watery round his genitals.

Oh, how he could, couldn't he? Right then!

Oh, how hopeless Sofia was with any piece of household equipment but a bed (and sometimes the sofa, and occasionally a chair). And, oh, how the rest of her was marvellous, too, right down to her mules!

But, all he said, was: "And did you find it?"

"What?"

"The bloody coal-scuttle!"

"Don't swear, then! Yes, I did. Suddenly remembered I'd seen it while I was dusting this morning— "

"—Dusting!"

"—next to the sideboard, and I found it was still there so I needn't have moved all this, anyway. That's the worst of having a system. You can forget how it works."

Jonty let his eyes float up to the topmost limit of their sockets, trying to look like a religious personage in a Renascent painting, and blasphemed mightily to himself for a moment or two.

Then, aloud, he said: "What did you want the coal-scuttle for? Want to paint it like that soup there? It could do with a coat of that!"

"What do you think? For a fire, silly!"

Jonty looked at the grate. It was empty, except for a lot of fine, beige coloured ash.

"Where's the fire, then?"

"Oh, yes! You see, we've got no coal. I thought it was full but it wasn't. I looked downstairs, but that sack is finished, too. So I thought I'd get on with my painting instead."

"I see! The Sofia-logic of that explanation is un-assailable."

Sofia took a breath, about to reply.

Jonty held up a hand.

"No, don't go over it again! I DO see the inescapable and necessary connection between your painting and the bare coalhole! Who wouldn't? Which, of course, entails the reasons why all this—"

He swung his arm around in a baroque gesture of despair.

"——-is in its place."

"Are you in a bad temper?" asked Sofia.

She stood up and put her brush and homemade palette on the stool she had been sitting on. Her T-shirt inched up over her nude glutinus maximus.

Oh dear, why does she have to do it like that?

Physically and mentally, she sent him mad, but managed to do it in quite opposite directions.

At the moment, the physical seemed to be on top and Jonty had difficulty in stopping himself from whirling her onto the overtoasted linoleum, moving the T-shirt up a fraction or two and Oh, Holy J. C.! why did life have to be so complicated when it could just as easily be so straight-bloody-forward?

"No, I'm not in a bad temper," he said. "I'm not in any sort of a temper. I'm just a complaining stomach, looking for a wad and a cup of steaming Nescaff. I've been listening to old Redshins going on and on about a series of what are supposed to be poems written by somebody who's supposed to have been a priest who is supposed to have called himself John Donne and who is supposed to have slept in his coffin with his mistress and I'm just about ready to go up to old Redshins and personally stuff one of the University Bulldogs up his nose and tell him he's supposed to enjoy it; and what do I find when I get back urgently in need of sustenance? You, sitting in the middle of an auction room, without your panties on, painting something you should have warmed up for lunch. It's too much. Of course, I'm not in a bad temper!"

"Don't be disgusting! You know I'm wearing some. Look!"

Jonty marvelled at how the physical and mental madness could change places so quickly and how Sofia's resistance to the points he had just so cogently made seemed to have been totally demolished by her little coquettish display.

"I'm not falling for that!" he said, trying hard not to.

"Anyway, I thought you wouldn't mind helping me to put all this stuff back," she said, letting the edge of her T-shirt descend its fraction again. "I didn't want to strain something, did I?"

"You don't mind straining something of mine, do you? And on an empty stomach, too. Why didn't you strain some soup, or something?"

Sofia opened her big brown eyes and put contrition on her face.

"Oooo-er! I forgot all about –. Sorry! Honest! Look, I'll just run down and get us some fish and chips from across the road."

"Not like that, you won't!"

"Of course not, silly! This is just for you," she said coyly.

Then her face fell.

"I've just remembered. It says no frying today in capital letters."

"That's all I was waiting to hear. Redshins on John Donne and now NO FRYING TODAY. And I'm bloody STARVING – in capital letters! Oh, well, I suppose it's Hall again for some more of that stuff they import from Viet Nam, or somewhere."

"What's that?"

"Oh, Christ, never mind! Anyway, the bit you'd have strained moving this little lot wouldn't have mattered much."

"What?"

"It's the other bits you'll have to watch. I suppose, now, I'll have to get out of these jeans and put a jacket on and go and eat cold sausage-and-buggering-mash in a freezing Hall full of reject army benches and the noble buggering faces of dead dons who were dead even when they were a-sodding-live."

"What a terrible man you are! Why do you have to swear all the time? And – you're getting worse."

"Why I swear is a BIG BUGGERING QUESTION! And no wonder I'm getting worse."

"Why?"

"Oh, save me! I need an unlimited supply of charity and patience. Or another wife!"

"Why?"

Jonty collapsed weakly onto the linoleum, curled himself up like a hedgehog and started moaning softly to himself.

"Oh, no! I spend the last ten minutes telling her why, and now she says, Why! She hasn't heard a buggering word."

"Don't lie down on the lino. You'll get your clothes dirty."

"Get my clothes dirty!" moaned Jonty. "Oh, sod me! Get my buggering clothes dirty."

Sofia stood near him, straddling slightly.

He opened an eye and saw the sweetest –

"Don't stand there like that! You'll harden the wax in my ears – and – . GO AWAY! Put some panties on. I've got work to do. I must get changed. You're eroding my will power. You're spoiling my timetable. She's a harpie, that's what she is!"

"Poor lamb! Shall I make us a nice hot cup of Nescaff, and then you can go and have your cold ess-and-em?"

"Well, if you put it like that, how can I resist? What's the time?"

"Half-past."

"All right! But no more than fifteen minutes, mind."

While Sofia went into the kitchen, Jonty, still acting it up, tottered through the blistered door, along the landing to the bedroom to change into respectable clothing for Hall.

He didn't want to be refused entrance; he was hungry.

On first inspecting the flat for rent, his impression had been that the paper-hanger, at the time he had stuck it on the walls, had been drunk. Not only had he left small gaps of wall on view, but he had also chosen a paper covered in cabbages, carrots, peppers, egg-beaters, milk jugs, and other examples of kitchen-ware and produce. These were scattered over the wall in big clear images in very bright and unignorable colours, with plenty of shiny white paper between each object so that you could see them better. Jonty surmised that the paperhanger had mistaken the bedroom for the kitchen in his stupor.

But, on closer acquaintance with Mrs Cough, and judging by the way her loose covers fitted very loosely, together with her general ideas, she clearly was the kind of woman who could INTEND such an effect. It was, therefore, a toss-up between the two of them.

However, there wasn't much doubt about the wall-to-wall carpet, which had a very widely-spaced warp and very little woof. Or vice versa. Either way, at night, on urgent jaunts to the lavatory, you never knew when it was going to jump up, grab you by the ankle, and execute a permanent crippling-job. The paper-hanger could scarcely have had a hand in the choice of that, could he?

Then, there was the monstrous mahogany wardrobe which reached from floor to ceiling for almost the entire width of the room. Clearly, a Mrs Cough item. It sometimes made a good extra bedroom for Twaggin, who could stretch out full length in it and still have space for pillows and clothes, although he claimed it needed more ventilation. His considered opinion was that it had been used as a bird aviary at one time and hadn't been cleaned out properly since. He thought Mrs Cough could be the culprit, as she owned a lustful little blue budgerigar that whistled at Twaggin every time he passed by; so he preferred to sleep in the bath when occasion demanded.

But the real *coup d'oeil* was the bed. It was a large tetrapod with a loud rusty spring mattress that muttered to itself even when you lay dead still.

Jonty sat down on it now to pull off his jeans.

He swore it had designs on its occupants: whichever spot you chose to fall asleep on, you woke up in the egg-shaped crater in its middle. He told Sofia that it reconnoitered in the night, waiting, between snores, for its chance to scoop you into its belly with a triumphal scream of its rusty springs, quick as a flash.

Jonty had perfected a method of sleeping whereby he lay on his left shoulder with his right arm bent under the mattress, where he could hook his pyjama sleeve onto a loose piece of spring underneath. He then pushed his right knee a good way over the bed. This seemed to defeat the predator for an hour or two.

Nevertheless, by the time he was ready for his first sojourn to the bathroom, he found Sofia and himself heaped compactly in the bottom of the egg-shaped crater, and another little tear in his right sleeve.

The bed's final stroke was the headboard. The headboard was a mirror, starred here and there in the inimitable Cough-manner, but, nonetheless, a mirror.

Jonty had never stopped wondering why his landlady hadn't censored that bit, but she hadn't. In fact, she had told them once in a moment of weakness, her eyes going slightly misty, that she and her husband had 'slept in that bed', with a slight rallentando on the word 'slept'.

Jonty had immediately visualized Mrs Cough and Mr Cough in a position or two of high camp, not only trying to stop themselves rolling into a tangled ball, but also beadily watching themselves trying to prevent it.

Furthermore, there was actually an anglepoise lamp screwed to the wall above the mirror.

Oh, the secret life of Mrs Cough!

Whether it was Mrs Cough or Mr Cough that had actually intended all that, Jonty couldn't be sure, but he ruled out the paper-hanger as having had any hand in it: even he found the implications bizarre.

Jonty stood up, fastening the belt of his respectable trousers.

And this was the bed that Sofia was marvellous in, and in which he could see how many ways she looked marvellous, while she was actually being marvellous! He had no doubt that it was really the bed they paid the rent for.

At that moment, Sofia came into the bedroom to don her white slacks and Jonty felt the familiar washing-machine motion in his stomach as he watched her. Apart from which, he'd have been damned glad of a cheese roll just then!

"When's the party at the Master's?" asked Sofia.

"What party?"

"You know, that one at the Master's!"

"Christ, you mean that one! Why didn't you say so first off and then I'd have known exactly what – "

"—You're just being horrible to me today."

"That's because you excited me on an empty stomach after a pornographic lecture on John Donne. I'm only human you know!"

"Sometimes, I wonder! You haven't forgotten, have you? You've got to hire a suit from—"

"—Oh, sod me! You mean, one of his Scrabble efforts?"

"Yes. We had the invitation a fortnight ago."

"Now, I remember. Wednesday! The viewing trough of the week!"

"You rarely watch television."

"And no wonder! I daresay, Sir Leslie'll be stepping-up his Scrabble Party Schedule from now on, until some *avant garde* producer puts on another of those serials with characters swilling beer out of chipped mugs and saying 'Laik I was tellin' thee, lad...' with all the panoramic views of wash-and-shithouses that he and Lady Owens are so fond of."

"You're so coarse! Come and have your coffee before it gets cold."

"Instant senna."

"No, it isn't."

"Airedale-coloured."

"I like it."

"Well, that's all right, then. 'You belongs to them as likes it, and I belongs to them as doesn't.' Two distinct kinds of people. A marriage based on the clear understanding of the merits of instant beverages is bound to last."

"Pig!"

He made a grab at her.

"I want to prove it!"

"Later."

She avoided him and went out. He picked up his jacket, put it on, glanced at himself in Mrs Cough's headboard, and followed her, as hungry as ever.

2

Sofia and Jonty sat in the kitchen drinking their coffee in silence. For the moment, both were absorbed in their own thoughts. They were sitting at a small plastic-covered table and on tubular-frame chairs, a group of items that Mrs Cough called "my dinette set". (This was a detestable phrase that combined Jonty's distrust of people who rhymed things, and who used copywriter's double-speak.) The table had thin tubular legs, like the William Blake expert from Newnham and the chairs had padded seats, like the Elizabethan Stage expert from Girton. They were the only objects in the flat that post-dated the abdication of Edward VIII.

Anyway, mused Jonty, no matter how strong the similarities between Mrs Cough's kitchen furniture and the two scholars were, nobody with any sensibility could describe the inmates of Girton and Newnham as "the dinette set", could they? "The Patience Strong set", yes! Perhaps at the full stretch of probability, "The John Betjeman set"? For the ladies in question, however, you could exclude descriptions like "the Jet set" at once – on all three counts: it misled; it rhymed; it was journalese. Exactly where to place them needed working on.

Jonty tasted with distaste his coffee: it had the authentic jackass flavour all right. Sofia was drinking her mixture with noisy satisfied gulps. He silently reviewed his stock response of sending the manufacturers a short snappy note — advising them to get the animal put down as soon as possible — and then glared malevolently at Mrs

Cough's spongy wooden draining board, next to the sink. He began wondering how long the unwiped cups, saucers, plates, knives, spoons, saucepans, jugs, tumblers, mugs and pans would remain there unwiped, and then gave it up as non-productive. Two years of living with Sofia had given him a very clear idea of how long the draining period would be likely to last, and he didn't feel like facing an image of such clarity and unambiguity at the moment, not after an hour of bloody Redshins, who revelled in shades of shadows of equivocality.

"An Owens's Scrabble Party is the last thing I want to go to," he said miserably. "I've got to write an essay on 'The Influence of The Gun Dog in English Poetry' for the Reverend F.E.Mewey."

"You're joking, of course!"

"Well, something like it! And before the week's out, too. He won't take Sir Leslie's unremitting passion for Scrabble as an excuse. Oh no, he'll insist on me helping him weed the Thomas Grey garden or, worse still, attending Chapel, again!"

"This party won't be as bad as the others, will it?"

"Why not? Third year parties are always worse than the others. You know how it'll go: *her* endless twittering about antiques; *his* orotund inanities about the influence of Sexton Blake on Californian junkies. Doesn't improve at the third hearing, you know! And all that 'when-it-comes-to-the- crunch' kind of lingo. God! It makes my feet ache!"

"Yes! But this time he's inviting girl-friends AND the wives of third-years, isn't he?"

"Oh, is he?" Jonty's face brightened.

"Well, that's what it says on the invitation."

"Don't tell me the Owenses have had a fresh idea! Unfortunately, bint will affect the standard of my Scrabble. Mmm! Never mind, you can come as my girl-friend, if you like!"

"Not that again! We're married."

"What's that got to do with it?" asked Jonty in surprise. "We've been all over that, before. You KNOW why."

"Yes, I know. But, you've only got until Easter! What difference would—"

"—NO! We couldn't suddenly announce it, now, could we?"

"Why not?"

"You're asking that question again! Think of Lady Owens's face when she finds out. No, on second thoughts, don't think of all of it. Think of a bit of it."

"I wouldn't mind!"

"Think of all those tiny lines round her mouth, then. She'd press them into service, fast. Disapproval, shock, even pain, at keeping such private business private and out of the way of her long nose. She'd talk the Senate into giving me a Third. Couldn't risk it!"

Jonty shook his head vigorously, and sucked in his breath through hollowed cheeks.

"That's ridiculous!"

"Anyway, you know what she's like, don't you? Last time, Twaggin said she ambushed him in the bathroom and asked him if he didn't think it better for his health to wear underpants as well as jeans in the winter!"

Sofia laughed.

"I don't believe that! That's Twaggin's line. She wouldn't. She daren't."

"Well, she should have! I know Twaggin wears only jeans and no underpants in the summer; it ought to be true! That's the way she is. I shudder to think what she might ask if she found out about US. My God!"

Jonty picked up his plastic mug and, in consternation at his own thoughts, swallowed the contents in one go. He instantly regretted it. He was even more regretful a moment later, when Mrs Cough chose to arrive, unannounced, unexpected, unwanted, overdressed, overblown and overloud. One moment there were two of them in the kitchen. Then there were six.

"Why is my sitting-room in such a mess?" she demanded. It was her way of wishing them good day.

Jonty stood up quickly: he was in three minds about what to do. Barge forcibly into her floral stomach on his way out; accuse her of trespassing in her own flat and disturbing the peace of the neighbourhood; or, like a composite brass monkey, hear all, see all, and say nowt? In the event, he did none of these things.

"Isn't it always?" he growled. "It's part of the decor."

Mrs Cough tightened her lips and glared at him, but before she could reply, Jonty said: "Anyway, Sweetie-Undercut, if I'm to get bangers-and-mash in Hall, I must be off."

"What about me?" asked Sofia, looking significantly in Mrs Cough's direction with her eyes while still facing Jonty.

"Perhaps Mrs Cough would like to organise lunch for you both, now that she's here?"

Sofia pouted at him, her deep brown eyes looking hurt.

"I don't mind a peck at something small," said Mrs Cough, seating herself, uninvited, in Jonty's chair.

"There!" said Jonty. "What about a Surprise Pea?"

He went down the stairs two at a time.

After delivering Monster from the possible predations of Mrs Cough's hedge, without even so much as the customary kick to his rear sprocket, he carefully negotiated the loose tile, mounted and rode off. The town was full of bikes and gowns on bikes and students in gowns pedalling furiously to find seats for lunch in pubs. As he cycled along the edge of Parker's Pieces, he watched the usual mothers pushing their prams back to their tinned lunches and the secretaries granny-booting across the greensward, eager to nibble a lettuce leaf and a Provita. He waited at the traffic lights while a group of beefboys — with a lot of curly hair, Adonis-like faces, and shoulders like villains in a James Bond movie — walked across the road. They shouted and laughed and showed an overplus of teeth. These were specimens of the *Hearty Cantabria,* who spent their afternoons being shouted at by little men in white caps from the end of long thin boats, and descended in a direct line, Jonty felt sure, from the group that had thrown Oscar Wilde downstairs in the eighteen nineties for wearing his hair too long.

As the traffic-lights changed, he headed fast for the College Hall, where, turning right into Trumpington Street, he encountered another species of Cambridge fauna. It had only two members in this instance, walking daintily along in Regency clothes, frilly-fronted shirts with frilly cuffs and inbred bleating accents. Their faces were pale, they used female deodorants and manicured their fingers. Jonty had never been close enough to overhear what they said, but he felt fairly sure he could tell by their lotus-shaped hand gestures and desiccated bleats that they spent a lot of time reciting Matthew Arnold's 'Dover Beach' at each other, or specially modified versions of Longfellow's 'Hiawatha', and occupied *their* afternoons in compiling an anthology of 'Fag and Drag Cooking Rhymes for Jaded Flat-Mates.' He had named them 'The English Poodle Verse-Speaking Group' and one day, when he had the time, he intended to write their Constitution for them.

He felt decidedly glad to reach the rear gates of the College without having to think about any more specimens of Cambridge Groups before he had had his lunch. He propped Monster against the outside wall and walked quickly through the portal of the gardens.

As he went towards Hall, Jonty caught a glimpse of a head almost submerged among rockery and succulents. The Dean was at it again! Early today! Must be careful! Jonty skipped neatly off the path and into a bed of rhododendrons, where the cover was good, and reached the path furthest from the gardening Dean that led into the courtyard through a small arched gate. That's much better! He didn't feel like being handed a trowel on an empty stomach, or discussing the day's odds on the Dean becoming the next Bishop of Ely, or even getting the latest league positions of the Charity Teams fighting Deathwatch Beetle in the Cathedral roof. The Reverend F.E. Mewey was all right; but sometimes Jonty wished, in his most desperate moments, that the Dean had also got Deathwatch Beetle, and then wished he hadn't wished it, because, in his second year, the Dean had rescued him from his former landlady, Mrs Leatherem-and-hubby-Ted. No, fair was fair! The Dean was, on the whole, okay.

In the Screens, Jonty registered that no new notices had been pinned up, and read once more his favourite to date, which reminded Gentlemen that jackets and polo-necked sweaters were considered improper dress to dine in Hall in. Jonty made sure he was alone in the Screens before adding a new notice of his own. This one was directed at the Manager of the Refectory and purported –– Jonty had grown fond of the word ever since Jarrold had threatened him with it nearly three years earlier –– to be a plea from the heart of Lady Owens on a point of etiquette. It was going to be interesting to see how many answers it provoked before he felt moved to add his own to the public response.

Jonty turned away from the Screens and entered Hall for his bangers-and-mash.

When he came out, full but unsatisfied, he walked down the steps from the Screens into Old Court, which had buildings in it that dated from thirteen-hundred-and-something. They were certainly very mature-looking: judging by the amount of darkness they enclosed in their thick walls, they could have come from a less enlightened period. He passed a group of undergraduates wearing open-necked shirts, soft hats, deerstalkers, wellingtons and thighboots. They clutched fishing-rods and crowed and guffawed about what they had just read in the Screens. A very tall thin gormless-looking youth, with an array of flies stuck in the red band of his green trilby, asked, in a high voice: "I say, what are they, anyway?"

"What?"

"Aubergines!"

"They're egg-plants."

"You're having me on, aren't you? Eggs come out of hens, you fool!"

"I know that. But aubergines don't."

"Here – !"

Jonty passed through Maingate, out of earshot, into Trunipington Street before he remembered that he had left Monster at the rear. He decided to walk round by way of Fitzwilliam Street, in case he met the Dean, still gardening in New Court, and got himself shanghaied in the rockery for the afternoon. He collected Monster without mishap and mounted and rode to the University Press in Trumpington Street where he bought a copy of the *University Reporter*. He glanced at the first page and decided that a pint of beer would improve its contents no end. So he crossed Trumpington Street, rode into Mill Lane, and went to The Mill for one of the clear-glass large-handled tankards he preferred.

"The usual, Harry."

Harry drew the bitter.

"Sorry, for the froth. We've just cleaned the pipes. It's the gas, you know."

"Don't worry! It's only poison."

"There's some fresh cheese rolls, there."

"Not today, thanks. Just come from a Vietnamese lunch in Hall."

Jonty carried his beer outside and sat on the little stone bridge over the Cam. He looked around to see if Twaggin had had the same idea as himself, but he wasn't in the vicinity, so he settled the Reporter on the parapet to see what the University lecture timetable had in store for him during the coming academic year. He placed his tankard on its open pages to prevent the breeze flipping it into the river and began reading. Drinking the bitter made the lectures appear, if not actually nicer, a little less awful, and, under its influence, he was even able to look with tolerable tolerance on the hairy heavy-thewed group that was throwing one of its members into the refrigerated waters of the Cam.

Jonty turned in time to see the victim disappearing with a splashless plop into the deepest part below the lock-gates, and took another pull from his tankard, noting with pleasure the unruffled smoothness of the water where the Hearty had gone in. He turned back to his reading, hoping fervently that he'd just witnessed a case of manslaughter. The yoicks and bloodsport-type laughter continued for some time before a slight note of alarm crept into their vociferations; then, from the changed character of the disturbance along the bank, Jonty concluded that they had dragged something out of the water that was no longer interested in the game.

Jonty groaned aloud as he read the long list of lectures to be given by Redshins on the poems of John Donne. If it had been programmed as a long list by Donne on Theodore Redshins, it would have been a bit more than all right — noteworthy. As it was, when Redshins had finished his expositions, explications, analyses, commentaries and interpretations of the text in question, which he never finished soon enough, Jonty felt that reading the poems themselves was a bloody sight funnier than listening to Redshins making them more opaque, more unfunny, and more quirky than the originals already were.

'I s'pose that's what he means by saying he's driving us back to the text!' thought Jonty. 'God, I wish I was taking something called "An Introduction to the Aramaic of the Targums"; maybe I could change to the Oriental Languages Tripos? Or the Mathematical Tripos? What's this, for instance? "The Logical Design of Clitoral Computers." Now, that could work you into a lather all right! What? No, can't be! Oh!' Jonty laughed.

'No, sorry! It's 'digital', Digital Computers.'

Jonty had now had enough of the *University Reporter* and talking to himself. He closed it and found himself staring glumly at its cover page with the four nose-thumbing lions, in four little boxes on three legs with their four virile-looking tails rampant, steadily marching towards Trumpington. They were *passant gardant* and hurling silent insults as they went. Jonty thumbed back at them.

'How to Design Your Own Escutcheon,' he murmured.

He rose from the wall, rolled the *Reporter* into a tube, with the lions inside, and returned his tankard to Harry.

"Hey up!" said Harry.

"See you!" said Jonty.

He realized that the pint of bitter had not dispelled his feelings of peevishness and slight depression. He put it down to the last vestiges of his tiff with Sofia and her refusal to let him go to bed with her. He resolved to keep his eyes open and miss fewer opportunities in future.

...Yes; it seemed to be time for another therapeutic walk round one of the Fellows' Private Gardens along the Backs, didn't it? Which College should he choose this time? The one with the pisspot on the Chapel spire? No, that was too far, for now. What about that one with the stone carving over the gate that seemed to celebrate Peter Abelard mourning the loss of his balls? No, that was also a way off, near Market Square somewhere? Oh, God, what did it matter? All this history lying about could be oppressive at times. But, of course, he should have been thankful: it wasn't nearly as oppressive as Burke's, Charles & Long's had been, was it, which had had no history at all, only a past, and possibly no future?

Jonty was in a querulous mood and found it difficult to stop the argument going on in his head.

'So, what're you griping about?'

'Who's griping?'

'You are! You wanted to come, didn't you? You wanted the Bursary, didn't you? You got it, didn't you? And you got Sofia, didn't you?'

'Yes, I got it—them.'

'Well, then!'

'Yes, well, all right! Don't keep going on about it.

'Oh, God, I don't think I like finding out what I like and what I don't like. Why do I keep asking questions about things? I suppose I like finding out more than I like not finding out. Why doesn't somebody answer me? Why doesn't a Public Address System boom out the explanations from the tower on the University Library? Why don't these dreaming spires and warehouses of ancient wisdom tell us all about things? Why doesn't the Government, in the clotted tones of Edward Heath, tell us what the score is? Are we being controlled from outer space by beings with fluorescent green souls? Am I really me? Have I been taken over? Have I come off the hinge? Am I getting hysterical?… Oh, to hell with it!'

He stopped in his tracks. He looked at the college buildings, a little way off through the gardens; he looked at the stone, the colour of one of Jarrold's arrowroot biscuits, damp with spilled tea. He looked at the bare branches of the poplars and the places along the river where the banks of Spring windflowers changed the Backs to a dream of saffron teased by the premonitions of Finals and Summer, and he laughed aloud.

'You know what's wrong with you, my boy? No? I'll tell you. You're not drinking enough. Give up driving and drink more beer! Q.E.D.'

And with that satisfying thought he continued his stroll, in a far less agitated mood, along the Backs.

3

The remaining short walk to the iron-barred gate of the nearest Fellows' Garden ('Fellows! That was a laugh! You should see some of them tottering about!) almost dispelled Jonty's fear that he was an impostor trying to be Arnold Jonathan Godley. He could not ignore the recurring image of himself as a third-rate quick-change artist on a never-ending tour of the Northern industrial towns of the United Kingdom, scrambling out of one costume after another. The short walk almost dispelled both fears, but not quite.

Now, here he was in another role in Cambridge, scrambling over (from motives that were not entirely clear to him) a tall iron gate into a garden he wasn't allowed into. Well, except for one clear motive, which was to sit in a quiet place in the October sunlight and muse.

Yes, but why did he want to do it here? And what did he want to do it about?

He could have more easily climbed into the garden of the Owenses, couldn't he?

Yes, he could have.

Well, then! Why didn't he just go back to the flat and curl up in bed with Sofia for the afternoon?

What if he got caught by some fellow in the Fellows' Garden? Did he want to get sent down, or what?

'Oh, Christ, shut up, can't you?

'Just watch all the trees and shrubs and grass being themselves, can't you?'

Jonty made a strong effort to leave his introspection behind him. He looked around and got comfort from the sheer tangibility of the garden. It was certainly full of things that seemed to know a lot about growing up and growing down and growing in and out, and generally daffing and clotting about with twigs and branches, berried and unberried, leaved and unleaved, while making a lot of play with droves of varied colours.

To Jonty, things that grew were either *berberis* or they weren't. Plants which weren't *berberis* he had decided to call *snarfia*. It was as good a classification as any. If plants had berries, or looked as if they might have them – which seemed to be mostly reddish or purplish – then you could be pretty sure they were *berberis*. Otherwise, they were *snarfia*. The plainness of the taxonomy appealed to Jonty a great deal.

It appealed to him even more when he recollected that the Dean made his life a misery in the rockery trying to sort out in a dead language all the names of the things living there. His grasp of religious Latin didn't seem to help him at all, even though he probably was nearer God in a garden than he was in his study.

But, Jonty had come to realize that it probably showed the Dean's lack of interest in the problems of "the Thomas Grey garden" at any level. The Dean's abiding interest seemed to lie in *not* going on being Dean, in *not* finding suitable digs for the lodgement of undergraduates, and in *not* spending his afternoons in the rockery, but certainly in getting to *be* Bishop of Ely at the earliest possible date and in *going on being that* as long as he could make people believe he WAS the Bishop of Ely.

His apparent obsession with rock-gardening was maybe the Dean's way of NOT thinking too much about what he most wanted to think about. Wasn't it generally accepted that thinking about things too much was simply not all right? Look what happened to Hamlet!

Jonty had been so still during his meditations that a bird had perched itself on the back of the bench he was sitting on.

"Hello, Twerple!" said Jonty.

The bird put its head on one side and looked at him out of one luminous dark eye. It didn't seem afraid. Jonty addressed it:

"Twerple, how would YOU feel if your father was being forcibly dried-out, if you were intimidated by your wife painting soups all day half-nude, and if you didn't know who you were? Would you care?... So I should care? Human, Shmooman, what's it matter as long as it keeps rolling on? Okay. You listen to me, those jokes out of the Talmud just don't—"

But the bird flew off.

"'Christ! You call that funny? said the Twerple,'" said Jonty.

He'd been sure when he'd got the letter, telling him to present himself for interview in Cambridge, that the Bursary was what he wanted, hadn't he?

Of course, he had!

He'd felt like a stud bull with four pizzles and eight testicles; he had savoured his powers, as if they had stretched before him like a meadow full of heifers waiting to be served. He remembered the excitement and joy with which he had anticipated reading his letter aloud at Crehan's party, and, with luck, hoping to use it as an open sesame for a bit of serving of his own.

He had, he recalled, patted the letter into the hip-pocket of his jeans and arrived to find the small gravelled courtyard full of cars, the smell of petrol, and light splashing onto the short flight of wooden steps and forming its pool in front of the white door of Crehan's Pad.

Above the little platform at the top of the steps, a thick cloud of cigarette smoke had formed and loitered; it grew fluffy lustrous tails whenever anyone went in and out of it. As Jonty was going in, a big blonde girl, who had managed to get quite a lot of herself, but not all, into a woolly gaucho suit, came out onto the platform, stopped, looked at him with a little thrust of her large bottom that was supposed to be provocative, and said: "Well, he-ll-o, you, you lovely man!"

She seemed to be wearing a lot of liquorice allsorts on a string round her neck. She may not have been really high, but she was rising.

'And will your woollies stay woolly for long?' thought Jonty.

"Lovely man, my arse!" he said. "I'm a Liberal."

She giggled.

"If you say so, darling."

"I do," said Jonty, and went in.

All Crehan's expensive photographic stuff had been hidden away somewhere. The room was bursting with people, standing in groups, posing with and without drinks, laughing, talking, shouting, and conscientiously doing what people at parties are expected to do. "Suede and leather and Regge," Crehan had said. Jonty was sure he could pick out hessian, canvas, cotton, dimity, tulle, corduroy, feather, fur, and anonymous sacking – as well as acres of human skin, all of which seemed to be fashionable this year. Jonty was standing just inside the door, surveying the big room, listening, but Regge hadn't arrived yet.

He spotted Crehan on the far side, talking to – not – Oh, my sweet Jesus! —- yes, Dummock! And somebody – who? – Isabel – Alexis's friend, was with him! He waved, trying to catch Crehan's eye.

"Did you want me, ducky?" said a man in a Norfolk jacket, who had immediately sidled right up close to Jonty and whispered in his ear. Jonty stood back a pace and regarded him. He was wearing a polo-necked sweater under the jacket and a dusty, creased face above it that looked as if it had just been used in the latest scrimmage match for the league points. Jonty whispered back to him:

"Yes! Get me a drink, first, will you?"

"Certainly, ducky," said the man, and wove his way eagerly to a table laden with bottles.

Jonty went over to Crehan. Scrimmage-face could drink it himself. 'Who did he think he was? More accurately, what did he think I was?'

"So there you are, Arnold, old hen!" said Crehan, who smiled and jiggled his Adam's apple.

He was half-cut already. Jonty thought: 'It's not everybody who can do that when he's on the way to paralysis.'

"I'm looking for a girl named Sofia."

"I know you are, lovey."

Dummock just stood there, like a streak of wind waiting for a loophole. Isabel was also silent, and regarded Jonty serenely, waiting. Crehan's nostrils looked bigger and hairier than ever and he breathed heavily through them.

'Maybe he's doing a course?' thought Jonty. "I increased my bust from thirty four and a half to a full thirty eight in just nine weeks." He must be halfway through by now!'

"I wondered if you'd give yourself time off from – er – ," said Crehan, unclearly; then, clearly: "Have a drink!"

"Thanks! I'll get there!" said Jonty.

He turned to Isabel, and smiled as he thought of the letter in his jeans pocket.

"What's that dazzling wet thing you're wearing, Issy?"

"It isn't wet!" she retorted, pouting. "It's made of silk. A kaftan."

Its silver-grey colouring had rinsed the rustiness out of her hair and made it glow bronzely. He recalled how she had leaned her softness against him at a previous party and, unexpectedly, he felt a sharp pang of desire, like hunger.

"I bet you've got nothing on under that," he said, to cover his slight discomposure.

Isabel let go of her serenity and became interested.

"Lay your odds, sweetie!" she said.

"What about half an hour each way?" said Jonty.

Isabel made a laugh like a deep gurgle in her throat.

During this interchange, Jonty had been aware of Dummock stiffening gradually beside him. (Issy must have made the mistake of sitting up and taking notice of someone else during one of Dummock's tours of inspection.)

When Dummock was around and about he expected all females in the near vicinity to take up horizontal postures and await his inspection. That was one of the reasons Jonty hated his suits; it had been the main impulse behind his sudden compliment to Issy. Jonty turned to look at Dummock who stared back levelly. Dummock had the cast of a man who'd just become aware of a bad smell and found it came from someone he had been trying to get close to.

"He does it all the time," said Dummock, seemingly irrelevant.

But his Wellesian voice, wearing a conceit that had shrunk, was a little strangled.

Crehan turning in surprise to stare at him and, waving slightly from his feet like a stick-insect, inadvertently placed a foot with over-deliberateness on one of Isabel's, while he directed his nostrils at Dummock as if they were radar dishes. Isabel looked anxiously at Crehan's elastic-sided boot. Jonty pushed his glasses to the end of his nose, leaned slightly towards Dummock, composed a Mr Chips expression on his face, as if talking to a favourite pupil, and said: "What's that, my boy?"

"Whasswhat, old dear?" asked Crehan, blearily.

"You're standing on my foot," said Isabel, suddenly, and gave Crehan a slight push. Crehan staggered, recovered himself, and looked at her in hurt surprise.

"My foot!" she said, and pointed vigorously at it.

"Oh!" said Crehan blankly.

The distraction had given Dummock time to collect himself.

"Writing!" he said. "He's always doing it. Letters, obscene and threatening letters, mostly. Eh, laddie? Like the one you sent to Jarrold."

His arrogance had returned. With his weight balanced on one leg, he had thrust forward his pelvis, as if modelling a new line in jockey shorts.

'Who's been reading *Vanity*, then?' thought Jonty, and wondered whether he shouldn't risk leaping straight up in the air, both knees pushed as far under his chin as he could lift them, while letting out a lung-splitting Maori war yell, and come down with both feet on one of Dummock's hand-made shoes. But he decided to save that until, one day, he happened to be wearing running spikes.

"How d'you mean?" asked Jonty, "The one I sent to Jarrold?"

Isabel looked curiously at Jonty. He looked back at her with an expression that said: 'How did the bastard know about Jarrold?' Crehan was still struggling with his nostrils, trying to get the fuel-intake-mixture right before putting his brain into gear.

"Oh, come bloody off it, Jonty!" said Dummock, nastily.

"I'm not on it."

Dummock made a movement forward, changed his mind, and stopped. Despite the smoke-laden air, Jonty was dispensed a hefty draught of the after-shave that Dummock regularly used to annul the smell of stud-goat he generically carried about with him. Should he advise him to change to a more effective brand?

"It was all round Burke's, Charles & Long's," retorted Dummock.

'I bet it was,' thought Jonty. 'It's bloody strong enough.'

Dummock turned to Isabel to explain to her.

"I was at home and I had a call from Treblitt, see, who'd had a call from this Herbert at the Education Office, who said that friend Jonty had sent Jarrold an obscene and insulting letter, which he thought was actionable, and where was Jonty?"

"Jarrold would use a word like that – actionable!"

Dummock swung his cleaver-like face savagely towards him.

"Oh, so you admit it, do you?"

Dommock's after-shave hit him again, and Jonty wondered if Isabel liked it better than his pre-shave and whether she'd had a chance of finding out yet.

"I don't admit a thing, Dummock!"

"That's nothing!" said, Crehan, unexpectedly, who now appeared to have got his brain back into gear. "Arnold's good at writing things. You should see the recipe he wrote for—"

"—What did Treblitt tell him?" asked Jonty.

"How should I know?" replied Dummock, nastily.

"Now that you've got a little office with your name on the door, I just thought he might have told you, that's all."

Dummock seemed mollified by this reference to his new status, and replied lamely: "No, he didn't."

"Look, you lot!" said Crehan, all his jets and filters working beautifully now, "just forget all this in-fighting and get yourself some more drinks. Arnold, where's yours? Come on, old hen!"

Crehan took Jonty by an arm and started to elbow his way across, not at all gently, to the drinks table. Jonty noted with some disgust that, as soon as they left, Dummock began turning his attention on Isabel with all the subtlety of a searchlight. But then, it was surprising how many women liked searchlights. Maybe Isabel was one of them? His thoughts involuntarily switched to a picture of Jarrold phoning up about him.

'I bet his stomach was mewing like a litter of Siamese kittens when he did it! And old Styles would have left a warm depression on the velvet seat of his chair and a strong smell of bedrooms, after spontaneously combusting! I can just see it! But how did bloody Jarrold get on to Burke's, Charles & Long's, I wonder?'

He reminded himself to look into that one, sometime.

"You should watch Dummock, Barry. Him and Alexis are old – er – you-know-whats. By the way, where is Alex?"

"What?"

Crehan half-apologetically glanced over his shoulder at a dolly-bird. "Oops! Sorry, darling. Plenty more where that came from. Your dress all right? That's good!"

Crehan had entered the world again, and now seemed fully in charge of himself.

'Must have bin all that deep breathing.'

When he had finished flicking at the invisible drops of spilled drink on the girl's bosom, Crehan put his mouth to Jonty's ear and whispered: "Headlamps should be dipped in a built-up area! Grrrr! What were you saying, old duck?"

"Haven't seen Alex tonight."

"Oh, she's upstairs, still dolling herself up. She was late arriving."

They had finally reached the drinks. The long whitewood table was full of bottles. If they had been people, someone would have informed the Municipality on Crehan for overcrowding his tenants. Crehan's liberalism was not merely theoretical, one good thing about him.

"What'll you have? In descending order of potency, whisky, gin, beer, fruit juice, coke, water, nesscaff? We've got the lot, here. A pint of Vermouth, maybe?"

"Gin and orange. I'll get it."

"That's the spirit! Hee-hee! Sorry about the pun. No! Allow me."

Jonty watched Crehan sloshing too much gin into a too large tumbler without a murmur of protest. While Crehan searched for the orange, he listened to the chatter around him.

"—and he was dragged in by his sponsors."

"Sounds painful! Was he all right?"

"Look out for your underwiring, that's all."

"Are you Aries or Pisces, darling?"

"Neither! I'm a Bhuddist, you see."

"They tell me egg-production's down again. It's these blasted Concords, you know. Sonic bangs do something to their ovipositors. In some parts of the country, they lay fresh coddled eggs, I'm told."

Jonty turned to see from whence the last speech had issued.

A jumbo-stomached young man dressed like a company director (who seemed to have moved his eyebrows down to a more exclusive site on his top lip) was looking happily out of his bald eyes, with a very eager expression, at a short blonde girl, all curves, dressed in a white T-shirt that had ALL SYSTEMS GO printed on the back. No wonder he looked eager. She must have sensed Jonty looking at her, the way that type of female can, and turned round to smile at him. SNOOPY was printed on her bosom and a tiny but big-headed green Martian lounged in the region of her navel. Jonty was feeling irresistibly impelled towards lounging in the same region himself, when he sensed a touch on his shoulder. He turned to find Crehan offering him a full glass of G & O, and grinning widely at him.

"Now, now, lovey! Hands off! Her father's a parson."

"It's not her father I'm interested in."

"Mebbe not, old lad, but he'd be very interested in YOU if you did what you looked as if you were going to do."

"Did it show that much? I must be slipping."

He paused.

"Here! Did you say 'upstairs'? I didn't know you had one. Where are the stairs?" asked Jonty, peering about him.

"Sh-sh! Not so loud. It's just for the inner sanctum. I'm still converting it. It's full of whatnots – tools and paint and shavings. Wouldn't do to bruit it around, old duck."

"How'd you get there?"

"Outside, at the back. Set of steps to the hayloft. Satisfied? Maybe I could show you around?"

"Sorry!" laughed Jonty. "Didn't mean to quizz you. That reminds me."

4

Jonty put his glass down. He took the letter from his back pocket.

"Look at this!"

After a slight pause getting the letter in focus, Crehan read it quickly.

"Why, Arnold, old hen, that's marvellous! They liked it! Interview. Great! End of January. After all you said about it being crap!"

"Just luck! It was the way he died. Eighteen double whiskies in a row. So he claimed! New York. Lecture tour. You know the hoo-haa! Otherwise those of the dreaming spires had never have heard of him. Just think! Me carried into Cambridge on the coffin of a Welsh poet! I must be growing a new set of ears."

"What? Ears? What have ears got to—?"

"—Forget it, Barry. It's a theory I'm working on. Earomancy! Oh, Jesus H.C!"

"Whassamarrer?"

"See that stumpy little man with a face like a beanbag? He's trying to seduce me."

Crehan looked around at the man in the Norfolk jacket. "Oh, you mean Ambrose! Don't worry! I'll head him off for you."

Ambrose suddenly spotted Jonty and started to wiggle his away across to them, balancing two full glasses of liquid in front of him like a juggler.

"It's too late! He's nearly on us," replied Jonty.

"Where've you been, darling?" asked Ambrose. "Looking for you for ages. I've brought you a drink."

Ambrose sounded husky with anxiety. Or something.

"Thanks, but I've got one."

All the beans fell into one corner of his face and it sagged, dolefully.

"Oh!"

"Never you mind, Ambrose!" said Crehan. "Put it down there. Thassright. Arnold'll drink it later, won't you, duckie? I've got somebody who wants to meet you, Ambrose."

Ambrose cheered up. "You have? Where?"

"This way!"

Crehan winked at Jonty and went off with Ambrose wiggling behind him. Jonty blasphemed thankfully and swallowed his drink in one go.

He made his way again to the little porch outside. The girl in the gaucho suit had gone. People were still arriving. But, now, there was hardly room to walk between the cars to Crehan's Pad.

Jonty walked round the building to the back. You never knew when you might need a flight of stairs, did you? Oooer! He stood still for a moment. He didn't oughter 'ave drunk it in one go, oughter he? The night air had made it worse.

'I'm not under the affluence of incohol,' thought Jonty, putting out a hand to steady himself on the wall for a moment, 'as some thinkle peep I am.'

Suddenly, he found himself sitting at the bottom of a flight of wooden steps. What in the name of the Plymouth Brethren had Crehan put in that drink? Jonty wondered hazily if it had felt drunker in the bottle than it did in him?

'I should have stopped him, the sly sod!'

He heard a door opening, followed by scraping and shuffling sounds, and then someone started to come down the wooden steps behind him. A woman! He ought to get up, but he felt better with his elbows on his knees and his face in his hands, watching the world through the cracks in his fingers. A pair of boots with a lot of buttons on them stepped into the oval of light he was gazing in at the stair-foot, then Alexis's voice said: "Oh, it's you! What are you doing here? Why aren't you inside at the party?"

Jonty managed to lift his face from his hands and look up at her. She looked beautiful.

"You look beautiful," he said.

"Why, Arnold Jonathan Godley, I believe you're drunk! You've never said that before. Anyway, it's sweet of you. Thanks!"

He reached out and touched her skirt. "All that expensive leather. My! Yes. That sod, Crehan, slipped me a Mickey."

"What?"

"Finn. After I told him about the interview."

"What interview?"

"I got an interview for Cambridge. The essay!"

"You mean the—? Oh, Arnold, that's wonderful."

She sat herself beside him on the steps.

"I'm so glad! Here, let me—"

She leaned over and kissed him on the mouth: "Congratulations!"

"Mmmm! Thanks! You taste like one of them cigarettes they smoke by mountain streams."

"Why you—!"

"—No, I didn't mean it the way it sounds. Honest! You've put all my gonads in a tissy, doing that. You taste as no self-respecting female has a right to taste. That's what I meant."

She laughed.

"Who's self-respecting? When're you going? For the interview, I mean?"

He told her and added: "You shouldn't have your hair tied back like that."

"Why not?" she asked, with a hint of irritation.

"Because it suits you. Worse than that. It suits me."

"My, you are a changed man, aren't you?"

"I know! It's the Mickey. I'm not myself. I'm lonely! I need a shoulder to cry on. Why don't you and me just slip upstairs and—"

"—Ah, no, not me, sweetie! I've just spent ages getting the effects right and I'm not going to spoil them, now. Your timing's wrong. Thanks all the same!"

"That's what happens when you get mistaken for a pouf! Your timing goes. It's humiliating!" he said, miserably.

"What ARE you talking about?"

"Never mind! Give us another kiss, then."

"That small thing, I can do... Is that better?"

"Much."

They found themselves sitting close in silence, just listening to all the party noises that were beginning to grow in volume. After a while, Jonty said:

"Do you know a girl called Sofia, that Barry—?"

He stopped. Alexis had begun to laugh.

"What's funny?"

"You are! Is that what's making you so nice and complimentary? Frustration! Humility! Defeat! And I thought it was me!"

"Don't be silly! It WAS you." He paused "Well, it's you as well. As well as me, that is. And do you?"

"Yes! I know her. She should be somewhere about. Here, I mean."

At that moment, Isabel came hurrying around the corner of the building. She was breathless. She stopped in surprise when she saw them sitting in the half-light.

"Well, well! What a funny place to – to – ." She looked with apprehension over her shoulder.

"Oh, dear!" And bending over Alexis, she added in a fierce whisper: "Alex, you've GOT to rescue me from your friend, Dummock! He keeps wanting to. And in public. He's explored the inside of my kaftan, twice! And he absolutely reeks of—"

"—The Age of Capricorn?" suggested Jonty.

Isabel laughed.

"That as well. Oh, Cripes, here he is!"

The appearance of Dummock striding resolutely round the building sobered Jonty instantly. He stood up firmly.

"I can kick his face in, if you like?"

Isabel put out her hand to restrain Jonty, but before she touched him, Alexis had taken over. She got up and walked towards Dummock, saying: "Hullo, Smedley! I've been wondering what had happened to you."

She took his arm and began to lead him away, but he was anxious about something, and kept glancing over his shoulder. Jonty knew who he was anxious about. So did Isabel.

When Alexis and Dummock had gone, Isabel and Jonty looked at each other and laughed.

"What shall we do now?" asked Jonty.

A voice that was hurrying round the corner towards them said: "Drink these! Alex said you were here. I've brought you one each."

It was Crehan. He held out two cornet-shaped glasses as long as umbrellas.

"You must come back to the party, old dears. We need you."

Jonty groaned.

"Is it some more of that lense cleaner you're so fond of?"

"No, duckie! Pure Daquiri, with a smidgeon of lemon juice. Try it."

"Will it make me drunk?" asked Isabel.

"Of course!"

"Then I'll take it. I feel like getting drunk."

"That's the way, lovey. Give in to it. Parties are for giving-in at, aren't they, Arnold?"

36

'It's funny, the way Crehan has given up litotes, these days. Perhaps the price has gone up?' thought Jonty.

"Well, some parties are," he said.

"This one is," said Crehan, emphatically. "Come on, lovers!"

And he led the way back.

5

As they strolled towards the little wooden platform, Jonty was tipsy enough to feel some disappointment that he had not gone for Dummock at once. However, he consoled himself with the expectation that, during the course of the evening, he would come across an ashtray full of soggy butts which he could empty at a suitable moment into Dummock's glass. Failing that, he would take up the lotus position in a corner of Crehan's Pad and *will* Dummock's bow-tie to burst into flame, singe off his eyebrows and turn his nose black. Jonty smiled at his fancies. But, Dummock was worth better.

'I'll try being nice to Isabel, instead,' thought Jonty. 'That'll fix him!'

Inside, it was as hot as a baker's oven.

"Ugh-ugh! Come over here! There's that Ambrose man again," said Jonty. "Quick! He's looking for a camping site."

They sat down on a chest with a leather top, near some windows with slatted blinds, and hid behind a group of people with very long hair. Isabel's colouring was really rather grand, wasn't it?

"You know, I used to think you looked like a cigar-store Indian! I don't know why."

"Don't you mean a squaw?"

"No! An Indian: that's how you seemed. You know, a little bit unfeminine. But, of course, you're not in the least."

Jonty reviewed all the reasons Isabel had for not being that, and she watched him reviewing them.

"I'm glad you've noticed! Took you long enough, though."

She gave another giggle.

"You want to watch that stuff! It's got alcohol in it," said Jonty.

"I know. It's the best way to take firewater. Me heap big thirsty! I don't believe you've ever seen an Indian."

"Of course I have!"

"Where?"

"At the flicks."

They both laughed. Jonty wondered if she was heap big hungry, too. He leaned towards her and took an opportunity to peer into her cleavage, which was nicely made for peering into. She didn't mind at all.

"I'm glad I found you, just now," said Isabel. "Our Smedley IS rather a handful, even at the best of times."

"And this wasn't one of the best, eh?"

Jonty was hoping that she would begin to elaborate on exactly what he was a handful OF, and, in the absence of such information, was considering offering his own carefully considered views on the subject, when she added: "I wish Alex would drop him."

Jonty was both surprised and disappointed by this remark. He felt the need acutely for her to be more specific about where and into precisely what Dummock should be dropped; but he let his surprise prevail.

"What don't you like? Her playing about with him, or him playing about with her?"

"Neither! I don't like HIM. He's a hard pushy man who wants to take all and give nothing. As long as HE gets on, everybody else can—"

"—Sod themselves, eh? With a bit of assistance from Dummock to complete the operation. I know. He's always on the prove. You know what he does—"

He told Isabel about Dunmmock's passion for a good game with his homemade chessmen.

"I'm not surprised," she said, and added irrelevantly, "He's awfully conceited."

Jonty wondered what the association was between his chess and his conceit. Of course, it was probably the feminine mind, which, at certain times of the month, could quite easily connect two or more things that not only seemed disparate but actually were. However, in this case, Jonty felt that Isabel must be right and the limitation had been his, for there clearly was a connexion between conceit and Dummock-dress, Dummock-humour, Dummock-nastiness, and so on. Why hadn't he been fully aware of it before?

"You know, you're right, Issy! I've always thought of it as lust, or sadism, or cruelty, but I think you've hit the target there. It's part and parcel of his ego. Clever girl!"

"I worry about Alex. He's the wrong kind of man for her."

"I wonder! Is there a wrong kind for Alex?"

"Don't be bitchy!"

"Of course, I know she finds some men more all right than others, but—"

"—Alex is a very nice person. She can't help being a bit, you know, turned-on sexwise," said Isabel.

It was true. Alexis had been very nice about his interview, and even nicer in not asking him for the money he owed her.

"Anyway, her father's a bit funny. If you had a father who – or, rather a lot funny."

She giggled. "Why can't you say 'a lot funny'?"

"I can! A lot funny!" answered Jonty.

"No! I mean—"

"—I know what you mean! Him, funny? Besides having an income of several million a year from selling second-hand oilcloth and old clothes from his stall in the Rag-market – which is one of the least funny things I've heard in a long time – he's got a beautiful unfunny grogblossom pitted like an over-ripe strawberry and nearly the same colour. And it's starting to get runny."

"You ARE revolting! I don't mean that kind of funny, funny-runny," she said, and giggled, "I mean funny-queer."

"What? Like Ambrose?"

"No! Worse!"

"Yes. He's got a thing," she giggled nervously, "about his own daughters!"

"What? I don't believe it! You mean he tried to—?"

"He didn't just try! He did! AND her sister!"

"Oh, God! When? How often? Where? Why?"

"They hush it all up, of course! And I'm only telling you now because I'm a wee bit tiddly and – well, you're you. Don't you, for God's sake, say anything to Alex, will you?"

"Not a soul! But are you sure you're not me and we're both sober and you haven't imagined everything?"

"Are you doubting me?"

"Of course not!"

"I knew you were nice underneath it all. There!" she said, and kissed him.

He kissed her back. Afterwards, she giggled again. She was doing a lot of that, wasn't she?

"Lovely! Drink up! Who knows what you might not do later?" he said. Then, he added abruptly, her meaning only just having penetrated: "Hey! What do you mean – underneath it all? Underneath what?"

"Don't be sordid, dear! I was telling you about Alex. When she was twelve. And her sister was fourteen. When it all came out, there was a frightful row. But it was hushed up! Ever since, he's been on the bottle."

"And you think that explains her…? It's Freudian, hey?"

"Maybe it's not! What if she just likes doing it, not only a lot, but too much? With anybody?"

"Well, she does, of course! But there's more to it than just sex."

"Just sex! Hers is just-sex-plus."

"Don't you think a thing like that would make YOU a teeny-weeny bit queer?"

"MAKE me queer? I AM queer, so I'm told!"

They both laughed.

"But funny-queer, not sexy-queer!

"Who knows?"

"I know!"

"Well, that's that then! How is your booze? Just tilt it up a bit more. That's it. Thanks."

Jonty took her glass and retrieved his half-full glass from the floor beside the kist. He could mend it with soda. He didn't want to be blotto for what he had in mind. If Isabel turned out to be Geronimo in disguise after all, he might have to start fighting for his scalp, which wouldn't rule out the possibility of her collecting prepuces as well. He stood up.

"I'd better be off – like a Jewish foreskin! Shan't be a tick."

But he knew he'd never become kosher, because unlike some, he felt that, if he'd got one, he must need it; so, whatever else he was willing to give away, he had resolved to keep that... No; it wasn't fair! It must be the drink talking... Isabel was much gentler, and much much nicer than he'd ever thought.

Somebody had switched on Crehan's hi-fi and people were making themselves inconspicuous by joining those who were jerking, twitching, bending, shaking and generally proving that something had gone wrong with the evolutionary process in the middle of the floor. A form of muscular dystrophy, Jonty had decided, but the pop-world called it go-go. Jonty, with his arms held wide, balancing the glasses, attempted to reach the drinks table. A girl backed into his arms.

"How'd you do?" said Jonty.

But she was clearly gone-gone and didn't hear or notice him, and jiggled out again. Then, he was given a hefty bump from behind. He turned to see a fat middle-aged teenager in cavalry twill trousers and a scarlet shirt, who was trying to start-start and never would-would.

"Don't worry!" shouted Jonty, "You're better off as a has-been-been!"

The man stood stockstill and stared at Jonty. Suddenly, there was a sputter on the tape, followed by a silence, in which everybody stopped and then Jonty managed to reach the drinks table. Just as suddenly the music started up again, this time on the regge tape.

When Jonty got back with Isabel's glass (full of a very potent liquid), she was half-sprawling on the leather top and had sprayed her long burnished hair out on each side of the kist in two glittering shields. Men standing by and going past the spot were regarding her with knowing looks. One little man, with a small worried brown face, had seated himself on the floor at one end of the trunk, and was trying to make it appear that he was interested in reading a booklet called 'How to Get Rid of Tense Nervous Headaches'. But Jonty wasn't fooled. Jonty knew about disguises. Another man, with very muscular instincts, eyes like two bruises and a cigarette drooping from a corner of his mouth, stood gazing at her speculatively.

'Oh, no, you don't, mate!'

Jonty pushed obtrusively in front of him. Without even a hint that he had noticed Jonty, the man eased his way through the crush of partygoers to seek fairer prospects. Isabel wasn't yet aware that Jonty had returned, so he took a moment to look at her, really look at her. How on earth had he once found her unattractive? A line from a poem he admired came into his head: 'Thetis of the shining breasts.' God! Under that wet-look garment of hers, they were shining all right. But he hoped *she* wouldn't cry out in dismay, when he—

"—Oh, there you are!"

She sat up, and the two burnished shields of her hair fused into one; her shining breasts separated dutifully.

"You looked as if you'd passed out," said Jonty.

"No! I just feel – Oh, I don't know! – relaxed and free and happy and—"

"—I hope you're free."

"Is that mine?"

He nodded. She took it from him.

"Oooh! What's in it?"

"Gin, mostly."

"That all? I suppose I can drink it, then!"

"You know," said Jonty, "what surprises me is that I like you and I like being with you."

"Arnold," Isabel simpered, "you do give me the most charming compliments!"

"Do I? I mean— Well, you scared me."

He saw her surprise and added, as he sat down beside her: "Well, be reasonable! You're bigger than me."

At this, the little man on the floor at the end of the kist, came out of his camouflage. He peered over his treatise on headaches, stared at Jonty for a moment, and then went back to his booklet, muttering to himself.

"I'm not! Let's see! Come on, stand up," said Isabel.

"See!" said Jonty, to the little man. "She agrees with you."

She put down her drink, shook off her shoes and pulled Jonty to his feet.

"Now, back to back!... See!"

Jonty took his hand from the top of his head. "Yes, you are. About a finger."

"Well, that's nothing!"

"It's better with your shoes off."

"Well, I'll leave them off."

"No, I don't mind. Not now. Anyway, I've got something to show you. Put them on again."

"What?"

"Come and see."

6

While Jonty and Isabel had been fooling about measuring their heights, he had spotted Dummock going full-steam out to the little porch, towing behind him the girl with the Martian on her navel. Jonty had a clear notion of where Dummock might be towing her for blast-off, and what kind of cargo he intended to put on board. Jonty's ashtray and bow-tie ideas and being nice to Isabel were not now, he felt, adequate to the occasion. Even if administered simultaneously. What, then? He didn't know, yet. But he knew the thing to do was to get away from all these people, somewhere he could think – which prompted him to propel Isabel in Dummock's wake.

As they made their way across the crowded floor to the porch, the little man watched them enviously over his booklet. Jonty said, "Excuse me!" to Isabel and nipped back smartly, to whisper in his ear: "Special offer! I know where you can get a set of six flame-proof casseroles – cheap!" The little man blenched and his lips began to move soundlessly. Jonty returned to Isabel, took her elbow and manoeuvred her through the doorway, onto the porch, and into the yard.

"What was that in aid of?" asked Isabel.

"I was just telling him something his best friends wouldn't," he said.

"Oh! Did he niff a bit strong?"

"I thought he seemed pretty grateful for the tip!"

"Oh!" she said, again. "Fancy being grateful!"

Jonty glimpsed Dummock edging and shuffling through the parked cars, pulling the girl by the hand as he went. Was he trying to leave, by any chance? No – that was going to be difficult, unless his car was parked at the end of the yard with a clear run out. Ah, got it! Much more likely that he was looking for a suitable station waggon to stretch out in, or something better. Jonty now felt very glad that he'd discovered Crehan's flight of steps, earlier. He had thought then that they might come in handy, and they had, hadn't they? He steered Isabel towards them.

"Shhh! Don't clop, lovey! Go up on your toes."

"I can't. My feet won't work properly. What're you hushing me for? Oops! My drink keeps spilling itself."

"Shush! There they are. Over in the corner."

"Who? Where are we going?"

"Don't shout! Dummock and his floozy. Look! They're getting in that car, right in the corner. See?"

Jonty and Isabel now stood on the wooden landing at the top of the flight of steps. They were in deep shadow and could scarcely see each other's outlines.

"So?" When Jonty didn't reply, Isabel asked again: "What do you want me to do about it? Shall I just stand here and sympathise with her? Will that do?"

"Come on!"

Jonty took her hand, opened the door with his free one, and drew her inside. He felt for the light switch, but his fingers met only the smooth pine of the wooden walls. He took another step forward, but she resisted behind him.

"Arnold Jonty! I won't move another step. I can't see a thing! If you're trying to seduce me, I refuse to go any higher. My head isn't fit to climb on roofs with, and, in my case, we'll slide off."

Jonty grinned to himself in the darkness. He turned and put his arms around her, firmly, and kissed her, gently, thoroughly and sexily. He could feel that she was still holding her drink.

"That's better," she said. "Now, I know where you are!"

"It'll be better still in a little while, and you'll know exactly where I am, then. Don't go away! I'm going to look for a light. Drink your drink."

"I am drinking it."

"That's a good girl!"

Jonty took a step forward in the darkness, using his arms and fingers gingerly, as antennae; and another step, and another. His fingers touched a wooden wall, directly ahead of him. Odd! He waved his hands about; his right hand encountered air and space. As his eyes grew accustomed to the dark, he discerned a diffusion of dim light to his dexter side. There seemed to be lightish oblongs or squares along the length of the building. Then, the picture put itself together in his brain.

On his right was a short corridor, with windows looking into the courtyard. That accounted for the shimmer of light. On his left, along the length of the corridor, he found a number of half-finished rooms, separated by wooden partitions from floor to ceiling, with window-frames overlooking the other side of the courtyard. The first two rooms were littered with tools of one kind or another – planes, chisels, hammers, pots of paint and small buckets of putty. The third room was partly furnished with a bed, dressing table, and two chairs. The window-frames had been glazed; a platoon of photographic floodlights stood to attention near the window. Lights must mean electricity – somewhere, surely? He tried switching on the lamp nearest the dressing table, but nothing happened. Then, his eyes fell on the shape of a torch. Just the thing! He tried the switch. It worked.

As he made his way back to Isabel, he wondered why coming up here had seemed to be a good way of getting back at Dummock. It was certainly a good way of reaching his objective in the Isabel-project, and perhaps that was reason enough in itself. But Jonty felt vaguely that it wasn't. He ought to be able to employ the circumstances and situation more conspicuously to the detriment of Dummock. But he couldn't see how and it nagged at him.

Could the Dummock-intention be a cover for the Isabel-intention, and not the other way round? He supposed it could; especially as he had recently discovered, through his reactions to first Alexis and now Sofia, that he was like other people in being different from what they imagined themselves to be, and like them in being different from what they wanted to be. To further complicate matters, he wasn't yet sure how or in exactly what ways he was different from what he thought he was. But it would just have to wait and make the best of waiting.

And as he reached Isabel waiting for him at the end of the corridor, he realized just how vibrant and welcoming that best could be.

After some time, he peeled himself away from Isabel and led her back to the room with the bed in it. He switched off the torch. Light drifted across the courtyard from the party and filtered through the window, together with shreds of regge music, laughter and voices. She sat down on the bed and sanguinely finished her drink. He could see her shape and movements but not her expression.

"Oooh! It makes things go up and down and wave about. It's lovely! Give us another kiss."

Jonty was happy to oblige. She began to relax, letting her weight fall backward onto his arms, and then onto the bed, pulling his weight upon her. It was a signal he shouldn't ignore, and yet he withheld himself. But he continued to kiss and caress her until her geography became familiar under him.

'Oh God, why was it all so bloody predictable? Why did girls ALWAYS have to have an effect on you? Even more to the point, why did they always have to have THIS effect?'

Why was his libido getting up and strutting about and waving its fists at his clear resolve to do something spectacular about Dummock? And he hadn't been careful, had he? No, he hadn't.

Dear Mother,

This is the first news you've had from me for some time. Help me! I'm almost in bed with a tiddly-eyed girl who knows what she wants and seems dreadfully intent on getting it. My problem is: Should I help her to get it now, or later? She would prefer it now; me later. The sequence I would prefer is, first, offer to get a new battery for the torch; second, do something to Dummock; third, do something to her. She would reverse the order and forget Dummock and the torch altogether. Should I go along with this and do something to her right now regardless? Is life always full of problems of this sort, or do they change substantially as you get older? Wish you were here, but glad you aren't. The weather's lovely except for the smoke and the regge music.

Your loving son, Arnold.

"Isabel! Adorable and irresistible dolly that you are, I must get up for a minute. Sorry!"

"NOT NOW!"

"I must! Bad time, I know. Nibble, nibble! Mmmmm! Delicious!"

"What for?"

"Guess!"

"Dearest Arnold, what an inconsiderate man you are, to want to do that at this very minute."

"Be much worse if I stayed, I assure you! Shan't be long. Don't go away!"

He disentangled himself, got up and took the torch from the dressing table. He had remembered seeing what he wanted on a worktable in one of the unfinished rooms.

'Ah, there it is, you little beauty.'

The idea had come to him as soon as he had finished the letter. Good old Mum to the rescue again!

He went to the end of the little corridor, opened the door on to the wooden landing, stepped out, looked about him and, seeing that the coast was clear, closed the door quietly to tiptoe down the wooden steps.

He rounded the corner and surveyed the car-packed courtyard. There was no-one about. They were all in the party. A noise like an excited football crowd came out of the open doorway of Crehan's Pad and the smoke eddied and swirled even more thickly over the little platform outside. Squeezing between the sardined cars, Jonty pussyfooted across the courtyard to the corner where he had seen Dummock and the girl.

There wasn't much light, but that was all to the good. After a brief search, he located the old-fashioned Aston Martin they had locked themselves into. It was a black, two-door model. Good: that would help matters a lot.

He peered carefully through a side window: there was a flash of white skin as they moved. They were in the luggage space behind the two seats. The chalky blur of the girl's T-shirt hung over the padded leather back of the passenger seat. Judging by the slight rocking of the bodywork, they wouldn't be interested in what was going outside for a long time yet.

He ran his fingers around the reel of packer's tape he had brought from among Crehan's tools. It was wide and strong and sticky, a favourite of furniture removers for sealing their cardboard cartons of crockery, strong enough to bind an elephant!

First, he went from the front to the back of the car on the passenger's side – bonnet, doors, body – rearward; then round, behind and across the boot; then from back to front – body, doors, bonnet – on the driver's side; then round and across the radiator grill, until he arrived where he had started. Excellent!

The car now had a wide stripe of buff-coloured adhesive along its length on both sides, and on front and back. It looked quite decorative! He did it all again, lower down. Now, there were two broad stripes binding the vehicle. Even more decorative! He then went over the doors and roof, sealing all the cracks vertically, horizontally, diagonally and at random. It was one of the most thorough jobs he had ever done. He grinned and chuckled in the darkness.

Once, he heard a startled whispering inside the car when, as he was doing his Toulouse-Lautrec walk along the bodywork, he had lost his balance and banged his hand lightly on a wing. But, after a moment, the slight rocking of the car began again. When he had finished, the Aston Martin looked like a circus property. He hooked the empty cardboard core over the front bumper and left, feeling well-pleased with himself.

He went back into Crehan's Pad, avoided Ambrose, gave the girl in the gaucho suit a quick peck under her ear, waved to Alexis and Crehan across the room, got two more drinks (a very strong concoction for Isabel) and returned to climb the wooden steps again. He made his way to the room with Isabel in it, put down the drinks and switched on the torch. Isabel was still there, but she was fast asleep. Not even the torchlight on her face disturbed her seraphic expression.

"Shit and derision! What does she always have to go to sleep after a few drinks for?"

He did various things that, under normal conditions, would have provoked immediate, unambiguous responses; but she made little ambiguous noises, and went on sleeping. He stopped doing them.

He considered doing other things, but some uneasiness of mind prevented him. It would be better if she were conscious, wouldn't it? That first time with Alexis, for instance, wouldn't have been the way it was if he had gone on being drunk: it might not have happened at all. A man HAD to want it and want it quite a lot before he could do it, AND you could tell when he wanted it, which was more than you could say for a woman. A woman often looked as if she didn't want it, when she did; and looked as if she did want it, when she didn't. Moreover, even if she did, she often did not want to show that she wanted it.

At least, that's how it looked to Jonty from his vantage point of inexperience and inebriation, at the moment.

'You simply can't tell, one way or the bloody other!' So what about Isabel?

Jonty was decidedly in favour of women you could tell with, and he had a shrewd idea that Isabel was a woman you would categorically be able to do that with.

'Well, that seems to be that, then, don't it?'

His quandary at an end, Jonty wondered what to do next. While he was wondering, he discovered one of Crehan's fancy dressing gowns hanging on the back of the door and covered Isabel with it. Then, he sat on the foot of the bed and drank his drink.

This fogged up the wondering process a bit, but somehow clarified the notion that he hadn't finished doing to Dumnmock all that could be done. Somewhere near the centre of the idea was Crehan's little platoon of lamps. Why? As he drank, his logical faculties, over-deliberate, tiddly as himself, asserted themselves:

'Lampsh are for giving light. Light is for seeing with. Therefore, these lampsh are for seeing with. That seems pretty unashay – unassailable so far, and jusht as good as this "therefore-all-men-are-mortal crap". Yes, but to see what with?... With?... Was that 'with' functional, or was it hanging around for undeshira – undesirable purposhesh? To see what? Answer: whatever there was to see. And what was there to see? Answer: treesh, buildingsh, people, carsh—

Carsh! That was it! Bugger me, yesh! Ash clear ash daylight; or it very shoon would be.'

He got up unsteadily, and went to the lamps near the window. Yes, the car WAS visible in that far corner from this side of the building after all. Good! Three floodlamps would be enough, surely. He directed them at their target. Okay, what's the next step? Plug in, and whoosh! He stopped dead in the middle of the floor and struck himself on his forehead with his open palm.

"Fool! Sho much for your logic!"

Ripe as he was, he had clean forgotten the lack of power. But he was convinced, nevertheless, that Crehan, being the kind of man he was, wouldn't have had a set of floodlamps and a bed set up if he hadn't been able to make use of them. Would he? No, he wouldn't!

He scrambled uncertainly about the room with the torch. He would not! Eventually, at head-height, behind the dressing table mirror, he found a panel set into the wall, with several sizes and shapes of holes in it. Just like Crehan! Wouldn't bend more than he had to.

Hazily, he sorted out the cables in the lamps and got ready to push the plugs home, but the holes kept getting bigger and smaller and moving to different sites in the panel. Then, he found that by holding them still with one hand he could push in the plugs with the other. After a short bout of feinting and clever footwork, he managed to get them all into place.

"Nine... three... two... zero... blast off!"

Three brilliant swathes of light cut out their paths to the old-fashioned newly-striped Aston Martin. Jonty picked up Isabel's untouched drink, gulped half of it and took it to the window with him. Woozy as a moth, he peered out.

The car was as brightly lit as if on a film set. Was it still rocking rhythmically? Had it stopped now? He couldn't quite make it all out. Was Dummock reaching frantically for his hand-made shoes, or had he kept them on?

Jonty made an enormous effort to control the pupils of his eyes and, between the heads of the bystanders, he managed to focus for a second or two on Dummock's startled face and the girl's, both trying to peer into the light, and their unclothed shoulders. The girl wore an expression that suggested she was making kitten-like mews, but it was all in dumb-show. Was that vague figure Dunmmock, struggling at a door handle?

Jonty tilted back Isabel's long glass, finishing the drink in one go. It did funny things to his eyes and thought-processes. He began to chuckle to himself and found he couldn't stop.

Down below, a group of people came on to the little platform for air, saw the spectacle, and began to talk quickly and loudly, until they were all gabbling like turkeys. One by one they began to laugh. Jonty began to laugh also; softly at first, then more and more loudly. People were now pointing and waving their arms in the air. A group of partygoers came out to see what the fuss was about. The turkey clamour increased. Soon, they were all laughing. It seemed to Jonty that everybody at the party was laughing, and he found himself rolling hysterically about on the floor. He couldn't stop. His throat ached. His head ached. He was dying with laughter.

'They can't get out! They can't get out! They...'

The liquor had reached his vital centres.

A moment or two later, Crehan came half-running, half-stumbling up the wooden stairs to find out what was happening to his precious silver elements, and discovered Jonty, luminous with drink, snoring softly, curled up at the foot of the lamps, smiling like a priest in a brothel, who, after twenty years in his Order, had turned his coat, achieved his first orgasm and fallen out of bed in surprise; Isabel, seemingly his trifle, was sleeping seraphically on top of it.

"Damn and blast his eyes!" said Crehan urgently, and turned off the lamps.

Without wasting another moment, he went down again to save what was left of his party, and to quieten the noise that had now risen to rowdy proportions. He didn't want his neighbours complaining to the police; that would seriously change the altitude of his profile. Oh dear, no, laddie!

By now, a small crowd had gathered round the car to twit and impede and delay the couple, while ostensibly peeling off the strips.

Dummock wasn't at all grateful for finding himself a prisoner in the car with the parson's daughter and a green Martian. Every so often, his efforts won applause, and a great roar would go up from the watchers, as if he was about to kick a try from fifty yards out, minus his boots and jock-strap.

Then, the owner of the car arrived: it turned out to be the character with two bruises in place of eyes, who had been calculatedly weighing up Isabel's wares in front of the kist. He was not only large, but hairy and obscene and threatening; and he made it clear that, if Dummock didn't hurry up and get bloody dressed and get out of his buggering car, he was willing to do things to Dummock that would seriously alter his future prospects in several directions at once.

He didn't seem to understand, even when it was pointed out to him, that Dummock was trying to get out of his car; and he had to be held back when both lovers finally emerged from the protective ring of their well-wishers.

Moreover, he hairily observed, that Dummock, unless he desired to go away stoneless, could get all that bleeding sticky paper off his sodding new cellulose finish, faster than immediately!

Dummock promised to do so with alacrity.

There was a lot more shoving and backslapping and laughing and swearing and shouting; but, in the end, people were persuaded quietly to depart. After all, it was late. Dummock and partner faded away with the others. Cars revved, gears crashed, horns hooted, wheels shunted, and people goodbyed each other, again and again. Finally, only those who would stay the night, Crehan's closest friends, were left.

That had been nearly three years ago.

Although Dummock-baiting was perfectly all right – and would always be so – Jonty felt sorry about the car. Would he think twice about doing something like that now, wiser, older,and married, as he was? He hoped so. He hoped that he'd improved since then. For Sofia's sake, he hoped so!...

Jonty looked around him.

Here he was, musing like an old pensioner in the Fellows' Gardens of Corpus Christi! He could see the spires of King's College Chapel. There were certainly music-makers there and dreamers of dreams.

They were certainly a long way from the sea and you could hardly call the Cam a desolate stream! And they'd lost a few worlds in their time, but had they forsaken them? Judging by the Association of the Commonwealth it didn't look like it. Here I am moveless and shakeless among the movers and shakers! Ah, well, it was therapeutic, wasn't it, sitting among the twerples and the snarfia, and it had given him a chance to digest a jug of Harry's best bitter and a Vietnamese lunch – no mean feat for any set of digestive organs. But, for the nonce, there was work to be done; hey-ho and jug-jug, back to the Bard!

Jonty left his bench in the winter sun, regretfully.

As he went homewards, he smiled wryly at the recollection of the way Crehan's party had ended for him. It must have been some time after things had all quietened down that he awoke to find himself still on the floor near Crehan's lamps. He wanted to go to the lavatory and he had felt cold. A full moon had arisen. He had stumbled down the silvered steps half comatose, darkened the glistening patina of the earth as he relieved himself and, preparing to stumble up again, his eyes already closing in sleep, he had felt his biceps gripped tightly. He had opened his eyes sufficiently to see Crehan holding him upright.

"Now, now, old hen! Careful does it!"

He had felt himself being guided up the wooden staircase, and along the corridor.

"Here you are!" whispered Crehan. "You'll be all right, in here... No! This one. That's it! She's waiting!"

He had swayed his way back to the bed by feel, undressed, and climbed in beside the sleeping girl. As he dizzily put his arms around her, she had moaned and grumbled slightly, but did not awake. Booze really put her out; a few mouthfuls and she was away. He remembered Dummock and smiled shapelessly. As he turned her gently over, he wondered why, earlier, he had thought it so important for a woman to be conscious while it was going on... and why it didn't seem nearly so important now... and... and...

7

He had been the first to wake. It had been light, too light. Even now, this morning, nearly three years later, he remembered exactly how his mouth had tasted and his stomach had felt on his awakening – as if he had just eaten a hearty breakfast of steaming owl-pellets and followed it up with a gallon or two of hot effluent, and where were Crehan's lamps and why was there no dressing table, and why did the room look strange? How did he get there?

A terrible apprehension had surged upon him as he realized that he did not know who he was waking up with. Who was lying beside him? He turned his head slowly. Dare he look? He would have to find out, sometime, he knew. But – the humiliation! The embarrassment of it!

Oh, Mother!

His stomach lurched, juddered, stopped, shook, until the washing-machine motion got properly under way, and he felt sick. It was the first time he had seen her at a party and only the second time in his life. Oh, God! Was this the way people got their heart's desires; or only Jonty-like people with Jonty-like desires?

He sighed deeply. Sofia!

It had changed his life. It was that moment that had brought them together:

Crehan had got a lot to answer for; and that moment, which had brought them to this breakfast this morning in their flat. Such are the furnaces and furnacemen that forge our destinies! And Jonty was made aware, once again, of the tea he was drinking. He had drunk two cups without really noticing them, lost in his memories; but he looked at the colour of his third cup in disgust. It was Sofia's Mark Two all right. It was altogether more powerful than her Mark One, which was an infusion of water, tinctured with iodine, and very suitable for reading the newspaper through. However, Mark Two was opaque. Jonty had never enquired how she brewed it, but, judging by its colour, he suspected that she stood a shovelful of horse-dung in a bucket of cold water overnight, boiled it up in the morning, and added a grain or two permanganate of potash just before pouring. The miracle was that it tasted nearly all right. Why, he simply couldn't understand.

Since they had married, half a year ago, he had shown Sofia several times, at her own request, how to brew a good cup of tea; yet she still produced these Mark One and Two versions in about equal proportions, often on the same day, and sometimes within an hour or two of each other. And always she professed not to know how it came about. It really was extraordinary! Patterns of this kind seemed to be utterly characteristic. Her lightly boiled eggs were similar instances. These, you were able either to drink through a straw or crush into granules with a hammer. What would her Mark Three tea be like – a ready-mix of quality tips and dried eggs, perhaps; would that give you Instant Egg-Tea Flip? Being Sofia's concoction, it would probably taste just fine.

"1 see we're on Mark Two this morning," said Jonty.

Sofia ignored this remark and went on reading her newspaper and drinking her instant coffee – Oh! no tea for her – in large slurping mouthfuls. Jonty regarded her with some perplexity? Why was she so good in bed and so bad out of it? Last night was a case in point. She had been just as marvellous as usual – undemanding, noisy, but ultimately satiable – and he felt fine, apart, that is, from the disc he seemed to have slipped through hooking himself over the edge of the bed. But, nevertheless, it had been one of his triumphant nights: he hadn't been sucked into Mrs Coughs' crater once. Now, here was

Sofia being unmarvellous again at the breakfast table. It was very puzzling.

"I made you some toast," she said, without looking up from her newspaper.

She had two types of this, too. The Jaguar-E model was a fast, low, slim-line job that was almost matt white on one side but smooth on the other. She seemed to have warmed it over sufficiently with a hot iron for the butter to soak in and turn the coachwork a golden yellow. Her Ford-T toast was quite different: ugly, black and noisy, which managed to bend itself into a horseshoe under the grill. If you tried to butter it, it snapped at you and broke into little pieces of black mosaic, suitable for an undertaker's bathroom. But Jonty had denied himself a visit to the shop floor to watch these models come off the production line; he had decided to stay at a distance and sniff.

This morning, it was the turn of the Model-T. He picked up one of the pieces of black mosaic and swallowed it quickly. There was no point in trying to butter it or even taste it. He drowned it painlessly in a gulp of Mark Two tea.

"What did Hacking Cough want yesterday?" he asked.

Sofia's large brown eyes, heavy with morning news, looked at him in the unfocussed way she had when she wasn't interested, and sometimes when she was.

"What?"

Her eyes wandered back again to the newspaper.

"Cough! What did she want?"

There was a pause while Sofia finished off the column she was reading.

"Oh, the usual! I paid her and she went away."

"I hope she marked it up in the rent book. Did you have to stand to attention while she inspected the barracks?"

"No! She was all right. She helped me to put back the furniture and said she might decorate the sitting room for us."

"Oh, Christ! We'll have to put her off that."

"Mmm!" she assented, and went back to her coffee – slurping and reading.

Jonty leaned over and moved the plastic hairbrush, still full of Sofia's lusty black hairs, a little further from his toast – athough which contaminated which was anybody's guess. It was habits like these that made him wonder why he had married her, for, despite the earthiness of his own upbringing, Jonty was strongly fastidious about ordinary hygiene and habits.

People were such bloody mysteries, weren't they? Here she was, displaying two of her best points in that unzipped red-towel dressing gown, ignoring him while she did it, and adding new speckles of instant coffee to the embroidery of stains already there, while being both desirable and repulsive at the same time. How could she do it?

Did she want to test his marital vow to cherish her, no matter what; or was she trying to strengthen his self-restraint for Sundays?

Of course, he had no objection to the unzipped bits in themselves; it was what they were surrounded by, what provided their matrix, so to speak, that he minded. The bits he liked best about Sofia were emphatically the ones she had grown up with and had had no hand in the growing of.

He supposed it was all owing to the gigantic cock-up which people like Aunty Wordsworth were prone to call 'nature's wisdom'. THAT was at the root of it all: THE BIOLOGICAL URGES v THE REST. The bits that Sofia herself was supposed to have control over – like cooking, and tidying-up, and living with people, and having will-power, and all that kind of stuff – just made him want to stand on top of Hacking Cough's rusty gas-stove and jump into a steaming pot of Sofia's Mark Two type tea.

How could she be so bad at this sort of thing, when she could sit in front of her easel and be so good at that sort of thing? At the same time, being superb at possessing what, actually, she couldn't help having? Were the unintelligent bits more intelligent than the so-called intelligent bits, as D.H. Lawrence must have asked somewhere? Did 'Life' have nothing to do with 'Art'? And if it didn't, why didn't it? He wondered if he could request Kingmaker to devote a complete lecture to answering those beauties, sometime!

"Oh, God! Give us another cup of that Mark Two, will you, beautiful?"

Sofia did not answer, but began pouring tea with her eyes still on her newspaper. Rather than watch her performance, Jonty decided to fetch the mail. He got up and went along the dusty landing and down the barrack-like stairs. He returned, holding a couple of letters.

"This one's for you," he said.

Sofia took the envelope without a word, bit off one corner of it, inserted her finger into the hole, ripped along the flap, withdrew the sheet of blue notepaper and began to read. Jonty winced. He took a clean knife and slitted the edge of his own letter.

'See what I mean?' he asked himself. He also began to read.

"Arnold! You know what?"

"What?"

"Alexis is getting married."

"Who's she marrying – her father?"

"Don't be such a beast! It's Barry. Next month. She wants us to go to the wedding. Oh, Arnold, LET'S!"

"I can't. I've got Finals this term. You know what that means."

"You wouldn't mind, then, if I – if – ?"

"No, not at all!" replied Jonty, with alacrity. "I could drink real tea and eat real toast and cook real boiled eggs, then. Think of that!"

"Pig!"

"How long for?"

"About a week, I suppose. All right?"

Jonty agreed at once. He had already seen that it would give him a chance to stay in his rooms in College, instead of pretending to stay in them, and he could make a point of letting the Dean *perceive* that he was staying there – as per College rules for all undergraduates: minimum period, one year. But, of course, he'd have to be careful how he did it; he didn't want the Dean to feel so well-disposed towards him that he'd receive an invitation for one of those excruciating teas, and upset his peace of mind before Finals.

"Oh, Arnold, I do love you!"

There she was again: Sofia being Sofia and making Sofia-type remarks. Had she no idea that, put like that, in that sequence, her answer sounded insincere? How did she find it so easy to reveal the true spring of her feelings by hiding them behind remarks like that? Next time, he would say 'No!', and wait to see if Sofia replied, 'Oh, Arnold, I do love you.' If she did, he'd certainly have to revise his – but, she wouldn't, would she?

"Who's your letter from?" asked Sofia.

"Me old Da'."

"How is he?"

"Pretty well. He's eating better and sleeping better and drinking better. They've started him on a new kind of cure. Very progressive, it is."

"For his drinking?"

"No! His gambling. Listen to this! *'We've got some new quacks since I writ last to you, with a lot of progressive ideas, and one of them is a bloke who goes under the name of Brown, and he's made a few changes, I can tell you. He reckons that, if he puts all us who've got the gambling bug in a special wing where you get waited on hand and foot and they let you put bets on to your heart's content, all day and every day, you'll get sick to the back teeth with it, and pack it up and never go back to it. They call gambling a sickness, you see. They say it's addictive, like sniffing glue. And they won't let you win real money. That's what he calls his cure. Some cure! The strange thing is – some blokes have really packed it in. But not me! Having the time of me life! More addicted than ever! Not only that, I've worked out a new system for the football pools. How's the studying?...'* See? As I said, the old man's fine. Then, there's something about the rest of the hospital routine. You know! And he asks me to remember him to you."

"It does seem a funny cure, doesn't it?"

"Based on the well-known principle, I suppose."

"What's that?"

"Too much is as good as a poison."

"Think it'll work?"

"Not in his case. If they make my Dad normal, he'll be ill. He's never been normal in his life. He LIKES gambling – the way you like sex."

"That's not the way I like it. I don't do it all day, every day, do I?"

"That's a point. WHY don't you?"

"Don't be silly!"

"What's silly about that? You could work your way towards it. You've never tried it!"

"How'd you know?"

"Ah, like that, is it? Right! Here's the plan! Get a stock of food and booze in for the weekend, and we'll lock all the doors to keep Mrs Cough and Twaggin out, and we'll have an orgy. It'll be good practice towards a daily timetable. Agreed?"

"By the way, what's happened to Twaggin? He hasn't put in an appearance for the last day or two."

"Ignoring my proposition, are you? He's got himself tied up with a new floozy. Don't worry! He'll be around before long. What time is it?"

"Nearly eight o'clock."

"Oh, God, is it? I've got to get round to my rooms before the bedmaker starts in. 'Bye-'bye! Don't forget lunch. Or the year. Or me."

Jonty grabbed his gown from the hook on the landing as he went, two at a time, down the stairs. Outside, Monster was still champing his way steadily through Mrs Cough's nude privet hedge. He'd have to hurry if he wanted to beat his bedmaker to the tape, though.

8

He arrived at the College quite out of breath. After propping up Monster in the racks outside the Wren Chapel, he ran to his staircase in Old Court, went up the stairs two at a time, threw open the door of his room and rushed in. Thank heavens she hadn't come yet! His bed was still neatly and tightly made. He went through his drill of pulling the blankets off the bed, rolling them into a ball, then unrolling them, then tangling the sheets together with the blankets, then untangling them, kneeling on the mattress, bouncing on it, thumping the pillows hollow, and generally trying to make the bed look as if it had been in its regular nightly punch-up. He had just finished, and was putting on his shoes again, when the bedmaker came in.

She was of such a nondescript appearance that people easily ignored her, or overlooked her – that is, until she opened her mouth to speak, when she was quite unstoppable.

"Oh, you've been at it again, have you, can't think what you do in bed, it's the worst bed in College, I have to take knots out of your bedclothes every morning, you ought to report yourself to the Dean, me lad, and ask him to get you looked at, it ain't normal for a young man like you to sleep so restless."

And so on. Jonty stopped listening. He stopped listening every morning, at roughly the same point. He walked over to a rust-coloured and very battered armchair in front of the fireplace, and sat down. What was the dratted woman's name? It was one of those disyllabic designations that ordered you to do something unpleasant, like Floggit or Bashitt. Jonty felt he should be able to remember its bizarre possibilities with ease, but couldn't. When he addressed her, he got over the difficulty by sprinting through the first syllable in a kind of stumble, and strolling leisurely along the second with emphasis. She never seemed to notice that he didn't know her name.

"Good morning, Mrs ——it! How're you today?"

Jonty inquired in the middle of her peroration. She never told him, and he didn't want to know. It was just part of the morning ritual.

"I've been making beds for ten years in this College and I never seen a bed like yours before, an' I don't want to see another, my husband says he thinks you must have cake-and-arse parties in here every night, but I told him you don't look the sort that's fond of cake, you aren't are you, I never seen no cake left round here, no crumbs nor nothing, I said I think it's the lad's nerves, he's got that look, little with quick eyes, and he looks worried, with spectacles and a tash, and I said to my hubby, that lad's got secrets, he's always in a hurry and he breathes quick, or my name ain't Else Stickett."

He knew it was something with an 'it' on the end, although, actually, on a quick re-assessment, it wasn't just her surname that was imperious; her entire name sounded like the last word of a crude ultimatum: "Rhubarb, rhubarb, rhubarb, or else stick it." Something of that variety. No wonder there had been a ring of great familiarity about her name from the moment she had first pronounced it. He must have heard it a thousand times before in a thousand questionable contexts, before even setting eyes on her.

"I shouldn't wonder if he don't let the room out to lodgers who get up very early, I can't think he gets up early himself and what puzzles me is even when he's just got up, and I go in to make it, the bed ain't never warm, and how do you explain that, I says, an' he says praps he's got poor circulation he says, an' I tell him his circulation looks all right to the naked eye, except he's often a bit flushed round the gills, besides looking worried, as if he's running two lives, but anyway it's a real puzzler, ain't it? There! Now, mind you do as I tell you, me lad, an' pop along to the Dean for a cuppa tea, a Seidlitz powder an' a holy chat!"

She had stopped her running commentary. Jonty sighed with relief. Her grammar always made him feel uncomfortable. Her last set of injunctions made up only the second sentence of her entire rebuke.

Had she been reading Thomas Wolfe, or by any chance, the last chaper of 'Ulysses'? Now that Mrs Stickett was preparing to leave and continue with her career of making beds elsewhere, Jonty breathed another sigh. He felt that she knew something, and her morning performances were exercises in obliquity; but he guessed, also, that if Mrs Stickett did know what subterfuge Jonty was carrying out, she wasn't going to tell the Dean. And even if she dropped a few hints one day while in the Dean's chambers, the Dean still wouldn't, in all probability, know then, because the Dean was the kind of man who often didn't know, even after he had been fully informed of things.

Jonty, clothed, lay down on his newly made bed, imitating the Dean's spinsterish enunciation, as he did so. "Oh, I see! Are you SURE, Jonty? Mmm!....? Well, I certainly have no recollection of any mention of –? Perhaps I should make a note of it?"

Mrs Stickett popped her head back round the door.

"What was that, deane?"

"Oh, nothing! Just thinking aloud, Mrs Ess."

"See the Dean, mind!"

See him! You couldn't miss him! If you didn't fall over him in the Thomas Grey garden, he called you in for consultations. And, of course, he hadn't made a note of anything. The next time you met, he would be under exactly the same weight of misunderstanding, incomprehension and misinformation as before. It was actually easier to live up to the kind of person the Dean thought you were, and do the sort of things the Dean believed you did, in the way the Dean was convinced you ought to do them, than it was to start moving the Fitzwilliam Museum, a brick at a time (weekends only) into the city centre of Darlington. (If Jonty had had a choice, he would, rather than trying to change the Dean's perceptions, have chosen the museum project.) Jonty felt that the Dean was really to blame for the pantomime he had to go through every morning – except on Sundays when Mrs Stickett didn't come in. It all arose from one of the Dean's bricked-in prejudices about undergraduates in his College.

"You see, Jonty, I believe that all gentlemen in *statue pupillaris* benefit greatly—"

'—Why can't the silly old goat say students?'

"—from spending at least one year in College."

'And doesn't he remember that I stayed in College in my first year, anyway?'

"It builds up – how should I put it? – a sense of corporate life, yes, yes, a sense of—er—community, an awareness of the needs of other people. Don't you agree, Jonty?"

Jonty was acutely aware of how staying in College presented endless opportunities for NOT fighting or drinking, but FOR singing, practicing the French Horn on Sunday mornings, staying up late, keeping awake all night, lying in bed all day, practicing the vibes on Saturday nights, having women, taking drugs, clandestine drinking, climbing into College, climbing out of College, getting fined, practicing the saxophone on Wednesday nights, keeping cats, dogs, mice, bears, or breeding canaries, fish, fleas, silkworms, or hamsters, as well as providing opportunities FOR attending Chapel every weekday, obtaining exeats, seeing tutors, meeting the Dean, eating in Hall, attending Chapel on Sundays, listening to musical tendencies and religious ambitions, playing the organ for hours at a stretch on any bloody day of the week, meeting the Dean, helping in his rockery, and generally going along with him and his world-view.

Oh, yes, he was aware of all that!

"Yes, I see your point, sir!"

"I'm so glad! I can see we can get on well together. You're nearly at the end of your second year, now, aren't you, Jonty?"

"Yes, sir!"

'Well he HAD got that right! Lucky guess, probably.'

"Will you have another cup of tea, Jonty?"

Jonty hadn't had any, yet. The cups were sitting on the tray, as pristine as when he had first entered the Dean's chambers, and THEY were still sitting on the Dean's leather sofa which was far from pristine.

"Thank you, sir," he said.

It sounded better than calling him Dean Newey, as all the American students did, or *Mister* Newey, or Rev., as had happened on one or two horrifying occasions with students from the Deep South. Jonty watched with fascination as the Dean picked up the teapot and moved it determinedly in the direction of the sugar-bowl, tilting the pot slightly so that puffs of steam came out of the spout, like morse signals.

"And having spent one year in lodgings with Mrs Cough – er, yes, an unfortunate business, that – I expect you're anxious to come into residence, aren't you?"

The Dean seemed to be on the point of emptying the entire pot into the sugar when he abruptly changed course and swooped towards Jonty's cup.

"Oh, I'm terribly sorry! Was it hot?" asked the Dean, blandly.

Jonty was imagining large blisters rising at an alarming rate on the tender insides of his thighs from the scalding patch of tea on his trousers. He dabbed at it, gingerly, with his handkerchief. But, with great restraint, he said: "No! Not at all! Don't worry, sir."

"Good," said the Dean, and he didn't.

After filling Jonty's cup and ensuring that he couldn't add milk or sugar until he had drunk some of the steaming fluid in its undiluted form, Jonty watched the Dean waving the teapot vaguely over the table, looking for a space to put it down in. Twice, he tried to wedge it into a space about two inches square between his own saucer and a plate of toasted scones that Jonty had been eyeing hungrily for some time and hoping one of which the Dean would offer him. When the Dean seemed about to make a third attempt to squeeze the teapot between the scones and the saucer, he suddenly switched his attention to a slightly larger location at the end of the tray. Then, noticing with some surprise, the site from which he had first taken the teapot, he, bewilderedly, restored it to its rightful position.

"So we can take it that you're willing to come into residence in your third year? I'm not sure that I shall be able to secure one of the larger – er – but I'll certainly not allocate you one of the very tiny rooms. You wouldn't want that, would you? No, I thought not. What about two – er – smallish rooms? Not small, but smallish? Yes! That's most satisfactory, I think."

Jonty looked around him. The conversation might not as well have taken place. When the time came round for rooms in College to be allocated, the Dean had quite clearly forgotten all about his intentions to give Jonty two smallish chambers. This wasn't one of the tiniest, it was true; however, it WAS one small room. It had just enough space to swing a cat in; but it was large enough to pretend to occupy, and to have to pay for. It provided him with a handy hideaway between lectures, and Mrs Stickett, and a cubbyhole where he could boil a kettle and make tea that was quite unlike Sofia's Mark One & Two types, or the incense-flavoured China-green variety favoured by the Dean. So he had something to be grateful for.

'In fact, what about a cuppa, right now?'

Jonty got up to put the kettle he always kept filled on the gas-ring. That done, he settled back on the bed again, musing.

During his second year at Cambridge, their relationship had deepened and grown. In the long vacation that had followed this interview, Sofia and Jonty had decided to marry. Since that catastrophic night of Crehan's party nearly three years ago, they had discovered their mutual need for each other's company, and, after discussion, had decided to take the plunge as soon as Sofia had finished her course at the Birmingham College of Art. Vacations were in progress at the time, so Jonty had written immediately to the Dean to inform him of their intentions, and to request permission from the College to live out of residence for his final year up. Sofia and Jonty had gone up to Cambridge a few days before the beginning of the Michaelmas term in order to find themselves an apartment somewhere in the town. That was when they had met Mrs Cough and agreed to take her flat. They were installed by the time the new term had opened. Jonty went at once to the College to see the Dean for confirmation of the arrangement.

The Dean denied all knowledge of everything.

"You say you sent it to me in the middle of the long vacation? Most extraordinary! I don't usually lose such things, you know!"

'I know. You just deny they ever existed,' thought Jonty.

"What did you say was in it, Jonty?"

Perhaps, NOT wanting to receive the information he was being given afflicted the Dean with psychological deafness, or with psychological idiocy? What made him ask the question for the third time?

"It informed you about my proposed marriage, sir."

"Oh, did it? Your marriage! Mmmm! I don't wish to – er – er. Just sit down for a moment, Jonty, will you? I'll look through my – my – "

'—List of hints on how to have beautiful habits?' suggested Jonty in his mind.

"—my – er – filing cabinet."

The Dean hated this kind of problem. Apart from the fact that it banged hard against one of his most cherished convictions (the celibacy he demanded of scholars), it confronted an ingrained superstition about periods in residence demanded of undergraduates, besides forcing him to take time out from his mulling over becoming the Bishop of Ely as soon as possible. It was, therefore, unsatisfactory from all points of view.

When the Dean returned from consulting his filing cabinet, he said, with animation: "No, nothing! Your letter didn't arrive, I'm afraid. But about this – er – er – . Perhaps you ought possibly to – er – think again – or even – er – postpone – your decision to – er – marry. Of course, I AM in favour of – er – . But, in your position – . I believe you are up here on a – er – a College scholarship, aren't you?"

'You don't believe it. You KNOW it.'

"Of a fixed amount, I suppose? Yes. Well, I'm awfully sorry about all this, Jonty, but – "

'—All what?'

"—but – I'm afraid that, at this late stage, I am quite unable to arrange lodgings elsewhere. Your room is ready for you in College. All possible vacancies with landladies have been taken. Besides, you know, Jonty, all the details, all the ARRANGING would have to be – er – done, actually done, AGAIN. You do see this, don't you, Jonty?"

Jonty wasn't sure that he saw what the Dean saw, but what Jonty saw he saw only too well.

"So – for the moment – your decision to get – er – married – "

'—It is no longer a decision, you old twit! I AM.'

"—Well," said Jonty, "it isn't exactly a decision, sir. You see – "

"—Oh, I am so glad!" interjected the Dean, quickly.

Jonty went on to explain, but he knew that the Dean wasn't listening by the way he was filling his pipe. He did it with unforgettable concentration, scowling at each strand of tobacco as if it had legs and was trying to dodge his compressive fingers. Until the final conflagration in the bowl of his pipe, he was as deaf as one of his own scorched muffins. When Jonty finished, there was a moment or two of silence while the Dean sucked the matched flame up and down on his pipe. Then, blowing out a huge cloud of smoke, he said: "Yes. All right, Jonty. Leave it with me, will you? I'll – er—"

'Take a course in Pelmanism?'

The Dean was lighting his pipe again, a truly unnecessary operation; and when Jonty finally left him, he was almost entirely invisible, obscured by the clouds of smoke he was emitting – which Jonty presumed was the object of the exercise.

Some time later, when Jonty met him accidentally in the Thomas Gray rockery, the Dean had apparently forgotten the whole matter saying "Room all right, Jonty?", and never referred to Jonty's marriage again. Jonty had been deterred from returning to it for fear of being treated as the Dean claimed he had once managed poor old Wilson Knight.

Well, it stood to reason, didn't it? Who would want to be behaved towards as if he had just demeaned himself in the Junior Common Room, clad only in academic dress? It was for some obscure reasoning along these lines that the Dean confessed to being quite unable to read the Shakespearean criticism of G. Wilson Knight, which Jonty lapped up like a cat lapping up warm milk.

The handkerchief in Othello seemed to weigh quite heavily in the Dean's assessment of both the character and critical acumen of Professor Knight. Why wasn't his reasoning at all clear to Jonty? Once, earlier, when he had been in his first year, and more innocent, Jonty had tried to draw out the Dean in conversation on the topic All he could get out of him was: "Poor old Knight!" and the Dean's renewed offer of a cold scorched muffin and another cup of incensed tea. Jonty had realized, then, that his curiosity had too big a price-tag attached to it.

Later, Jonty described it all to Sofia.

"So you see – ? The Reverend Newey finds the idea of an undergraduate appalling, in itself. But a married undergraduate is unimaginable to him; he starts smoking and preparing for blast-off to

Alpha Centauri. I think we'll just have to hang on to this flat, and keep it all quiet. Anyway, to explain our marriage to the Bursary Board – No, I just don't fancy going through all that. Shades of Jarrold and feckless! They might even cancel the scholarship!"

"You're ashamed of me, aren't you?"

"Why should I be ashamed of you, sweetie?"

"'The flat is like a pigsty.' That's your refrain. 'Can't ask anybody but Twaggin,' you say."

"That's not true! There are a number of down-and-outs who'd be only too pleased to—"

"—You're so unfeeling and selfish and – and – you don't think I should spend any time painting, do you? You want me to devote myself to looking after you, that's all!"

"Sounds wonderful!"

"Oh, YOU! You're so bloody patriarchal! So piddlingly Victorian! So crashingly Miltonic in your views about marriage! You've got the mentality of a Middle-Eastern caliph in the Sinbad era! You haven't even got up to Ibsen and Shaw and the Emancipated Woman, never mind Women's Lib! And as for Simone de Beauvoir – "

"—Showing off your Comprehensive School education, are you? I thought you were an Art Student!"

"Patronizing sod!"

They were sitting in the kitchen, and Jonty was doing his best to ignore, velveteened with mould, the grey wedge of cheese on the dresser, the crust of fossilized bread in the bin that smelled like a disused brewery, the mummified slice of tannin-coloured lemon on the draining board, and the half-jar of marmalade that was quietly furring itself in the cupboard; but it certainly wasn't easy, and having to listen to Sofia highlighting his weak points, like that, was making it all the harder. In order to bolster himself up and better withstand her taunting, he put himself into a posture he had seen in sepia-tinted photographs of Victorian gentlemen with large families. He tried to convey that he was wearing a big beard, a black-skirted coat, a celluloid collar, and controlled a household of subject females.

However, it wasn't working very well, for she went on: "That's right! Just the pose. You to a Tee: full of egotism. Yes! Always going on about authority. All bluff! Ha! You're so nigglingly conventional, I want to throw up when I think about it. So bloody MORAL! Why SHOULDN'T you tell Newey? Why SHOULDN'T you tell Twaggin? Why SHOULDN'T you tell the Bursary Board? Why SHOULD you tell the – . Oh, what's the bloody use? I'm wasting my time!"

There couldn't be any doubt that she was mad at him, could there? It was another of their patterns: her insults; his clowning; then her tears, followed by their peace negotiations in the bedroom. It was all so bloody PREDICTABLE! Still, he shouldn't grumble; the sexual bits were absolutely marvellous, weren't they...?

"You DO see, don't you, sweetie?"

"I'm not YOUR sweetie!"

"My lovely Sweetie-Undercut!"

"Shut up! And stop pawing me!"

In the end, Sofia agreed. But her reluctance was tangible. She said "Yes!" like a nun who had just been propositioned by the Prior for the umpteenth time: Yes, Prior!" she said, "Yes."

Jonty was quite satisfied with the arrangement. It allowed him to pass as celibate with the Dean without actually being celibate, while enabling him to put about among the undergraduates the rumour that he kept an established establishment and had an adoring mistress. Such an image increased his standing with people like Twaggin, who firmly believed that marriage had been invented for the sexually under-equipped; and Jonty liked having his standing increased. That was how it had stood at the commencement of the Michaelmas term and how it was standing now on the last stretch to Finals.

Mind you, there had been one or two ups and downs! Oh, yes!

Like that period in the middle of the Michaelmas term, when his standing had started to sink to its knees under the spotlight of Twaggin's suspicion that he and Sofia were actually married: all due to a few careless remarks of Sofia's! But he had managed to put it right with Twaggin by strenuous lying. Now his standing was utterly vertical and Twaggin treated him as a friend again. That is to say: he ate Jonty's food, borrowed his money, kissed his wife, drank his beer, tore his pillowcases, offered free advice, slept in the wardrobe, utilized the bath, and gave long recitals in a growling bass voice on the use of symbols in pornographic art.

It wasn't everybody who could claim Twaggin's friendship.

Jonty stretched and yawned on the bed, and smiled at his thoughts. It was odd, wasn't it, that Twaggin and the Dean had turned out to be allies in their common refusal to acknowledge that Jonty and Sofia were truly married.

But, on reflection, was it really so odd? After all, when it came to religion, the Reverend F.R. Newey had a very worldly and practical approach to it, especially when it concerned his own preferment to a Bishopric. And, Twaggin, when his own cause and comfort were at stake, had a very religious approach to that, and was just as diligent in his observances of it as the Dean was. They were brothers under the skin!

True, the Dean didn't have a beard like a damp straggly haycock, thick spectacles, and a joke nose. But he COULD have had; and it wouldn't have made any difference to the way people felt about him. In fact, if there was any truth in the aphorism that outer beauty was a sign of inner grace, he SHOULD have looked like that. Had Creation slipped up somewhere; or had the Reverend Newey had a face-job and disguised himself? That would explain why Twaggin looked like Twaggin and Newey didn't: Twaggin had no time for disguises. Yes, there was probably more to this Twaggin-Newey alignment than met the eye!

Take, for instance, the first time Newey had ever seen Twaggin: he didn't bat an eyelid. That was incriminating, in itself. Any normal person batted more than an eyelid on first acquaintance. After the first bat, they usually went on to make three hundred and sixty five not out, and on the fifth day they were still batting, and, often, for a long time after that. Some people, in fact, went on batting just as long as Twaggin was about. But not the Dean! Oh, dear, No! His appearance didn't faze him one bat. And what about the way he acted? Twaggin's behaviour was even more eyelid-batting, but the Reverend Newey never blinked once. It was a conundrum he would have to give more thought to.

Now, he must get up.

9

Jonty rose from the bed that Elsie Stickett had recently talked into shape and went down his staircase into the courtyard.

Jonty's Staircase was in Old Court, near to the Porter's Lodge, and fairly close to the Lecture Hall in Mill Lane. Twaggin's staircase was on the far side of New Court, near the Waterhouse Library. Jonty wondered if Twaggin was going to attend Kingmaker's lecture today, but there was no sign of him. Twaggin usually attended all of Kingmaker's performances. Should he go up and remind him? Maybe, he was still in bed; or simmering in a large tubful of very hot water in the communal bathrooms, from which he would eventually emerge, prawn-pink, and proceed to unguent and pommade himself. Better not! It wasn't a pleasant process to watch.

As Jonty approached the main lodge, he saw the young Porter on duty, with whom he was friendly. He passed through the gates, making a rude sign to the young man as he did so. The Porter made a much ruder sign back, and grinned at Jonty. Jonty returned the grin.

He crossed Trumpington Street, walked to the right a little way along it, and turned left into Mill Lane. As he strolled the short way to the Lecture Hall, he amused himself by recalling one of his introductory memories of Twaggin.

It had been at a lunchtime sherry party given by the Senior Tutor, a mild and learned man, of impeccable manners. Jonty's impression of Twaggin's early hirsute period was of a scented, large, untidy hayrick with an enormous appetite for little round salted biscuits. After disposing of several hundred of these, and doing away with a decanter and a half of Senior Tutor's best Spanish sherry, he had taken up a posture suggestive or a vervet monkey in a pulpit and disagreed stridently with Senior Tutor's interpretation of an episode in Homer's 'Odyssey' (on which Senior Tutor was an acknowledged expert).

Twaggin had bayed at him in his formidable baritone that he would send round a good book on the subject by a man he had once met in a pub. Such was the politeness of Senior Tutor that he had filled Twaggin's glass yet again with his excellent sherry, thanked Twaggin humbly for his offer and said he would look forward to the book's arrival. Afterwards, Twaggin emerged from the sherry party acting like a triumphant aboriginal rainmaker exhorting the heavens to open (a manner in which he conducted himself on even the most sedate of occasions), and flung his arms about and shouted:

"I've never even read Homer! 'The lyf so short, the craft so long to lerne', what else could I do?"

"What craft?" asked Jonty.

"It's a quotation!" protested Twaggin.

"I know. Chaucer? What craft?"

"Well, if you insist, polemics and invective."

"Oh, so you're going into politics, are you?"

They both laughed and from that moment on, Jonty and Twaggin had been firm friends.

The Lecture Theatre was full. All Kingmaker's lectures were given to packed audiences. Undergraduates came by the hundreds. This phenomenon probably owed little to his reputation of 'Great Critic' and much to the insulting observations his lectures were peppered with, the range of which was impressive. His targets ran from University colleagues and administrative personnel to television idols, editors of literary weeklies, purple hearts, white-tile Universities, the

75

Sunday Observer, a well-known academic who wrote children's stories, current best-sellers, the BBC, conurbations and T.S. Eliot.

Or, alternatively, his popularity could have been related to his habit of throwing out, from time to time, guesses about the nature and content of forthcoming examination papers. The likelihood was that in the present run-up to Finals, his audiences would increase.

However, the increase in attendances certainly wouldn't be related to the clarity of his delivery and subject-matter, because when he was working on a new set of Lecture Notes – which seemed to be most of the time – he mumbled incomprehensibly. His audiences always recognised this as a signal that he was doing a fresh study of the prescribed author, and looked forward to a series of lectures that shed darkness on darkness. All that emerged from such performances was Kingmaker's tortured but sincere view that the author in question was worth looking at – advice that most of his audience carefully avoided following, preferring to stick to the published commentaries rather than to the originals they commented on.

When Kingmaker was fully comprehensible, which was rare, and which occurred only when his current studies had been completed, the audience disagreed with his views. No, it was his asides, his acerbic wit, the flashes of vituperation and the calculated lightning of his insults illuminating the impenetrable core of the lectures that packed them in. And he certainly packed them in.

Jonty looked about him. They were sitting even on the steps and in the aisles of the tiered lecture theatre. Luckily, he had managed to get a seat at the back, near the entrance doors, high above the lectern.

Kingmaker was late as usual, and Jonty had filled in the period of waiting by finishing off his reply to Lady Owens's query about aubergine knives and forks. It was just about done when Kingmaker came in. He was panting noticeably. He had ridden from his home in Cherry Hinton, wearing, at this time of the year, a long herringbone overcoat, on an old bicycle that looked like a damaged bit of brass bedstead several sizes too large for him. The handlebars were very high, and the saddle was very low, and he dismounted by leaping off it before it had a chance to crush him underneath it.

He had taken off his overcoat outside the theatre, and put on a tie for the lecture. (He ordinarily wore a brown leather waistcoat and an open-necked shirt; he hated ties almost as much as he hated the *Sunday*

Observer). He strode, panting, down the steps to the lectern. Under one arm, he carried a sheaf of notes, handwritten on what appeared to be greaseproof paper, and, on the other arm, his frayed herringbone overcoat.

Jonty was observing Kingmaker with interest yet again.

He wasn't at all what Jonty had expected a Great Literary Critic to be. For one thing, he was small. For another, he was thin, almost scraggy, giving the impression that his limbs were short lengths of string knotted at strategic points to nobbles of bone. For another, his face was gaunt and he had a bald head with a short fringe hanging like a dung-coloured skirt at the back of his neck. His pate reminded Jonty of a crown of Spring rhubarb trying to force its way through a halo of horse manure. And, lastly, his adenoids seemed to give him trouble.

How all that reconciled itself with his lofty and incisive diatribes was very puzzling.

Kingmaker placed his overcoat on the table beside the lectern, unscruntled his scruntled-up lecture notes, put them in front of him, folded his arms, leaned on the lectern, looked down, and began in his breathless, scarcely audible, adenoidal voice, to address the sheaf of notes before him.

He enunciated his words prissily and thriftily, like a grocer who wanted to be a church warden. Once he looked down, he never looked up. All those faces frightened him.

"...and I keep reading about people who want me to explain my ethical allegiances. If I wish to use an explicit moral judgment, do I have to explain my ethical allegiances to a particular system? I say – No, I don't!..."

'Hear! Hear! Explaining ethical allegiances is a mug's game,' thought Jonty. 'Especially if it's the kind of – "

"—It HAS its definition, in the context, in relation to the particular illustration. And after all, it has taken the writer the whole book to ESTABLISH the context, hasn't it?..."

'I suppose it has. If not the whole, certainly a large part of it....'

Kingmaker was a master of the art of querulous self-defence and Jonty guessed that he had got some leeway before Kingmaker recollected what it was he had come to talk about. Jonty had heard all these stratagems before, and in his first two years of study he had made extensive notes on them so that, at a later date, he could subject them to some rigorous study along psychoanalytic lines.

So, Jonty settled into composing his questions for the new type of examination paper he was thinking of submitting to the University Senate. After long consideration, Jonty had decided the rubric that would head his paper would read: ANSWER AS FEW OR MANY QUESTIONS AS YOU LIKE. (THE MORE THE MERRIER. THE FEWER THE BETTER). TIME: ALL NEXT WEEK.

He was, thus, at the stage of beginning to formulate the questions and had got as far as the first one or two. He owed his first to a don from Girton, although she was quite unaware of the fact. At present, it read:

"D.H. Lawrence's art makes bad things memorable." Discuss.

A rumour currently going the rounds among the undergraduates was that, a few years earlier, one of the globose but passionate scholars of that distinguished College had blurted this out at high table one evening, after drinking a glass of unaccustomed wine in the presence of E.M. Forster, who was also unaccustomed.

Whether it was the strangeness of the writer or the strangeness of the wine that went to her vital centres was still a matter for speculation. But it was a memorable judgment, and Jonty had exerted himself to work a strong flush of embarrassment into the wording, as a tribute to its author, but he had found this quite impossible to do. In the end, he had decided to let it stand in its virginal form and simply add the one word 'Discuss', because of the very large scope it would provide, as a question, for the underground elements of the student body.

Jonty turned to the wording of his second question. His aim, with this one, had been to extend the field away from the usual, tight-gutted and inbred collection of nit-picking preoccupations with piddling topics that the current team of resident dons seemed to favour; in a word, to work towards a more inspiring and intelligent paper than had hitherto climbed out of the cellars of the University Press.

He wasn't sure he had succeeded, but, in its present form, it read:

"'Not only were great things done in his/her age, but it was he/she who did them.' Illustrate from the life of Mrs Pankhurst or Lewis Carroll or Neville Chamberlain."

Strangely enough, another of his questions Jonty owed to Kingmaker himself, whose high-pitched adenoidal whine had now reached his bit about receiving only one review between the covers of *The New Statesman* during the last twenty or thirty years, and THAT had been disparaging.

On the earlier occasion, Kingmaker had been in the middle of a diatribe against the B.B.C., when he suddenly interpolated an anecdote about a colleague who was being a nuisance at the current meetings of the Examination Committee, of which Kingmaker himself had been unexpectedly elected Chairman after many years of being assiduously passed over by the University Senate. Kingmaker had been quite outraged at the plea made by this colleague for a question of his to be put into the Eighteenth Century paper of the English Tripos. Kingmaker had then given his imitation of someone spitting out orange pips after a sharp intake of breath – which served him in place of a laugh – and had come out with:

"Yes, it's true! 'Write a criticism of "The Rape of the Lock" in Pope's metre.' No; I didn't invent it. I couldn't!"

This was a gift that Jonty had taken with both hands, so there it was, neatly packaged into his model paper.

However, the difficulty he was wrestling with at the moment had to do with the dirty-minded lecturer on Donne, Theo Redshins.

Jonty was struggling to formulate a question that acknowledged the man's distinct and undeniable PHYSICAL presence in the University, while, at the same time, conveying clearly to all that his MENTAL presence was not only irrelevant but invalid, and probably immoral.

A question on Donne there clearly had to be, because Donne, like Redshins, was out there somewhere; but it had to be one that Redshins wouldn't have the faintest idea how to mark. After much thought, Jonty had settled on a formulation which, although not perfect, was infinitely preferable to the prurient crossword queries thought up by Redshins:

"Je me demande, par ma foi, ce que nous faisions, toi et moi, avant d'aimer." In what ways is this passage reminiscent of John Donne, or John Donne of it?

On reading it through once again, Jonty felt that, despite all his efforts, a touch of the Redshins interrogatory technique had crept in towards the end; but he decided to leave it as it stood, nevertheless, because he had a shrewd suspicion that Redshins couldn't de-code the French.

Jonty was brought back from his cogitations by a reference to William Morris and Queen Victoria that he hadn't heard before. Kingmaker was still, unfortunately, on the prolegomena to his subject-of-the-day, but this did seem to be a new story. Morris, it appeared, had been summoned to carry out a spot of painting and decorating in one of the Royal residences, and the Monarch had intimated to him that she wished it all done out in pastel colours. Morris is reputed to have drawn himself up very straight and replied:

"Madam, if you want dirt, you can pick it up in the streets."

At least, that was Kingmaker's version of the incident, although – give him his due – he didn't actually claim to have been there at the time.

Kingmaker, however, WAS claiming that the incident illustrated the relation of art to life in some way; but Jonty had difficulty on this occasion in following the tenuousness of his argument, despite the fact that it was a topic Jonty was fond of. He must ask Twaggin about it. If he wasn't able to explain it to Jonty's satisfaction, he would have to wait until Kingmaker's own fondness for the topic threw up the reference again, as it certainly would.

Jonty paused: was that the expression? Could a preoccupation with a topic that was lifelong, and that drove Kingmaker from sheer excitement to become as inaudible as a bat, be described in terms of affection? No, fondness wasn't the word. More like obsession. Wasn't that what he was exhibiting at the moment, addressing the surface of the lectern in adenoidal earnestness? Jonty strained his ears to catch what Kingmaker was saying.

"The term 'moral' comes up BECAUSE the criteria are challenged. If they were not, the term would not arise. We try – at least, SOME of us try – "

Here, Kingmaker gave a lift to his shoulders, lowered his crown of Spring rhubarb between them, sucked in his breath, closed his lips (preparing to compose them for his sardonic smile), smiled, opened them and said:

"—SOME of us try to bring the values to bear on literature that we use in life. The two are, in fact, inseparable. So – "

Suddenly, a neck-stiffening but subdued screech started up in the lecture theatre.

Kingmaker stopped, stiffened and froze where he stood. It sounded to Jonty as if someone was trying to write with an empty beer bottle on a blackboard that had been electronically amplified. Could it be Twaggin?

But he knew the sound was human. His teeth began trying to get up and walk out of the hall. The audience was dead quiet; no-one moved. The screeching continued, gradually getting louder and louder. Although Kingmaker's little pile of greaseproof papers was still clearly visible to him, he hadn't moved, struck by alexia; and he bore an expression that was utterly vacant, as if all the meaning had leaked away from the pages and dribbled onto the dais under his feet.

The beer-bottle screech was turning into a scream and getting louder. Jonty turned round to find from whence it came, but could see only other students now beginning to do the same, craning and twisting, on rubber necks. Then, everyone was rubbernecking, vigorously; only Kingmaker was immobile. He'd followed up the alexia with an impressive bout of aphasia, giving a good imitation of a man who had managed to forget not only the English Language but also most of the conventions of social behaviour.

The screaming was now dreadful, filling the room, paralyzing the mind, freezing the body, like a device used by Martians for immobilizing their enemies. Then, instantly, the screaming stopped, and halfway down the tiered theatre, a large fair-haired man slowly toppled sideways and slithered to the floor between the ranks of benches.

There was a sudden burst of rushing and scuffling around the unfortunate student and, in a little while, the prone figure was carried up the steps to the swing doors at the rear. As they passed, Jonty saw the froth on the mouth of the stricken man.

Kingmaker was goggling at his notes, his mouth working soundlessly, shivering. He could have been in the early throes of a similar attack himself.

The three men and the unconscious victim had passed through the doors and left them swinging slightly, but still the audience waited to see what Kingmaker would do. Kingmaker did nothing.

The silence pressed into Jonty's ears like fingers, almost less bearable than the terrifying scream. Unless the impersonation Kingmaker was giving of a clogged-up faucet could be considered as 'doing something'. Little gulping, gurgling and swirling noises began to issue from his throat and rise into the hushed air. His bald pate glistened with sweat. He began to smooth down the fish-and-chip paper his notes were written on in short jerky strokes. Presumably, he was trying to continue with his lecture, as if nothing had happened, attempting to bring out yet anothex moral nuance from the long caravan of such nuances that was wending its lonely way across the desert that stretched between contemporary literature and contemporary life.

But Jonty decided not to wait in order to find out exactly how the next oasis could be reached.

He got up and left.

Outside in the sun, the epileptic had been stretched out on the low concrete parapet that bounded the University lecture theatre. His eyes were open, his hands were clasped behind his head, and he was looking normal and fairly comfortable. A few students were gathered about him, chatting, or just lounging, sympathising by their presence, proximity and silence.

Jonty was surprised to see that Twaggin was one of these, but still his usual flamboyant self. Today, he was wearing an academic gown, according to the rule for attendance at lectures, and a black bearskin, according to the rule that forbade the wearing of all headgear with gowns, except mortar boards. The bearskin had belonged to an uncle who had been in the Queen's Coldstream Guards, but that didn't cut any ice with the University Senate. He looked as if he was wearing two beards: one, shiny and groomed, growing upwards, and the other, faded and scruffy, growing downwards. In between he was wearing his joke-nose and spectacles.

A canvas plaid holdall half-full of empty beer bottles stood on the concrete beside him.

As Jonty approached, Twaggin, in his growling baritone, announced to all in general and Jonty in particular:

"*Some* of us bring to bear on literature," and he paused, to give his disparaging laugh, the one that sounded like a series of backfires from a six-tonner in the Mersey Tunnel, "the values we use in life."

A number of those around him laughed, too. The fair-headed youth had now recovered from his attack and, as Twaggin was speaking, he had raised himself from the horizontal to sit on the parapet. He spoke to Twaggin.

"That's the second time it's happened in one of Kingmaker's lectures. I think his adenoids must affect me. Wave lengths, or something."

"Well," growled Twaggin, "it couldn't be his adumbrations on Henry James. They don't affect anybody."

"Is he still chuntering on?"

"He'd stopped when I came out. Throat wouldn't work. Don't worry. Kingmaker's ideas produce visceral reactions in a lot of people," said Twaggin.

The youth smiled. Somebody had gone back to see if Kingmaker's lecture was continuing. He returned and announced to everyone:

"He's holding his notes up to the light, trying to decipher one of the vinegar stains."

Twaggin had picked up his holdall of beer bottles and taken them across to a stretch of wall that was in the sun, where he sat down. Jonty joined him.

"I didn't see you in the lecture," said Jonty.

"I was late. I sat at the back."

"Oh! What did you think of it?"

"I think I've already made my comment," he said, portentously. "Let's talk about something else."

"Okay! Have a look at this."

Jonty gave him his draft of the reply to Lady Owens on the question of table etiquette.

Twaggin seemed to have exhausted his powers of concentration for the day. Without reading more than a word or two, he began offering Jonty his advice on how to rewrite it. He seemed to think the style was wrong. Or something.

While Twaggin droned on, Jonty lost interest and looked about him.

Those who had gathered sympathetically about the epileptic were drifting away one by one.

Kingmaker emerged from the building in the middle of Twaggin's monologue, but Twaggin was peering closely at Jonty's sheet of paper and talking, quite unaware of Kingmaker's exit.

Kingmaker looked as if someone had taken a pair of pincers to his nostrils and pinched them together even harder than usual; the wings were white. He pulled off his heavy tweed tie. He opened his collar wide, and inhaled deeply. He began to wrestle with his herringbone overcoat, which appeared to have put a half-nelson on him.

Finally, he managed to get it on and stepped up onto the low parapet to mount his bicycle that stood in one of the iron stands provided. He failed; the bicycle leaned away from him. He tried again and this time succeeded in mounting the saddle, and balancing himself with one foot still on the wall. Then, he dropped his gown and had to dismount, retrieve it, and go through the process again.

At last, he was ready. He rode away, along the building, towards Mill Lane, his gown flapping from the handlebars. Twaggin still hadn't noticed him.

"Okay, thanks!" said Jonty, suddenly.

He removed his draft from Twaggin's mauling grasp, stood up, and said: "See you!"

Sofia had informed him haughtily that she wanted to spend the day painting, so he had decided to use up the rest of the time working in the University Library.

When he left, Twaggin was counting his beer bottles.

10

After his day's work in the University Library, Jonty emerged to find that it was raining. He wrapped his gown tightly about him, climbed onto Monster, and started to pedal disconsolately back to the flat. Jonty didn't like rain. He firmly believed that Britain had far too much of it, together with pollution and the Trade Unions. To cheer himself up, he started writing another letter in his head, one that he had been putting off for some time. It was to the Managing Editor of a large Publishing House. He thought he had, at last, worked out a reasonable approach. The rest he would have to leave to the inspiration of the moment.

Dear Sir,

I am riding through Cambridge, on a wet evening and a bicycle, with a headache, some brilliant ideas and a sense of frustration. I have started compiling an anthology of Dog Poems. Would you be interested in its publication?

Its provisional title is: An Anthology of Gun Dog Poetry. This will appeal to three audiences: (a) people who like gun dogs; (b) people who like poems about gun dogs; and (c) people who like anthologies about anything. Of course, it goes without saying that it will appeal to people who like all three at once. Also, depending on the selection, it might appeal to people who like poetry.

If the sales are good, and they will be, – considering the passion shown by the British Public for anything on four legs – you might like to consider following it up with an anthology of cat poems, mouse poems, hedgehog poems, *und so weiter*. Personally, I believe this trend could be profitably exploited to include insects and other species; but how fond the reading public is of literary insects, you would know better than I.

The insect concept can, of course, be extended to include people, and I've got my eye on a few already.

I am offering these brilliant ideas to you on behalf of the Dean of my College, who is the originator of all of them (except the last), as I feel the public should be made aware of the calibre of thinking that goes on in this ancient seat of learning. His generic name for this sort of thing is: A Study of Animal Imagery in English Poetry. My name for him I am, at present, withholding. I am also withholding my own name in case you contact the Dean.

Yours truly, Thoedore Redshins, M.A., Ph.D., University Lecturer in Pornographic Poetry

P.S. The signature above is a pseudonym.

Despite the rain, Jonty reached One Dust Road in a glow of satisfaction. He avoided the belligerent tile, stabled Monster in the wet nude privet hedge and clumped up the unlighted staircase to the first landing.

At the top, he fell over something that made a noise like a bottling factory. Jonty rubbed his shin vigorously, hopping and blaspheming in the direction of Mrs Cough's kitchen.

The sitting room door opened and a wedge of light fell out like a slice cut from a big piece of yellow sponge cake. Sofia stood in the doorway, wearing a pair of floppy white slacks and a black vest, watching him. She was clutching a newspaper.

"My poor lamb! Let me kiss it better. I thought you'd fallen downstairs."

"Leave it alone! Shin-kissing is sexy. What's that hairy bastard left his bag here for? Where is he? I want to stuff his beard up his nose. Why are you clutching the *Daily Express*?"

Jonty limped into the room and sat down in his wet academic gown. Sofia knew which questions to ignore.

"He's downstairs, frightening the spinsters. He's come for supper."

"Hard up again, is he? What's happened to the light?"

"What light?"

"On the landing."

"Oh, that! Twaggin ate it."

"Ate it!"

"Yes! He's just met a man in a pub who told him how to eat light bulbs and he wanted to try it."

"He can eat his own bloody light bulbs. Why doesn't he eat his bottles? He's got a big bagful of 'em. We'll have to get another," said Jonty, gloomily. "I'd better go down and collect him."

"I'll get some supper. Bread and cheese and beer suit you?"

"Lovely! Can you dry this off for me?"

He indicated his dripping gown. Sofia took it between thumb and finger into the kitchen. Jonty went downstairs.

"Twaggin," he called. "Where are you, you bastard?"

"Here," rumbled Twaggin.

Jonty went into the front room that overlooked the nude privet hedge. It was used by the Cough's as a junk room. Twaggin was sitting in the darkness on an old armchair in the bay, supping beer straight from the bottle, and waiting to pull faces at the spinsters who stopped to read the three-year old notice of the Brahms concert stuck on the window outside. Rivulets of raindrops ran down the glass, disappeared for a few moments behind the notice, and then, reappeared, glistening in the lamplight.

"There won't be many spinsters out tonight, Twaggin. It's raining."

"What did you kick my holdall for?" asked Twaggin.

In turn, Jonty ignored his question.

Twaggin liked to watch the expressions of the spinsters reflected in the glass of one of the windows as they tried to read the notice by the lamplight. When he got drunk enough, he invited them in for a beer, or sex, or a discussion on Brahms.

They never accepted.

"Sex with spinsters is no good, anyway," growled Twaggin. "They always want you to marry them. Although they like Brahms."

"They wouldn't if you asked them in in the daylight," said Jonty.

"What? Like Brahms?"

"No! Want you to marry 'em."

He detected the edge in Jonty's tenor.

"Why don't you sit down and have a beer?" Twaggin's baritone intoned, as if it were a piece of recitative in an opera.

"Thanks! Sorry I can't offer you another light bulb."

Twaggin also ignored this remark, pointedly, and picked up an already opened bottle from the floor beside his armchair and offered it to Jonty, who sat down on a packing case to drink it.

"Brahms they like."

"Beer?" asked Jonty.

"Not much. Sends them to sleep. Reinforces all their inhibitions. I can't stand spinsters asleep. Too quiet. Spinsters should be awake, jittery with frustration, yearning for what they're quite unfitted to enjoy. A contented spinster is a contradiction in terms. Look at Tom Eliot. 'Gin, inhibitions and prurience produced The Waste Land. Discuss'."

Jonty laughed.

"I'll steal that one for my new exam paper! Let's go upstairs."

"Why?" asked Twaggin. "I'm comfortable here."

"Sofia's pouring out the supper."

"I've been thinking about George Eliot," said Twaggin.

He seemed to think this a good enough excuse to remain where he was.

"What? As a spinster, or a novelist?"

"And about Minnie Nathcoutts."

"You'll make yourself ill, thinking about Minnie in any way at all."

She was the Nineteenth Century Novel expert from Newnham, a straight, rectangular woman, who looked like a well-used folio stuffed full of old documents.

"I realized today why she gives people the impression that she's eroding with time," growled Twaggin.

"Does she? I didn't know she gave me that impression."

"Her mind, I mean."

"Oh, that's different," said Jonty.

"Her mind – if that's the word – her mind is what's left," said Twaggin, pompously.

"I beg your pardon!"

"What's left of a promontory, that was once a country completely inhabited by George Eliot, now surrounded by the sea of the twentieth century. Hence, the impression of erosion. But the real question is – why did you kick my bag? And I ask that advisedly."

Jonty could see that Twaggin had been working on the geography of that pronouncement for some time, and he was damned proud of it and he didn't wish to give Jonty a chance to examine it, or modify it, or disagree with it. Hence, the red herring about his bag. Jonty decided to let him keep his pride intact.

"Because you left it in a bloody silly place," said Jonty.

"Oh!" said Twaggin.

He considered the explanation for a moment, seemed to find it quite satisfactory, and said: "Let's go up, then."

When they reached the sitting room, Sofia was sitting in the hearth on a cushion, warming her back and a half-eaten cheese roll she held in her hand on one shoulder. She was still reading a newspaper which she held in the other. Without looking up at them as they entered, she said:

"The food's on the table. Listen to this! There's a firm of solicitors in County Sligo called Argue & Fibbs. Would you believe it? And they're trying to trace somebody called the Reverend Sammy Lickorish, last heard of in Cambridge. You two don't know anybody called that, do you?"

"That?" said Twaggin vaguely.

He looked at Jonty and winked.

"Yes! Mr That. It's a common enough name, Twaggin," said Jonty.

No, fools!" said Sofia. "Lickorish."

"Not unless it's one of Newey's aliases," said Jonty.

Twaggin lowered himself onto a cushion on the other side of the hearth from Sofia. He rested the shoulders of his long trunk against the warm tile surrounds of the fireplace, and stretched his short-thighed legs out in front of him, sighing luxuriously.

Jonty sat down in front of the fire on a pouffe that reminded him strongly of one of the classics lecturers, on account of the way it had one shoulder distinctly lower than the other. He had named it Botts, in honour of its archetype. He placed Botts so that he was inclined towards the heat and began to admire the way Sofia's thighs and hips filled up her slacks as opposed to he way Twaggin's left a lot of room inside for other things. Was that something to do with her being female and him being male? Or rather to do with her being Sofia and him being Twaggin? It was a nice point.

On consideration, Jonty was inclined to think it had more to do with Twaggin being Twaggin and Sofia being Sofia than anything else. Twaggin, clean and perfumed as he always was, tended to half-empty his clothes rather badly most of the time, whereas Sofia, clean and perfumed as she mostly was, tended to fill hers out rather well all of the time.

'And most of it belongs to me,' he was thinking, when Sofia suddenly forsook smiling at her cheese roll and looked up as if to say something to him, but, on meeting his expression, asked, gooseberry-faced: "So, what are you smirking at, Jonty?"

"Smirking! That's an alluring sexy smile, that is!" he said.

Sofia sniffed, loudly and derisively. Under her breath, she murmured, "Simpering, then!" and folded her arms over her breasts.

'I only hope she knows they're mine,' thought Jonty.

"Sofia," growled Twaggin through a mouthful of cheese roll, beer and whiskers, "if you're going to start making sexual advances to Arnold, I'm going away. On the other hand, if you're going to start making sexual advances to me, he can go away. Which is it to be? Speak up if you want to save our relationship."

Sofia looked at Twaggin.

"Shouldn't it be the other way round?" she asked with a smile on her face.

Twaggin sat up very straight. He held his beer bottle against his heart and intoned: "Madam! My impulses are not in the least perverted."

"No! I didn't mean – . Oh, yes!"

She started to giggle.

'Stop it!' thought Jonty. 'Who's Gauleiter around here? *At ease!* Go back to reading your newspaper.'

Tomorrow he'd have a notice up in the kitchen, which announced in big black lettering:

GIGGLING AT TWAGGIN'S JOKES PROHIBITED ON ODD AND EVEN DATES. BY ORDER.

"Do you know why I was late tonight?" asked Twaggin.

He started waving his arms about and twitching his nose and catching his breath in short little gasps, and generally going into a sitting-down rainmaker's act. This kind of performance was usually a prelude to some kind of social outrage.

"No! Why were you late tonight, Mr Bones?"

Twaggin ignored this. Twaggin was as good as Jonty's father at ignoring things, but not as good as the Dean.

"I came round to see you about seven – "

"—That's funny!" said Sofia. "I haven't been out."

"—I wheeled my bike round the back, as usual, and put it in the Cough's shed, came upstairs and made myself a cup of that cocoa you keep lying about and read your newspaper."

"How extraordinary! I never heard – "

"—I must have been here about an hour when a tall thin personage with grey hair and a tweed skirt came in and told me to get out or she'd call the police!"

"Who on earth – ?"

"—What did you do?" interrupted Jonty.

"I invited her to sit down and have a cup of cocoa, and I'd tell her about the Brahms concert and discuss her chances of marriage."

"Was she a spinster?"

"Almost certainly. She went out threatening to turn her dog on me. I thought I'd better retire and come back later. Before I could get up and go, she returned with a minute Pomeranian on a string that just wouldn't shut up. I poured the remainder of my cocoa over it. But it seemed to like this and it lapped it all up. Then it nearly went crazy trying to lick it all off its ears, at which point, the grey personage got hold of a hefty-looking fry-pan. It was at that moment I began to entertain suspicions."

"You mean, apart from the one that she didn't want you there?" asked Jonty.

"Yes, that's it! I began to suspect that she might – have right on her side."

Jonty reflected that Twaggin had avoided the rhyme nicely.

"Whatever made you think that?"

"I suddenly perceived I was in the wrong house!"

"Oh, God!" moaned Sofia, weakly.

"So I retired as gracefully as I could, giving her a standing invitation if she felt any strong impulses for revenge, to come round to One Dust Road and do the same in your kitchen. I hope I did right?"

"Oh, quite!" said Jonty. "But it's rather different here. We don't have a Pomeranian. I'm not even sure we have a frying pan."

"Don't be ridiculous!" said Sofia.

"It's in exactly the same position as your house," pursued Twaggin. "In fact, it's exactly the same house. But it's in the next street along."

"Quite! Same difference exactly! But don't worry, Twaggin. Rain does that! It makes houses all look alike."

Sofia folded herself up, laughing helplessly.

"I thought – ha ha! – Arnold was the – ha ha! – only one who did things like that."

"I do hope I shall never have to go through such an experience again," Twaggin boomed, with heavy irony. "In order to calm my nerves, I wrote a short request to the Dean that he offer up some prayers next Sunday in Chapel for my Tripos results, and I'd subscribe a small but useful sum to his Church Fabric Fund. On a strict Guarantee-or-Refund basis, of course!"

"Of course."

Twaggin was giving out his Mersey Tunnel laugh, when there was a light tap at the sitting room door. It didn't open fully, but became slightly ajar, and then, quite suddenly, Soapy, Twaggin's current girl, had slipped through it into the room, like a post-card through a letter flap. Quick, quiet, now you see her, now you don't! It was Soapy's usual manner of going in and out of doors. Then, just as swiftly, loud as a spider in a bag of flour, she was sitting beside Sofia. Twaggin was still laughing.

"Hello," she whispered.

11

S ofia and Jonty smiled at her in greeting. She was wearing a black cat-suit. Her limbs were long and skinny and she folded them under her neatly. As she sat, she gave Jonty the impression of a craftsman folding up a carpenter's rule. Everything about her was in direct contrast to what was about Twaggin, who had just finished going through his Mersey Tunnel routine, and was now peering through an empty beer bottle like a telescope, pretending he couldn't see her. Soapy ignored him in return.

"Have some beer and cheese," said Jonty.

"No, thanks, really. I ate on my way, after work."

She had a little-girl voice, and she watched you for a prolonged time after she had answered, blinking her long-lashed eyes, like a cat when it is slightly peeved.

"How's the job, then?" asked Sofia.

"So-so! Tiring."

She worked in the centre of Cambridge as a waitress in a restaurant, near the Market Place, that sold dozens of kinds of soup out of long rows of huge steaming tureens, and kept live laying hens in banks of wire-framed cages, and displayed huge blown-up black-and-white studies of selected parts of the human body all over the walls.

Soapy, blinking, watched Twaggin trying to push his tongue into the neck of his bottle of Tolley beer.

"Have a Tolley, then, Soapy?" asked Jonty, slightly uncomfortable with the half-rhyme of the two words.

"All right! Thanks."

Jonty got off Botts, went to the table, took a dumpy of Tolley's best ale, opened it and gave it to her.

"Would you like a glass?"

"Please!"

Jonty wondered what had attracted them to each other: Twaggin, loud, active, filling up a lot of space untidily, hairy, flamboyant, with, on the surface, as much tenderness as a rugby boot; she, skinny, compact, reposeful, occupying space with skill and economy, unhairy, and, apparently, shy as a wren.

Twaggin was pretending his tongue had got stuck in the bottle. Everybody looked at him: Soapy, blinking; Sofia, proudly, the way mothers watch little boys, caught short, piddling in the gutters; Jonty, with absorption, hoping Twaggin's tongue really was stuck. But it wasn't. Twaggin pulled it out with a loud lascivious plop.

"I've decided," boomed Twaggin, "that this Tolley bottle is the precise shape of the Reverend Newy's mind. Only little things will go through the neck without getting stuck; unless they're quite formless, like beer, and will take up the shape of the bottle. You've probably noticed that all Newy's ideas are either tiny or liquid. Anything sizeable gets stuck half-in and half-out of his mouth, at the neck; otherwise they're quite formless and flow, while he's talking, in all directions at once. This obviously accounts for the breaks, hiatuses, knots and gaps in his homilies. What do you think, people?"

Twaggin looked up and peered through his thick lenses at nothing in particular. Once again, Jonty had the impression that a false nose and spectacles had been balanced on a mass of some little-known variety of lichen.

But, through the glass, Twaggin's eyes were very blue and very alive and very intelligent. Twaggin examined each of his three companions in turn. When his eyes reached Soapy, he said:

"Oh, hello, girlie! When did you arrive?"

Jonty interpreted this remark as some kind of elaborate objection to Soapy's way of going through doors. She looked at him amiably, smiling and blinking, her lips together, her rather large square chin held forward. She didn't speak; she watched him, blinking. She didn't feel in the least challenged by Twaggin. Jonty suddenly realized one of the qualities that had attracted him to her. She was just what he needed; she soothed him, like a pet cat, by being herself.

"Why are you called Soapy?" asked Sofia. "I've often wondered."

"It's a childhood nickname. My name's Sheena, really."

"Oh, that's a pretty name!"

Twaggin snorted into his bottle.

"My father used to call me Soapy because I was always so grubby and, apparently, I flatly refused to wash. Used to scream the house down when my mother scrubbed me."

"My father didn't call me anything. He wouldn't admit I was his," said Twaggin.

"My poor darling!" said Soapy. "What a shame!"

Sofia looked across at Jonty with an expression of triumph on her face, which puzzled him.

What kind of Sofia-logic was at work now?

Because Jonty didn't know what better to do, he decided to raise his eyebrows, try to look like George Robey, the music-hall comic, and waggle his head. Sofia turned away abruptly and spoke to Soapy.

"My father used to call me Foocumber!"

"I didn't know that!" said Jonty, in surprise.

"There's a lot of things YOU don't know!"

She tossed her head so that her breasts jiggled. Jonty watched Twaggin watching them.

What have I said now? Her needle's jumped round to 'stormy' all of a sudden. Have I studied Soapy's earlobes for a little too long? Did

I assess the width of her pelvis too openly? Did I peer at her crutch too obviously?

"Why did your father do that?" asked Soapy, looking at Sofia.

"Oh, I was mad about cucumber and that's what I called it!" she laughed with delight.

"She still is," said Jonty, "as long as it isn't curly. Positively Freudian."

"What's that supposed to mean?" asked Sofia, belligerently.

"How's the beer?" asked Twaggin, suddenly.

Twaggin got up and helped himself to another Tolley. When he came back, he sat down in his place, lifted his knees, stuck the dumpy between them, rested his chin on it and began staring at Sofia. Half the bottle had disappeared inside his beard. It was clear what he had in mind.

'Is he aware,' thought Jonty, 'that his pose emphasizes the length of his trunk, the shortness of his thighs, and the lustfulness of his thoughts? Or is it accidental? Or was it possible that he'd had his thighs shortened deliberately to heighten the continual parody of life that he aimed at? If so, he'd slipped up somewhere in his thinking, because thoughts like that don't go with thighs like his, nor do they go with me. He can stop watching my floozy and watch his own. Or else....'

Soapy was smiling at Twaggin fondly and blinking her cat-blink. Sofia looked mutinously at Jonty: it made her brown eyes lose their shortsightedness. Despite her aggressiveness, Jonty quite enjoyed the experience; it was so rare that she actually focussed on him.

Her lips were apart and there was a slight flush on her cheeks, which might have been due to the beer. She turned away from him and smiled radiantly at Twaggin. The effect was immediate. Twaggin put down his beer and stood up.

"I have never been in favour of the elaborate rituals developed between the sexes as a prelude to the act. I much prefer the thing itself."

Twaggin had put this out in the form of a general announcement over his public address system; but he followed it up with a special message to Sofia several decibels quieter.

"Sofia! I'm sure we see eye to eye in this matter?" He said, holding out his hand to her. Sofia stood up and took it.

"We can find out, can't we?" she asked, and smiled sweetly at Jonty. "After all, Arnold doesn't own me, does he?"

As they went out, Twaggin managed to trip over his holdall, which he had moved to a spot beside the door.

"He should be careful," said Jonty. "I might get up and throw all his beer bottles out of the window."

Soapy laughed and clasped her knees.

The savagery of Jonty's intentions towards Twaggin were, at the moment, so rampantly obscene that he didn't trust himself to formulate them.

'But who can blame Twaggin?' he mused desperately. 'He is at her mercy. Sofia has deliberately manoeuvred Twaggin into this as a retaliation for my recent victory in the We-Can't-Tell-Newey-We're-Married campaign. Whatever she says or does to the contrary, she WANTS me to own her. She WANTS me to throw Twaggin's bottles into Mrs Cough's front garden. She WANTS me to tell Twaggin the shortness of his thighs is offensive, the length of his trunk indecent, and that the two together are an example of the Theatre of the Absurd and that even Twaggin himself couldn't have invented them without outside assistance! She wants me to—'

At this point, Jonty had great difficulty in keeping the image of Twaggin out of his mind, strutting about naked and ducklike, in front of Mrs Cough's mirror, showing Sofia the length of his beard, and preparing to set Vesuvius smoking on Mrs Cough's bed.

He looked desperately across at Soapy squatting contentedly in front of the fire. She was basking in the warmth, oblivious, like a cat. As an immediate counter-offensive, why shouldn't he...? He made a sudden lunge at her across the tiles, knocking Botts over as he did so. The force of his attack caused Soapy to roll sideways still clasping her knees.

Then, he was lying half across her, his weight keeping her knees against her chest. He moved to one side and she started to unfold, obediently, pliably, silently, like a carpenter's rule. He clasped her to him and kissed her, forcibly.

Her lips were deliciously soft and sensual, quite unlike her body, and her body quite unlike Sofia's. Her chest was nearly flat, a boy's, with almost undetectable swellings, a couple of tiny buttons under the knitwear. He could feel the ridges of her ribs and the projections of her bones at her pelvis. The whole of her corrugated body was enclosed in the cat-suit.

'I'm an amorous launderer, mad with passion, fondling a washboard!'

Only her lips and the nice fresh-air smell of her skin, as if she'd been hung out with the washing for a while, made the experience acceptable.

'She's certainly learnt a lot about ablutions since she was a little girl, hasn't she?'

Feeling embarrassed, he sat up and said: "Sorry about that! I just couldn't help it!"

"Don't apologise. I liked it!"

"Good God! Did you?"

"Yes."

"Why? I just attacked you."

"It's flattering – being attacked."

"Women! I'll never understand women!"

He snorted. "I'll never understand ME!"

"Of course you will," she said soothingly.

"No, I won't! I keep FEELING things. I get angry with people when I don't expect to. I get jealous. One minute, I'm quiet and placid, like a cow, and the next, I want to start a punch-up. I even want to clobber inoffensive people like old Newey! I'm primitive," he said woefully.

"Everybody feels things," crooned Soapy.

"You can't expect me to believe that! You mean that Newey actually FEELS things? You mean—"

He stopped himself, disconsolately.

"See? I started doing it to you!"

"That's all right! I don't mind, dear."

"No, it isn't all right! You're gentle! You're forgiving!"

"It's all right. Really!"

"All right! If you say so, it's all right. Okay, okay! Look, then! What do you see in Twaggin?"

"Philip? Oh, a lot."

"What?"

"Well, he's very gentle for one thing."

"Who, Twaggin? He can't cross his legs without kicking something over on the other side of the room. I mean – look at that bag just now!"

"Yes, but that's clumsy, not harsh! He's not like that in his feelings, and – and the way – he touches you! You'd be surprised."

"I wouldn't, you might! Touch me? But Twaggin – like that!"

"Yes."

Soapy laughed and stood up. Jonty noticed that her legs were set wide apart on her pelvis and left a space at the crotch, inside her thighs. He wondered vaguely if he should try resting his hand between them, and calculated that he could do it with a bit to spare on each side. She saw him looking and smiled placidly.

"That's how he is," she said.

"Well, why does Twaggin keep acting like Twaggin? I don't mind it, I admit. But a lot of people do."

"I know. It's partly because – because – well, it sounds silly, but I can't say it any other way – because he's embarrassed about things."

"Embarrassed? Twaggin? Now, you've just gone off the edge!"

"No! It's true! He's embarrassed about – well – being a Jew, for one thing. And – "

"—What difference does that make?"

"None! But he thinks it does, and so – it does. If you see what I mean. And about having no father. And—"

"—But he's got a father!"

"—about the way he looks. And about – oh! a lot of things."

"You seem to know a lot about him!"

"Of course! I'm in love with him."

"With TWAGGIN?" yelled Jonty, incredulous.

Soapy nodded, smiling.

Jonty was struck by the incongruity of it all: Twaggin! Of all people, Twaggin, not only being loved by a woman, but being loved by Soapy – who sounded no more than twelve years old and looked no more than fifteen. And Twaggin! Every day, he tried more and more to look like Archbishop Makarios – as if he'd spent the best part of a long life in the priesthood of the Greek Orthodox Church. Being loved by Soapy, wise Soapy! Extraordinary!

"I didn't know!"

Jonty shook his head, bemused.

"And yet you don't mind him going off with Sofia – and me trying to...."

"No, silly! That's just fun! He doesn't mean any harm by it. Nor do you. Anyway, I trust him!"

"Trust him? Why? He's in bed with Sofia, now, this very minute! You call that nothing?"

"No! I don't. But a lot of people do."

"Well, I'm not one of them," said Jonty, belligerently.

"Nor am I!"

"Well, what on earth do – ?"

"—Oh, Sofia's all right! Stop worrying! I expect, if you went in, you'd find them lying chastely on the covers, discussing George Santayana, or somebody."

"You really think so?"

"Of course!"

She laughed.

"You're a funny boy, aren't you? Sofia's no fool! She's just trying to provoke you."

"Then she's bloody well succeeded!"

He glanced at her shyly

"You know, Soapy, I like you."

She made no reply, but gave a slight curtsy. Jonty got up from the floor where he'd been lying since his abortive leap and went across to where she stood, placed his arms on her shoulders and, remembering to do it gently, leaned towards her and kissed her full on the mouth.

"That's nice," she said, when he'd finished. "You're improving."

"Thanks!" said Jonty, removing his hands from her shoulders. "Soapy, I can't tell you how good it is to know that Twaggin likes a certain kind of spinster, at least!"

"Oh, what kind?"

"Your kind."

"But I'm not a spinster!"

"You're not? Are you…"

"Yes."

"Who to? Or, if you prefer it, to whom?"

"Twaggin!"

"TWAGGIN?"

"Mrs Philip Twaggin, at your service!"

"Oh, my God!"

Jonty began to laugh. He went on laughing. It was quite a time before he could speak.

"Let's have a drink on it!"

"Let's!" she cried, and smiled with such delight that her whole body lit up with the radiance of it.

12

Ever since Twaggin's seduction of Sofia – if that's what it was – Jonty had been sleeping in his rooms in College. If the Dean had known, it would have pleased him enormously, especially as it meant that today, Jonty would not be late for the supervision he had been given for nine o'clock. Now, he was hurrying to get his breakfast things put in order before Mrs Stickett arrived: he had absolutely no desire at this time in the morning to listen to one of her unpunctuated perorations on undergraduate trends in night attire, or the general uses that they put the extra-large breakfast cup to. Mrs Stickett's volubility at early nosh was even worse than Sofia's wordless immersion in the William Hickey column every baptismal morning of their lives.

It wasn't Twaggin's escapade that had maddened him. It was the flat refusal of Sofia to tell him what Twaggin had got up to in the bedroom, and how exactly he'd got up to it, that had tipped Jonty over the edge. Not knowing what had gone on or not gone on was just what Jonty couldn't bear. So apart from merely wrestling with the college bedclothes in the mornings, he was now also sleeping in them nights – although he had not relished the suspicious looks Mrs Stickett bestowed on him whenever she found that the bed was not only dishevelled but still warm.

Jonty had been dying to know if Soapy had been right about Sofia and Twaggin's behaviour, and to be assured that he had nothing to be jealous of.

"I hope you enjoyed the experience," he had said to Sofia after Soapy and Twaggin had gone home. "Did he take his glasses off, first?"

"You're so coarse!"

"What's it like sleeping with Archbisop Makarios?"

"What ARE you talking about?"

"If the way he has treated Mrs Cough's lavatory seat is anything to go by, you must be black and blue. It was anything but ecclesiastical."

"You're obscene!"

"I found it leaning against the wall looking absolutely beaten. When I put it back and sat on it, it split down the middle."

"And pornographic! I think you must have an anal fixation."

"That's without mentioning the tile in the front path. It's disappeared completely. Soapy says that the Archbishop is very gentle in bed. Is he?"

"Oh! So you talked about us, did you?"

"Whatever gave you that idea? She only mentioned it as a comparison to my own superior technique."

"If you think you're going to provoke me, you're wrong."

"Not only that, have you seen Mrs Cough's kitchen doorknob? He only went in once. Now it comes off in your hand. I've had to climb down Mrs Cough's drainpipe twice to get out. I shudder to think what damage he'd have done if he actually had to FORCE an entry. That is, IF he had to do that."

"I don' think you've got a shred of natural delicacy, have you, nor any concern for my feelings?"

"Suppose I want to make love to you – and bits start coming off in my hand?"

"You're not going to! You can start sleeping in College, instead. You think you own me, don't you?"

"Don't be silly! We're married! I could get a – "

"—Oh, no, we're not! You've told everybody we're not. So we're not!"

Her large myopic eyes were actually looking at him again, but, this time, as if she'd just won the Women's Singles at Wimbledon without bothering to put in her contact lenses: a beautiful fast blind return to the backhand. It had beaten him all the way. She may not have been Little Mo, but she wasn't going to be hustled, was she?

"Look! That's only a joke. You know that. Twaggin and Soapy – ?"

"—Not to me, it isn't! But actually being married to you is even less of a joke. What do you think I am?"

Jonty firmly resisted the temptation to amplify the answer to this question, although it happened to be one of those he'd examined many times in his mind before. Was she ever going to get over that little deceit? It was only an administrative convenience after all! It enabled them to go on receiving the bursary instalments without questions being asked, didn't it? Wasn't it worth it? If she did intend to get over it – when did she? But she was very tenacious; you could see that from the way she kept on painting tins of soup in face of the full knowledge that she had nothing new to say about them; and, moreover, at times when she had chores to perform. She wouldn't even take his advice and start doing portraits of the packet variety, instead!

"Sofia! Go on, TELL me! What did you and Twaggin – ?"

"If you don't shut up, I WILL tell you and then you'll want a divorce."

"I might have to sue for one, in any case! Wifely insubordination."

"Pig! I never promised that bit. Remember?"

There had been a number of exchanges like that one and they all came to the same conclusion: exile for an unspecified period to the doghouse on C Staircase in Old Court.

The dog finished tying his shoelaces and got up with a sigh. He looked round the room: it didn't make him want to wag his tail. Obviously, it hadn't been constructed as a studied insult; but why was that window so small, so high and so opaque and inserted at the end of that little alcove, if it wasn't meant to provoke anger? And why were the walls so thick and heat-resistant if you weren't EXPECTED to suffer from cold-sores, chilblains and bronchitis on the first official day of Summer?

Why hadn't they known about built-in obsolescence in those days? Why weren't the University Authorities aware that what might have been all right for a lot of mediaeval monks with tonsures, cowls and loads of dedication, simply wasn't all right for a lot of 'mod' students with incredible haircuts, fantastic shirts, footwear, and no dedication whatsoever? Who wanted to be a monk, mediaeval or otherwise? For that matter, who wanted to be an undergraduate – especially when you had to go and read ALOUD an essay on 'The History of the English Gun Dog' to a clergyman whose library was made up of books about rock-gardening and the life-cycle of deathwatch-beetles?

Surely there must be something better in life than life? And, if not, why not? Hey?

To relieve his feelings of frustration, Jonty decided to pin up his now-completed reply to Lady Owens about etiquette; so he made his way in a slightly improved frame of mind to the Screens. Luckily, no-one was about.

He scanned the notice boards for anything new. Apart from the usual polite exhortations and routine warnings about jackets, exeats, meals in hall, unorthodox footwear and the general official bleatings from the University Senate, the only new one seemed to have issued from a group of people calling themselves the Outposts Group, who, apparently, had a meeting-place deep in the Bible Belt, north of the River Cam. It was announcing a contest against a Witness Team from Writtle, without saying what it was they were contesting. A number of impolite possibilities presented themselves for inspection, but Jonty confined them to barracks immediately.

His previous letter to Lady Owens had miraculously survived without defacement. Even Lady Owens herself seemed to have missed it, or it would have been removed – as well as Rupert, the Buttery Manager, to whom it had been addressed. However, judging by the undercooked improbabilities HE served up with sauce, he must be half-blind, anyway. On Twaggin's advice, Jonty had been reading the 'Poetics' recently, and Aristotle's dictum drifted into his mind: 'Likely impossibilities are to be preferred to unconvincing improbabilities.' That needed modifying for a start:

ANYTHING was to be preferred to Rupert's inventions, whether probable or improbable, likely or unlikely. Still, the general drift of the aphorism was clear and made it plain that old Aristotle knew a good plate of porridge when he saw one. Yet, Rupert was the man Lady Owens had chosen to write to for advice on etiquette! Talk about impossibilities!...

Now, where was Lady Owens's original query? Ah, there it was! He read it through again to see that he had framed his reply properly:

Rupert, Manager College Buttery

Dear Sir,

Would you kindly solve an etiquette problem for me?

Are aubergine knives and forks socially acceptable for eating aubergines?

There seem to be two schools of thought on this.

(Signed) Lady Owens

The Master's Lodge.

Jonty, satisfied that he'd remembered it correctly, was just about to pin up his carefully typed reply, when two waiters on their way from Hall to the Buttery steps on the other side passed through the Screens, laughing and joking noisily, undoubtedly amused by the excesses of Mr H. Rupert's menus.

He waited until they had disappeared down the steps before pinning up his letter. He placed it as close to Lady Owens's missive as he could and stood back to admire his handiwork:

Dear Lady Owens,

You're not kidding! I know at least six schools of thought on it.

Historically, aubergine knives and forks were introduced to the nineteenth century dining table by Victorian coal merchants, as part of their new-found opulence. As no-one

107

outside a mine owner had ever heard of an aubergine at that time, still less eaten one, their questionable social acceptance is explicable. (In the best French circles, aubergines were eaten with the first and second fingers used as a scoop.) The non-U image has persisted until today.

Aubergine knives and forks are an unnecessary expense and a bother to service. Incorrectly serviced, they have, on occasions, been known to explode – which is expensive in butlers. Nor does it improve one's wallpaper. If one doesn't own butlers or wallpaper, what in the name of William Morris is one worrying about?

If, my Lady, you know personally of someone who would make me a present of a set of Burke's, Charles & Long's steam-driven aubergine knives and forks, I'd be glad to use them for special occasions at High Table – when, for example, the Master had invited a Tory politician for dinner whom he didn't like.

Hoping I have been helpful, yours respectfully,

(Signed) Rupert of Hentzau Buttery Manager.

Jonty had just finished relishing the letter once again, when he heard the noisy waiters coming back from the Buttery, so he bent down to tie up his shoelaces. One of the waiters held himself in a posture reminiscent of the Dean. A weight of gloom descended on Jonty's bowed shoulders at the prospect of the forthcoming supervision.

'Maybe this is how a Holy Martyr would feel, forced to take part in a Witches' Sabbath? Or a witch forced to attend Holy Mass?'

He rose and walked dolefully towards the Reverend's chambers. Another Bad Day at Black Rock!

A little along the dim passage, he reached the door; knocking on the Dean's wood and went in. The Dean was out. Jonty's jubilation was irreligiously strong; but not quite rugged enough to overcome the joylessness of Newey's study, and, transomed as it was, the sanctum was even more joyless when Newey wasn't there.

So Jonty left. But the Dean would undoubtedly be back. Oh, dear me, yes! If only to one of those single-cylinder un-decoked pipes of his. Perhaps a walk round the Thomas Grey rockery to fill in the time? No. That wouldn't do at all. He might be out there, coaxing an alpine berberis into unwonted succulence and luxury. It wouldn't do to disturb intimate operations of that sort, would it? Towards New Court, then.

Quite a long way down the corridor from Newey's rooms, although still 'next door', on the New Court side, was the Dean's bathroom, the door of which sported the unashamed declaration – TOILET. This had appeared during re-decorations in Vacations while the Dean was on holiday. One of the painters, under the impression he was doing the Dean a favour, had painted the word on the door in large black unmissable letters. Unfortunately, the label frequently persuaded chance visitors to the College to stand outside, kicking and swearing at it when it wouldn't open. Ever since, the Dean had been forced to keep the door locked. It was a cause of great embarrassment to his Christian charity and he often forgot to lock it. He had forgotten today.

Jonty looked up and down the corridor to make sure he was unobserved, then went in.

13

He had been in only once before. The Dean, fuming, had invited him into the bathroom upon first discovering what had happened, just after Jonty had come up as a freshman, and they had spent the entire supervision there, while the Dean fulminated against the moron with the paintbrush who had defaced his door. He had propped the oak portal open with the bath mat, sat upon the edge of the tub, invited Jonty to seat himself on the john, and kept pointing out the lettering, along with a lot of other things, such as:

"It's quite impossible, you see Jonty, that the College would have authorised the painting of a euphemism as vulgar as 'toilet' on my bathroom door. In any case, I never asked for any kind of announcement. It's most disturbing!"

The mock gentility of the term 'toilet' offended the Dean deeply.

On the grounds of linguistic accuracy alone, he had to reject the misnomer. If you added social propriety to the matter, the unacceptability was total. He went as far as to specify the term 'lavatory' as superior in every way.

When Jonty, feeling he should contribute to the supervision in some manner, had put forward a claim for the term 'water closet', the Dean had conceded that, properly truncated, the intitals 'WC' were acceptable, IF, (and it was a big IF) anyone would be foolish enough to request a label to be painted on his own private facility!

"You do see that, don't you, Jonty?"

"Oh, yes, sir!"

Jonty had wondered at the time how he would have reacted to the common undergraduate term of 'BOG' in big black letters, but hadn't pursued the idea.

The supervision, which had seemed endless, terminated with the Dean's oft-repeated re-assertion that he would have the offending label removed "Double quick!"

Of course, he never had; and as time elapsed, it had become clear to Jonty that not only had the Dean NOT minded wasting his entire supervision analysing the linguistic and social solecisms of the term 'toilet', but now, after a couple of years, Newey had jockeyed himself into a mode of blindness so that he wasn't even aware it was on the door, anymore. It was just another piece of information the Dean refused to ingest; and Jonty had not been able to erase the feeling that it was some kind of Newey-type insult to be added to the Jonty-type injury of refusing to acknowledge his marriage. Now, he had a chance to redress the balance.

A wasted supervision was a wasted supervision in anybody's money!

In the bathroom, with the door closed, Jonty was in the middle of an operation using one of the Dean's Valet razor blades. He heard footsteps outside in the corridor and quickly changed to washing his hands in the basin and studying the persuasive innocence of his expression in the mirror. His Wyatt Earp moustaches didn't help the act very much, but that he could do nothing about.

The footsteps passed by; he dried his hands and went back to his scratching.

"The moron with the paintbrush" had put another label over the Dean's hot water tap. Jonty was trying to rectify that at the moment. He stepped back to admire the effects of his handiwork. It now said HOT DRINKING WATER in place of NOT DRINKING WATER.

Ah, that would have to do! Even though there was a kind of shadow around the aitch, the general message came across well enough.

The next stage would be trickier. It would have to be carried out in the open corridor. However, if anyone passed by, he could lean on the bathroom door, read his essay and pretend he was waiting for the Dean.

In the event, no one came and, after some careful and delicate scraping, Jonty had managed to remove a painted letter without damaging the white enamelled surface underneath it. The door now said, boldly: TO LET.

Surely the Dean couldn't object to that? If he did, it would have to be on the grounds of inaccuracy rather than poor taste.

The third stage in the operation would have to be postponed until Jonty could get hold of a brush, a lettering set and some black paint, and until he could count on the corridor remaining vacant for an appreciable time; maybe an evening or a weekend? Jonty was going to provide the Dean with a message he would be able to object to on a number of heads, as yet unused: TO LET would be followed by KEYZ NEXT DOR.

At the very least, it would have the consequence, for a while, of taking the Dean's mind off his private ambitions and the deathwatch beetles in the roof beams of Ely Cathedral. Besides, the enormity of the spelling errors might even reconcile him to the late twentieth century usage of the word 'toilet' to designate a toilet.

You never could tell – and that was, for Jonty, the fascination of the experiment.

Jonty felt high. He was one of the lucky ones: he didn't need grass, or LSD, or a hookah to send him on a trip. He just needed the opposition of a Treblitt or a Jarrold or a Newey. After a victorious skirmish with one of them, he experienced a sense of elation that was as good as a shot in the arm.

At present, he was hooked on the stuff the Reverend F. E. Newey happened to be peddling: he felt like a mainliner, and no mistake! As Jonty made his way back to the joylessness of the Dean's chambers, he chuckled at his own fantasies.

The Dean had still not arrived. Could he be away much longer? Probably not.

He would find it easy to forget Jonty's supervision, but difficult to forget he needed tobacco, and it was highly unlikely that he would have remembered to carry all his smoking materials and implements on his person when he went out.

Jonty sat down to wait. He began to wonder what it would feel like to be the Reverend Newey, full of recollections but, at the same time, psychotically absent-minded: pursued by forgotten appointments and cravings for tobacco, jostled by hope for the re-establishment of the English squirearchy and nostalgia for his childhood, haunted by beetles and yearnings for preferment, beset by undergraduates for losing letters and muffing arrangements, obsessed by rock plants and hating words like toilet.

Jonty would have loved to know exactly what it was like in Newey's mind. As it was, he'd have to make do with knowing what it was like in his chambers, instead.

Jonty looked about him. He was surrounded by heavy, liver-coloured Tudor furniture, with the genuine and the mock jostling for dominance; there were several old-fashioned globes of the world, on stands; hundreds of books about geology, theology, entomology and the growing of xerophytes were ranged on shelves against the walls; various-sized pots of spiky succulents, of a nauseating eau-de-nil colour, were scattered higgledy-piggledy about the room; armoury and armorial relics of the Boer War advanced and retreated wherever there was space; pictures that had been painted mainly in shades of brown, placed in brown frames, and then varnished all over in brown lacquer, appeared anywhere the brown walls would hold them; finally, piles of undergraduate essays had been put wherever places could be found for them, which was virtually wall-to-wall.

The general sense of religious oppression in the room was heightened by the spiritual struggle going on, unremittingly, between the decorated ceiling and the undecorated floor as they attempted to close the gap which was kept steadfastly in place by the short secular stone uprights of the heavily leaded windows.

No radio was visible in the room, and it was doubtful if the Reverend Newey had ever seen a telly, let alone watched one. What a world! Jonty was glad he was only there on a visit.

However, Jonty was trying seriously to fathom the Reverend Newey.

Having made up his mind that the Dean WAS people, he felt the need to extend his experience more strenuously; Jonty's imagination being actively kinaesthetic, he stood up, there and then, in the Dean's study, and tried to BE the Dean.

First, he scooped out his chest, or rather, scooped it in, spoon-shaped; second, thrust his head and neck forward, turtle-fashion; third, folded his arms behind his back, yokel-wise; then, with a slight but permanent bend, stiffened his knee-joints, pensioner-wise; finally, while attempting to immobilize his toes, he stumped about on rigid, pushed-out feet, Newey- manner, muttering to himself with different forms of emphasis:

"I *AM* the Bishop of Ely. I am the *BISHOP* of Ely. *I* am the Bishop of ELY… I am *THE* Bishop of Ely—"

In the middle of Jonty's rehearsal, the Dean burst in, his neck thrust out characteristically over his dog collar. He stopped in mid-flight, putting his feet down like snowshoes, and glared at Jonty. He was brandishing a trowel and a little pot full of soil.

"Your posture is terrible, Jonty!" he shot at him. "Stand up, stand up for Jesus, as the hymn says! You'll injure your pulmonary system if you – if you – ! What's the matter? Are you all right, Jonty?"

Jonty was trying so hard not to laugh that it made him cough. He collapsed into a chair.

"I'm all right, sir! I was just thinking of something funny."

"You weren't talking to yourself just now, were you, Jonty?"

"Oh! Singing."

The Dean looked at him, oddly, quizzically. Jonty thought for a moment that he was going to suggest a group of his favourite hymns to go with the one he'd already mentioned, but he said nothing and put down the trowel and the pot on a pile of essays, while he patted himself all over. He began looking vaguely about the room.

"Mmmm! Wonder what I did with my pipe?"

"Here it is, sir!"

"No, not that one, Jonty! Needs a good scrape."

Jonty looked at the briar in his hand, knobbly with carbon.

"Oh! Does it?" he said disingenuously, returning it to its place on the arm of his chair.

"There! That one behind you, on the shelf. That's it! Thanks."

As Jonty handed it across to the Dean, he noted that its clotted interior was half-full of charred tobacco, otherwise it was indistinguishable from the empty, soot-choked bowl of the briar he had just offered him. As the Dean took the chosen pipe from his hand, checked its tobacco level, and found some matches in a pocket, he said:

"This one's a Petersen, you know!"

He looked at the S-shaped implement on the Dean's palm.

"Oh, is it?"

Jonty had no idea what he was talking about. Did the Dean perhaps give pet names to his pipes the way Jonty gave them to his bikes?

He sucked the Petersen vigorously into life. His expression was ferocious throughout the operation, and Jonty fancied Newey would have to watch himself in later life, or he could turn into a tobacco-reeking prelate who would frighten little girls in the dark.

"What was it you wanted, Jonty?" he asked suddenly, out of the cloud of smoke.

Without waiting for an answer, the Dean walked across to the tar-coloured mantelpiece and placed the little pot of soil that he had entered with, on top of it. The damp trowel he put in an out-tray, half-full of letters, on his desk. He began opening and shutting its drawers, synchronising his words with his actions:

"Pouch – pouch! – Where – did – I – put – that – pouch?"

The Dean seemed to have forgotten Jonty entirely; or was he putting on a performance especially for Jonty's benefit, to convince him he was in need of care and attention, or even hospitalization? No; the odds were against that.

Was he seeking sympathy? Possibly.

It was lucky he hadn't got more than eight drawers: the sentence was just long enough. Was he going through an elaborate subterfuge to distract Jonty from seeing that he'd suddenly remembered about the supervision? More likely.

Jonty wondered whether he shouldn't set up a counter-performance, to show he wasn't taken in. What about jumping up onto Newey's liver-coloured table with the thick knotted legs (who did they remind him of?), and giving a highly suggestive rendition of 'I wonder, by my troth, what thou and I did till we loved', based on Redshins's commentaries, and accompanied by a set of gestures that G. Wilson Knight would have applauded wholeheartedly?

Could he use a routine like that as a lead-in to the supervision he was supposed to have with Newey?

By the time Jonty had considered and rejected these alternatives, and mildly murmured, "Supervision – the Gun Dog era!" Newey had discovered his pouch in one of his pockets, had sat down, and was leaning back in a huge chair with padded side-wings, filling its seat and his Petersen pipe with ginger shreds of tobacco.

"What was that, Jonty?" he asked.

Jonty reminded himself to scrutinise the architecture of Newey's listening equipment, as soon as the chance presented itself. It seemed that his ears were largely dysfunctional and only there as some kind of eccentric decoration. Apart from finding out if he actually washed them from time to time, he might discover a relationship between Newey's character traits and their mass, contour and size, that would actually help him to understand the man. It was a last resort, but you never knew, did you?

"I've brought my essay on Dog Imagery in English Poetry."

"Oh?"

Newey looked at Jonty as he might regard a fast-talking salesman who was trying to sell him a job-lot of hymn books, ancient and modern, at the vestry door. Having thrown out the suggested topic while he was looking through a seed catalogue in the last few minutes of his previous supervision, he could have forgotten that he'd ever made it. He obviously found the topic quite absurd.

"I've entitled it 'The Influence of Canine Imagery in English Poetry."

"Oh?"

'Oh, so he's started oh-ing me again, has he?'

Under his breath, Jonty intoned: 'I oh! Thou ohest! He ohs! We—.'

Before he could decline the whole verb, Newey said, tartly: "It's a somewhat improbable topic, isn't it, Jonty? Most unpromising, in fact. Whatever led you to choose that?"

"Well, as a matter of fact – you did, sir!"

"I?"

Newey was quite incredulous. He busied himself with another pipe-lighting ceremony to regain his composure. Suitably enveloped in smoke, he felt more secure.

"You gave it to me at our last supervision. Don't you remember, sir?"

"Are you quite sure, Jonty?"

'Oh, J.H.C,' wailed Jonty in his mind. 'Here we go with another of those You-say-you-told-me-you-have-married? dialogues.'

"Shall I read it to you, sir?"

"Well, I suppose there can't be much harm in that, can there?"

Chuckling at the brilliance of his own repartee, Newey showed Jonty a line-up of rounded ochre-tinged teeth, similar to the lichen-covered tombstones Thomas Grey had probably studied for his poem on a Country Churchyard.

After staring at them for a while, and trying to find a better metaphor, Jonty gave it up and began to read his essay aloud.

He had scarcely managed to reach his second paragraph before the Reverend Newey remembered an unattended-to administrative matter that simply couldn't wait. He made a brief apology and promised to return soon.

Abruptly, he left.

Jonty began to wonder if, in the meantime, there were any further alterations he could make to Newey's bathroom, but concluded that, for the moment, there weren't.

After a while, he put his feet up on the Dean's coffee-table and tried to make up his mind what colour it was. He settled finally on that of a pint of Black & Tan, without the froth. Exactly.

After fifteen minutes, the Dean had not returned.

"I do believe the sly old sod only came back for his baccy and pipe!"

Jonty was moved to sit out the rest of the supervision just where he was. He closed his eyes, serenely, and waited.

14

As he dozed, Jonty's mind went back almost three years, to the time he was a freshman. Twaggin had arrived clean-shaven, then. For a year before coming up, he had worked as a cab driver in his father's London taxi business and had been forbidden to go hirsute. Twaggin had said his father told him:

"Bald faces are better for trade! At least, your face bald is!"

Twaggin hadn't agreed with his father at all. He said he had replied:

"Not my face! It wouldn't encourage any trade if I shaved it down to the first layer of skin!"

Jonty was inclined to agree with him. Twaggin had thus, later, preferred to embarrass people with his exhibition of facial hair rather than embarrass them without it. But, even hairless, he had devised ways and means of making himself conspicuous. For example, his antics, in the first supervision Jonty had had with Newey, before Twaggin and he had become firm friends. He recalled it vividly. During his time in Cambridge, Jonty had had a number of different supervisors and many supervisions, but that first one had a very good chance of turning out to be the worst one; or the best, according to the way you saw it.

Twaggin had asked him: "What about taking a punt out this afternoon?"

It was before the event of the Sherry Party where he had corrected the Homer Specialist's view of Homer and he had not yet covered his face in hair. Jonty had found the request surprising, as they were both still trying to weigh each other up and were still in the early rounds. But he had answered civilly enough.

"Afraid I can't."

"Why not?"

"I've got a supervision with the Reverend F.E. Newey."

"Excuse me?"

Unusually for him, Jonty had not picked up the question mark in Twaggin's voice and had replied:

"Of course!"

But Twaggin had stayed, patiently studying Jonty's face through lenses as thick as the bottoms of milk bottles – and, at that time, the same shape and much cleaner.

Why didn't Twaggin go? Hadn't he given a signal that he must go somewhere urgently? What did he mean by standing about? Had he, perhaps, inadvertently offended Twaggin by mentioning Newey's name?

Then the penny dropped. He realized that Twaggin meant: "I'm sorry! I don't understand."

'But why,' Jonty thought, 'can't he say, "I beg your pardon," like everybody else?'

Jonty replied: "Surely, you have supervisions?"

"Not in Natural Sciences. We do Lab Work instead. Controlled experiments."

It was only in Part Two of the Tripos that Twaggin had changed over to literary studies.

"What's a supervision FOR?" asked Twaggin.

"A good question. I'll tell you when I know. He wants me to read him an essay."

"Aloud?"

"Aloud!"

"Can't he read, then?"

"Don't know!"

Jonty would have had to admit that, after three years, if he'd been closely questioned on the subject, he still wasn't sure whether Newey could, in any real sense, read; or what his supervisions were actually for.

He had, however, discovered that Newey used the students' reading aloud of their essays as a device for letting him concentrate on his own favourite obsessions. Indeed, the entire shape of Newey's supervisions was dictated by his desire to have nothing to do with undergraduates' essays, least of all in an audible form, but had most to do with his desire to satisfy more of Newey's desires.

Of course, he was only partially successful in this. Even Newey at his Reverend Newey-est couldn't prevent certain undergraduates getting something out of them, if only by accident. But Jonty had learned that he wasn't, by any examinable method, one of the lucky few.

"I'll come with you," said Twaggin.

"What?"

It was Jonty's turn to misuse an interrogative.

"Experimentally. Find out what gives."

"Newey might object."

"It won't hurt him, will it? Why should he?"

"It might."

"Excuse me?"

"Oh, all right!"

So it was settled. At two o'clock Jonty had gone along to the Reverend F.E. Newey's rooms, as arranged. Being a first supervision for Jonty, the Dean had obviously made an effort to be present, and on time.

When Jonty knocked, his smoky voice had said "Come in," promptly enough. He was actually sitting at his desk, in his wing-back chair, accompanied by his pipe, and seemed to be making an effort to look at an essay, which was placed on the blotter before him. A chair with a rattan seat stood in front of the desk, specially positioned for the initial interview.

"Ah!" said the Dean. "Arnold Jonty, I believe. Please sit down."

He indicated the empty chair. Jonty remained standing for a moment, while he asked his question. He was nervous and felt safer vertical.

"My full name, sir, is Arnold Jonathan Godley. Would it be all right, sir, if a friend of mine sits in on my supervision? He's doing Natural Sciences, and he's rather keen to see what goes on in – in – a – "

"—What is your friend's name, may I ask?"

"Twaggin."

"Is he a member of the College, Jonty? Twaggin. Don't recall any member of that –   Mmmm! Yes, I suppose it will be all right, Jonty. However, should – "

There came a loud rapping on the door. The Dean stopped mid-sentence. Before he could make clear what constriction he was placing on him, Jonty chose that moment to sit down in the chair.

"Come in," said the Dean.

Twaggin came in. Jonty immediately wished he hadn't.

Twaggin was wearing white shorts, a khaki bush-jacket, long white socks, and a battered Cecil Rhodes pith-helmet that looked as if it had been used for a variety of dubious purposes by persons other than Cecil Rhodes.

Twaggin said nothing. He simply stood a little behind and a little to one side of Jonty's chair.

Jonty said nothing. The Dean said nothing, but turned away from the sight very quickly and stared out of his mullioned windows at the Thomas Grey rockery. His lips were moving quite soundlessly.

Was it the pith-helmet, on top of the socks and the bush-jacket that was too much for him? Or was it Twaggin himself? Was the Dean swearing or praying?

Twaggin was grinning vacuously, straight at the Dean's profile. It was all quite silent, like a tableau of the absurd. Jonty wanted to roll under Newey's desk, clamp his knees under his chin, stuff his essay in his mouth, his fingers in his ears, himself into a knothole in one of Newey's drawers, and just laugh – silently – for ever.

After a time, Jonty managed to say:

"This, sir, is my friend, Twaggin."

The Dean did not reply, or even turn his head. He kept staring out of the window. He seemed to have stopped swearing, or praying. He seemed almost to have stopped breathing. He stayed quite still, as if he could not trust himself to move without shattering into tiny pieces. He did not even try to reach for his pipe. He was the same colour as the light that came through one of the stained glass windows of his Wren chapel.

Jonty felt helpless and sat still and watched him, compassionately.

No such paralysis afflicted Twaggin. He strutted, short-legged, round the Dean's desk and stationed himself behind his chair, near to a wooden model of an elaborate oriental church that was positioned on a sideboard. He stood rigidly to attention, his middle fingers straight as pencils, exactly in line with the imaginary seams of his imaginary trousers. He had a black bootlace coming from one breast-pocket of his bush-jacket to one corner of his mouth. He was sucking the end of it.

The Dean carefully prevented himself from squinting out of the corner of an eye to see what Twaggin was up to. He went on staring at his rockery. He said nothing.

Twaggin said nothing; he just sucked his bootlace.

Jonty's mind raced through a number of alternatives. Get up and run? Apologise? Hide under the desk? Frogmarch Twaggin into the corridor?

But discretion got the upper hand and Jonty decided to begin reading his essay aloud. It would, at least, break the suffocating silence.

"The question of whether Milton is on God's side, or on Satan's, in the great epic poem of 'Paradise Lost'…," he began, abruptly.

He read much too quickly, not even allowing the little meaning that was in his commentary to emerge – skipping the punctuation, muffing the quotations, and reaching the halfway mark in record time. Only then, did Newey's eyes even begin to blink.

Twaggin was still standing rigidly to attention, sucking his bootlace.

A big shuddering sigh broke from Newey's lips. He slowly turned his gaze away from the window, and began to fill his pipe from the pouch that had fallen, nerveless, into his lap. He kept on sighing until he had filled it with as much tobacco as it would hold – a convincing sign that he was not yet in control. Then, using his customary half-box of matches – a robust variety, like Scoutmasters' staves – he lit his pipe.

The ritual reassured him. He began to relax a little. He slanted slowly into his wing-back chair, looking vaguely in Jonty's direction. A lot of smoke escaped from his mouth to accompany the puzzled expression that escaped from his eyes. Jonty read desperately on.

"...With 'Literature & Dogma', Matthew Arnold established a tradition that many literary critics have since followed, the most notable of whom is..."

A loud rasping noise hit the air as the Dean began to clear his anxiety-dried throat.

It startled Jonty. A technicolour image flashed onto his inward eye of an old larangytical rooster, atop an enormous heap of dung, trying to chastise the dawn.

Obviously, he'd been reading too much Chaucer: he'd better cut it down!

"Would you like some tea, Jonty?" croaked the Dean.

A liking for tea was one of the few things that Jonty had in common with Newey so he accepted with alacrity, although their respective concepts of what tea WAS differed widely.

Newey got up thankfully and went through a heavy oak door on one side of the room.

Twaggin still stood to attention, fastened to his pocket with the bootlace, staring straight ahead of him. Jonty looked at him, but Twaggin refused to meet his eyes.

There came the hollow sound of water drumming into a vessel. Newey bustled back without so much as a glance at Twaggin or Jonty and put the kettle onto a gas ring in the tiled hearth.

His bustle was perceptibly slower than his normal pace, which was far from fast. He moved as if he had suddenly grown years older. To reach his desk again, Newey had to make a large half-circle round Twaggin. He did it with ease, without appearing to know he was there. He sat down, picked up his pipe and nodded to Jonty to continue.

Jonty began to recite again. As he read, he was assailed by a growing sense of unreality.

Matthew Arnold's ideas, and even his long sheeplike face, had seemed to have a certain aliveness and aptness when he was writing the assignment; but, now, confronted by Twaggin's bootlace, his Grock-like thighs and Newey's consternation, their vivacity had drooped, their relevance faded, and Arnold's image retreated into the sheepfold. Jonty felt that he was making a lot of noises that were strung together on a syntactical principle he couldn't discover.

Later, this experience had helped him to understand how Kingmaker had felt in the terror of the lecture with the epileptic student in the audience.

But why, now, was Newey forcing him to go on reading? Why didn't the silly Reverend Bugger object, and tell them to get the hell out of his study and not to come back again unless they wanted to be reprimanded, exorcised, fined, sent down and despised? Why didn't he insist, at the top of his voice if necessary, on drinking his religious tea and eating his sacrificial crumpets in God's peace and quiet, on his own? What was the matter with him?

Someone knocked on the door behind Jonty: thankfully, he stopped reading. Someone entered without the Dean's bidding. It was a College servant carrying a tray of tea things and a plate of Newey's favourite scorched muffins.

Jonty groaned inwardly and stared reproachfully at the script in his hand.

"Thank you, Mrs Stickett."

Jonty looked up, startled by the name. As she toddled past him to his right, her eyes were fixed with concentration on the milk jug.

'Another of her duties?'

Mrs Stickett, still concentrating on not spilling one drop of milk from the over-full jug, put the tea tray down very gingerly on the beer-coloured coffee-table to the Dean's left. As she straightened, her eye fell on the rigid and immobile Twaggin, still at attention outside the wooden Oriental church, behind the Dean's chair.

Jonty expected a heavy malodorous dollop of the usual admixture of gossip, chastisement, exhortation, and structureless English to fall out. But all she said was:

"My dear Gawd!"

And left quickly, shutting the door in a way that would have done credit to a silk worm in gym pumps.

Twaggin hadn't moved.

The kettle on the gas-ring began heartily puffing out large clouds of steam and rattling its lid. The Dean continued to sit in his chair, also puffing, deep in thought. Jonty looked over at the kettle. Condensed rivulets of steam began to run down the dark tiles of the fireplace.

"Shall I turn off the gas for you?" asked Jonty.

"Oh, yes! If you'd be so kind. Oh, no! Thank you. I have to make the tea," replied the Dean.

He put down his pipe, got up from his wing-back chair, made again his half-circle round Twaggin, reached the fireplace, turned off the gas, picked up the kettle, shuffled round, made his semi-circle once more, and walked past his chair and across to the tea-things.

He lifted the lid and poured boiling water into the teapot, after first pouring a little into the sugar bowl and onto the tray cloth.

After that, he put the kettle on the floor beside the table, looked at it, made up his mind that it wouldn't do, picked it up again, and went through his entire procedure for avoiding Twaggin to stand the kettle once again on the gas-ring, deciding once more it wouldn't do, removing it and placing it on the tiles of the hearth.

Then, he stood helplessly looking at it, as if he had forgotten what came next. So far, he had managed without acknowledging Twaggin once.

It was a remarkable faculty Newey had, mused Jonty, for ignoring what he found unpleasant.

"Shall we sit down, Jonty, and have some tea?" asked the Dean, still standing in the hearth and indicating the sofa that stood behind the coffee-table.

"Thank you," said Jonty, and went over and sat down.

The Dean, after repeating, yet again, the figure of his masquerade, joined him on the sofa.

The Dean reached tentatively for the pot, hesitated, and let his hand drop again to his knee. His fingers twitched, spasmodically.

At last, his politeness finally getting the better of his consternation, he managed to stammer:

"Er – would your – er – friend, Twaggin – er – like some tea, I wonder?"

Jonty looked across at Twaggin who still stood rigidly to attention, eyes directly ahead. He seemed to be sweating slightly under his Cecil Rhodes hat, but that was all.

"No, I don't think so. Thank you," said Jonty.

"Oh, very well."

A slight tone of annoyance, as if he couldn't find his hymn book, was in evidence.

The Reverend Newey was recovering.

When they had drunk, in total silence, one brimming cup of Newey's religious tea, and eaten one of the brown flexible discs that passed as muffins – heavily buttered, thank heavens! – it was officially time for Jonty to go.

Jonty stood up, firmly resolving to call Twaggin away; but, at the last minute, after the Dean had given him a strained, reproachful look and another essay topic, his resolution had wavered. The realistic time for him to go had been when Twaggin had arrived; and Jonty had sincerely regretted, on many occasions since, not having gone and taken Twaggin with him, if only for the Reverend Newey's sake.

But, all he had said, pusillanimously, was:

"Thank you for the tea, sir!"

And, free for a fortnight, aware of his cowardice, he had made his escape with relief, while Twaggin had been left there, still standing to attention.

Yes, it was one of his most ignominious actions, wasn't it?

Sometime, in some way, he would have to make it up to the Dean.

Jonty stretched with discomfort at the recollection of the episode, yawned, reflected that it had probably been the least enjoyable of Newey's supervisions, and one of the least informative, but one of the most revealing, nevertheless.

It was certainly more revealing than the one he was supposed to be at right now, with Newey out, conscientiously making another of his administrative ballsups.

Jonty took his feet off the beer-coloured coffee-table, in disgust.

Should he fill in the time by emptying the soil out of one of Newey's pot plants and into Newey's tobacco pouch? It was there where he'd left it in his haste to escape.

Or, should he rather leave an anonymous letter, conspicuously placed on his kettle, warning Newey to stop molesting Mrs Stickett in the College linen cupboards? Next time the Dean took tea, he wouldn't be able to miss it.

Or, maybe he should attempt a more ambitious impersonation of the Reverend Newey pretending to be the Bishop of Ely? No, he'd need a mirror for that.

Or, perhaps, go along to Newey's bathroom, remove the toilet-roll, and come back and brighten up the gloom of Newey's study with white paper streamers?

The trouble was, Newey would guess who the culprit was, and that wouldn't do: subversion by ridicule was far more effective when it remained anonymous. So, instead of simply going away, Jonty had just chosen to finish browsing through the *Woman's World* he had hidden under his gown, when the Dean unexpectedly returned.

"Good heavens, Jonty! What's that you're reading? I hope it isn't—"

"—I like reading the knitting patterns, sir!"

"What?"

"Linguistically, they're very interesting. There's practically no use made of deictics. This seems to be a characteristic of—"

"—What was that, Jonty?"

"Deictics, sir! They're—"

" —I see." said the Dean. "You're not referring to those tracts put out by rabid Non-Conformist Groups, are you, Jonty?"

"Not at all, sir."

Jonty thought he'd better try another tack.

"And there's an element of the detective story in them, too!"

"Really, Jonty? That's most interesting!"

Jonty felt very relieved at having thought of a sentence with the term 'detective story' in it; the Dean seemed to understand that.

"Yes," he went on, "you follow all the clues, and then you get the unravelling bit at the end."

"Unravelling! Ha, ha! Yes, that's very good, Jonty."

"Thank you, sir."

Well, if Newey thought THAT was good, there wasn't much he could do about it, was there? But it just showed the kind of puerile –

"—I hardly think there's much point in continuing our supervision now, is there, Jonty?" said the Dean quickly, looking at his watch. "There are only a few minutes left, I see – "

'Continuing!' thought Jonty. 'Continuing our WHAT? I don't remember starting it!'

"I suppose not! What shall I do with this?" asked Jonty, holding up his essay.

"What's that, Jonty?"

"My essay, sir."

"Well, you could... No! On second thoughts, leave it here, and I'll – I'll – . Don't write me another, Jonty, will you? It's too near finals. I think you would be better advised using the time to – er – to—"

'—Start mass-producing an inflatable, unsinkable, waterproof Tripos paper for everybody you haven't taught to swim?' thought Jonty.

"—er – REVISE. Mmmm? Yes, well, good luck for the examinations, Jonty."

"I shall need every bit I can scrape together."

"Oh, I wouldn't say that, Jonty!"

'You would if you'd had the Reverend Newey for YOUR Supervisor throughout the year!'

"I'm not a good examinee, sir!"

"Well, I did my best to frame the kind of questions that would help my students, Jonty. And I had a hand in three of the papers, you know?" he said, proudly.

"Oh, really, sir? Which were those?"

"I think those were the Tragedy paper, one; the Shakespeare, two; and – oh, yes!—the English Moralists paper," replied the Dean, counting them off on his fingers.

"I shall look specially at those papers, sir!"

Then Jonty muttered under his breath:

'Because if you've worked a question into the Tragedy paper on the life-cycle of the Deathwatch Beetle; and another on rock plant diseases in the English Fens into the Shakespeare paper; and one on University Administration into the English Moralists, I'm going to get a bloody starred first!'

"That's the spirit! That's the spirit! Well, goodbye, Jonty, goodbye! Now, where did I leave my pipe?"

Jonty left his final supervision on a characteristic note. He rather regretted that when the Dean came to fill his pipe, after a farewell like that, it wasn't going to be from a pouch bulging with John Innes Compound No 1 instead of his Balkan Sobranie Flake. Experience of the Reverend Newey's supervisions, in his first year, had been the reason that Jonty had soon started going to Kingmaker's tutorials, as well. When Jonty had explained this to Twaggin, not long after the pith-helmet episode, Twaggin had replied:

"I don't blame you! You know, he never even invited me to sit down?"

"You stood to attention all the time! He didn't know you wanted to sit down?"

"No! I mean, yes!"

"Well, then!"

"That isn't the point! He didn't even address any remarks to me!" said Twaggin, indignantly.

"Can you wonder? He was afraid."

"What of?"

"You, of course!"

"ME?"

"Don't shout! Yes, you. You didn't fit in with his reading. You should have made more effort to look like somebody out of 'Plain Tales from the Hills' and then you'd have been acknowledged. He likes Kipling. Instead of that, you looked more like a cross between Groucho Marx and Sanders of the River."

"I didn't know he liked Kipling," growled Twaggin.

"What happened after I'd gone?" asked Jonty.

"He just went on with his tea and muffins."

"What did YOU do?"

"Kept him under observation!"

"What for?"

"Well, I AM doing Natural Sciences, aren't I? I wanted to see how an organism of that kind reacts to stress. It was a controlled experiment. I didn't actually ENJOY it, you know. It wasn't funny, standing in that heat, listening to you jawing, me impersonating Groucho Marx!"

"You can say that again! How do you think I felt – trying to squeeze some juice out of John Milton?"

"But when he got up to refill his teapot, I engaged him in conversation on that Boer War muzzle-loader he's got hanging on the wall. We parted on the best of terms, you know!... But he's easily knocked off balance, isn't he?"

Jonty looked at Twaggin with astonishment. It was the first of a succession of such moments.

15

Spring had come to Cambridge. Jonty had seen two certain signs: Snarfia along the College Backs had started flagging him down with their bright yellow gestures as he passed by; and; it was becoming more difficult to get to the bar counters in the pubs.

Jonty had heeded both signs – first, by stopping occasionally to look at the yellow trumpets of the Snarfia nodding at him in the wind, and, second, by revising his Spring Term boozing programme. He hadn't yet filled in all the details of his alcoholic itinerary but the general directions were already mapped out: more and stronger beer, bigger and better tankards, oftener and longer at it.

In the meantime, he was testing a few details at The Locomotive, one of the additional taverns he had placed on his timetable. His companion was an 'urban, squat' Cambridge man – one of the clan who, according to Rupert Brooke, 'rarely smile' and are 'packed with guile'.

However, Jonty had found him surprisingly open and voluble, ready to talk about anything from sex to safety pins, without a hint of guile. True, he was urban, and he was squat; and the flat cap he wore on his large head made him look squatter than need be; and, so far, he hadn't smiled.

But, maybe he would, given time?

Nonetheless, he was companionable; he liked talking and, at the moment, he was holding forth on one of Jonty's favourite topics.

"Noo-ooh!" Flatcap was saying, "You don't HAVE to have froth on beer. And you can't get drunk on froth. I like the BEER. You get drunk on beer. You can't get drunk on froth, can you, mate?"

"Oh, I don't know!" said Jonty. "You probably could if you drank enough of it. Anyway, it tickles my moustache. I like that!"

"Stands to reason you can't get drunk on froth. Or they'd sell froth instead o' beer, wouldn't they, mate? Just think of it. A pint of froth-bitter, please! Sounds daft, dunnit? You'd start floating before you got drunk, wouldn't you? NOOO! I like getting drunk on liquid, not bleedin' bubbles! I like beer. It makes you FEEL drunk."

"As well as actually MAKING you drunk?" asked Jonty.

"How'd you mean, mate?"

"What you're forgetting is – beer doesn't have froth if it's not good. Beer without froth is flat beer, isn't it?"

"Ah, well, I s'pose that's right enough," admitted Flatcap, grudgingly. "But that's different, o'course! I ain't talking about flat beer, I'm talking about GOOD beer – without froth! See?"

"Yes, I see," answered Jonty, resignedly.

Flatcap probably had quite a lot in common with the Reverend Newey, if the truth were known.

"There's a difference."

"Yes."

"Must be! Stands to reason."

"Well, drink up and have another," said Jonty.

"Ah! Don't mind if I do. Ta!" said Flatcap, quickly handing Jonty his tankard.

Jonty got up and walked to the bar with the two empty glasses.

He had just finished his third pint and he was wondering how many more he would have to drink before he felt like facing Sir Leslie and Lady Owens at their Scrabble Party. He was tempted not to go to the Owenses at all, but to stay in The Locomotive drinking beer and talking with Flatcap, who not only liked DRINKING it, but admired beer in and for itself. Flatcap also liked talking with people who liked drinking-and-talking; but he particularly liked people who liked talking about beer-drinking as a self-contained topic.

What made it all so much a welcome change from the nit-picking gab of scholars like Redshins, and the hag-ridden prattle of anti-savants like Newey, was that Flatcap seemed to know something about brewing beer as well as just drinking it.

It was very pleasant indeed.

Jonty concentrated on holding steady the two frothy pints of best Greene-and-King's in front of him, and went back to Flatcap sitting at the iron table with the lion-pawed feet. He made a point of placing the tankards carefully into the wet circles they had already made on the tabletop, just to satisfy himself that he could do it.

"I did it!" said Jonty, sitting down, contentedly.

"So you did, mate," said Flatcap, grasping the handle of the tankard. "Ta and cheers!"

He took a small pull of the beer, which left a half-ellipse of froth round his mouth. He wiped it on his sleeve, and went on with his discourse.

"You see, mate, it's the Specific Gravity that counts in beer. That's what it's called – Specific Gravity. See?"

"Yes," said Jonty. "Cheers!"

"That's the part that makes you drunk. Cheers!"

Jonty noticed for the first time that the man's face was ginger, as well as the large cap he was wearing.

This time, Flatcap took a very large pull of the amber beer. He simply put the glass to his mouth, tilted back his head, and kept perfectly still: a study in tones of cinnamon? There were no signs of movement, no bobbings of his Adam's Apple, Crehanstyle.

But when he took the glass mug away, there was a thick frothy gingerish moustache on his upper lip, and very little beer in the tankard.

'That's funny!' thought Jonty. 'I didn't see any signs of swallowing going on. Maybe he's got special pouches in his mouth?'

"That's what a heavy beer is, see? It's got a lot of gravity in it. Gravity is heavy."

'He must have swallowed it or it would have swilled out onto his muffler while he was talking, wouldn't it?' thought Jonty.

"They don't put much gravity in a light beer, see?" said Flatcap.

"This beer's got a good head of froth on it," said Jonty.

"Gets up your nose," said Flatcap.

"But it's good beer," said Jonty.

"Better without the froth," said Flatcap, wiping it away with his hand at last.

"I can feel it making me drunk," said Jonty.

"Well, have another," said Flatcap, emptying his glass, "Finish the job off."

"I'm not sure I should," said Jonty, "I'm going to a party very soon."

"What, a drinking party? 'Cos if – "

" –No! A Scrabble Party."

"What's that?

"Scrabble's a game where you make up words."

"Make up words! You can't have a party making up words!" said Flatcap in great disgust.

"Sir Leslie Owens can!"

"Not with the kind o' words I know he wouldn't. Not after a good few pints o' this stuff! Where'd you write 'em?"

"We use cubes of wood. With letters on."

"Hey, better have another pint! If you've gotter start lugging pieces o' wood about,—"

"—No, they're small. About the size of sugar cubes."

"With letters on?"

"Yes."

"Believe in making life difficult, don't he? Sounds a funny sort o' game. Not like drinking."

"No! You place the cubes on a board – in squares."

"I'd rather put mugs on tables. Have another! It'll oil the wheels."

"All right! You've talked me into it."

"That is, if you want 'em oiled."

"Oh, I do, I do!"

"Well, drink it down then, mate!"

By the time Jonty had finished it off, his fourth pint, his wheels were beginning to run freely – like an electric clock on a soaring voltage.

Flatcap went to the bar, rolled up his sleeves, and returned carrying the two pints of frothy beer, which he put down skilfully onto the lion-footed table.

Jonty looked at his forearms: they bulged like Mrs Cough's thighs, but with ginger hairs on. Jonty glanced at his own arms: two peeled willow wands. The fifth pint looked too heavy for them.

'All that specific gravity,' thought Jonty, hazily.

"Cheers!" said Flatcap. "What if you can't spell?"

"Cheers!" replied Jonty. "You'd lose!"

"I can spell swear words."

"Not allowed!"

"Why not?"

"Rules! Only words in the O.E.D. allowed," said Jonty.

"Whassat?" asked Flatcap.

"Oxford English Dictionary."

"Ain't there a Cambridge English Dictionary? Of swearing?"

"Not yet," said Jonty.

"Should be! I know a professor from Jesus. I never seen him reading that dictionary. I did his garden for 'im. Used to swear something vile! Swore at 'is wife in the house, then come into the garden and swear at the flowers. O' course, the flowers took no bleedin' notice, but his wife used to cry something awful!"

"What was his name?"

"Little chap – with a big face, looked as if it'd been in a punch-up. Lived out of town a bit, Grantchester, I think."

"Oh?"

"Yes. Drat the chap! What was he called? Summat like – Thinshanks. No, there was a 'red' in it, somewhere."

"You don't mean Redshins, do you?" asked Jonty, in surprise.

"Ah, that's it! Redshins. Real filthy at times, he was!"

"That sounds like Redshins, all right! Just like his lectures on Donne, and just like him to take his sewer of a mind into the pastoral coyness of Grantchester. Just!"

"The wife's a nice little body! Runs a tea garden in – "

"—You mean that place in the village that does Oldee Worldee scones and teas?"

"Ah, that's her! That's what made him swear, see! Said it warn't right, the wife of a professor doing things like that – selling tea! Went right up and down the bleedin' alphabet, I can tell you!"

"He isn't a professor!"

"Well, whatever he is, then!"

'And that doesn't leave much room for doubt, either,' mused Jonty. 'So that nice little body is his wife, hey? And Redshins is the unwilling owner of a tearoom near Byron's Pool, is he? Well, well! What would Byron think about that? For that matter, what would John Donne think about it?'

Jonty felt strongly that it was the kind of information he should be able to make use of. Twaggin would certainly be intrigued by it.

"Listen!" said Jonty. "I don't know your name."

"It's Horatio, mate! But I keep it a secret."

"I know what you mean? I COULD call you Horace, instead?"

"That's bleedin' worse! Call me Smitty! Everybody does. What's yours?"

"I won't have another, thanks."

"Nobody's bleedin' offering! I mean, your name."

"Oh! Call me Jonty."

"Nearly as bad as Horatio, ain't it?"

"My first name's worse!"

"Join the club, mate! Okay! Jonty it is, then."

"I'll have to be going, Smitty. Got to get ready for this party."

"Ready? How'd you get ready for a Scrabble Party? Finish your beer!"

"Got to put a dark suit on. Can't go like this," said Jonty, looking at his rolled-up shirtsleeves and his greasy jeans.

"You must be jokin'! To make words up in? Go on – finish your beer."

"And a tie, and a clean shirt."

"I can lend you a few juicy words, if you like! But first, you finish your beer."

"Oh, yes! Shoes! I forget the shoes!"

"That's not all, you bleedin' forgot! So far, you got no trousers on! AND you forgot your booze. Now, about these words – "

"—It's okay. Really! I've got some juicy specimens of my own. Got to rush. Don't get drunk, Smitty!"

"I always get drunk. Cheers, mate!"

Jonty got up and walked a little unsteadily towards the solid swing-doors of The Locomotive. When he reached them, he turned about to wave a sociable goodbye to Smitty, but Smitty had already finished his own tankard and was now hidden by the upturned bottom of Jonty's half-finished one.

Jonty had never before met anyone who could drink as fast as Smitty. He was more proficient, even, than Jonty Senior; he was somebody to admire.

If, instead of the rag-tag-and-bobtail accomplishments Newey had collected, and that he tried, unsuccessfully, to palm off on his students – if, instead, he had gathered around him some know-how of Smitty's kind, he would have been twice the man he is. In Jonty's present hazy condition, he felt this most fiercely.

Jonty left Smitty hidden behind his beer mug and went through the swing-doors into the street.

Well, Rupert Brooke had been right about one thing – Cambridge men didn't smile, not as much as a quiver of the lips; but there was absolutely nothing wrong with Smitty's *esprit,* was there?

16

I t was only a shortish walk to the flat.

As he walked, Jonty realized that the four and a half pints of Greene-and-King's best bitter had heightened his sense of resentment towards the Reverend Newey.

He hadn't yet got over the way in which the Dean, so light-heartedly, had dismissed, just a couple of days ago, a whole term of absentee, near-absentee, and plain-bloody-useless supervisions. Throughout, Newey seemed to have been under the impression that the University Senate had chosen leaflets on Sexual Reproduction in beetles, Sangster's last year's Seed Catalogues, and some old issues of The Anglican Church Magazine, as set books for the English Tripos this year.

Ah, well!

At the very least, there must be a letter to Newey's Bishop in it, somewhere – a topic worth giving time to. Furthermore, Jonty was surprised to discover that Smitty's company had marginally increased his sense of ill-being at the prospect of the Owens's Scrabble party. Perhaps that was just the mood to play it in?

'I'll make up words that even Lady Owens will find embarrassing,' he resolved.

When Jonty reached the flat, he found Sofia wondering whether or not she should wear her quilted skirt to play Scrabble in.

"It's not suitable," said Jonty.

"Why not? And don't breathe so hard. 'Specially on me."

"We're not going to a Garden Party on the lower slopes of the Himalayas, are we?"

"You read that in Jack Tanner's Revolutionist's Handbook, didn't you?" Sofia scathingly retorted. "I've gone off Shaw."

"Remember! – Leslie Owens can't help being Sir Leslie."

"And I can't help being me! He might LIKE my skirt."

"And Mrs Owens keeps trying to be Lady Owens."

"Surely, she can't object to fashionable dress, can she?"

"All right, go as you bloody well like! I'll wear jeans and sweat-shirt, and be me."

"That's not the same thing at all! Anyway, you made me go to the trouble of hiring that suit for you."

"Where?"

"There!" said Sofia, pointing her finger.

Jonty looked mournfully at the dark attire, full of discretion, lying on the bed, and then looked mournfully at the bed under it, which showed, in its unmade state, an utter lack of discretion.

The contrast was depressing. It had seen too much of Mrs Cough and it would never recover its *savoir-faire,* no matter who or what lay on it in the future.

"Yes, and I wish I hadn't."

"Why? It's a nice enough suit," said Sofia.

"I tried it on. It made me feel like the President of the Association of Chartered Morticians," groaned Jonty.

"It's appropriate, then! You sound like him."

"All right! You wear your Indian quilt and I'll go as a Yak."

"No, I've changed my mind," said Sofia.

"You've what your what?" asked Jonty.

"Beer makes you so pugnacious and rude! More than usual! Do you know that? I'm going to wear my black chiffon dress, with a gold scarf, and a white pearl brooch."

"That thing with the neckline down to the navel and the waist hitched-up under the armpits?"

"Yes. Don't you like it?"

"Oh, I love it! But Sir Leslie won't be able to keep his protuberant eyes off your protuberant whatsits. It'll make him think of words like – "

"—I don't need examples!"

Jonty watched her stepping into her briefs: left leg first, then, sit a while on the bed, musing; the thick dark triangle of her pubic hair drew his eyes; at last, she lifted her right foot, paused a moment, stepped through, stood up, and pulled them over her hips. Oh God! It was moments like these that weakened him.

Who cared about the way she dis-brewed his tea, un-kept his house, impulsively invited Twaggin to sleep in their bath, furred up the marmalade, and painted endless portraits of tins of soup, when she put on her panties like this?

Jonty went across to where she stood beside the bed and smoothed her naked loins in long vertical strokes with the tips of his fingers. He waited for his libido to wake up, yawn, and come strolling out of its lair. But it didn't. It slunk about inside, growling.

He just wished he hadn't drunk so much beer, and spent such a long time drinking it – on top of which, he now had to go and exhaust life's forces at the Owenses, building up words, when there were so many better things to build up and to exhaust life's forces on. Damnation!

"Don't!" she said emphatically.

She walked away from him and began to get into her dress

So they still weren't married, eh? She had been just the same all day yesterday. Two MORE days of celibacy to be added to the five days' sentence up C Staircase already served!

To Jonty, it felt like a deprivation of Trappist proportions.

"But I'm not a bloody Trappist!" he blurted out.

"I know you're not," said Sofia, in surprise. "Who said you were?"

Arrested in her making-up, she looked at his reflection in the mirror.

"I'd rather go barefoot, with no jockstrap under my cassock, and fast through Lent, than have this carry-on."

"What ARE you raving about? I thought you'd crack, one day!"

"You've turned me into a twenty three year old stud bull with a stomach – or rather, four stomachs – rotating like spin-dryers. You can't keep me off my concentrates like this! The vibration will shake me to pieces."

"You haven't apologised for what you said about – "

"—What did I say about –?"

"—Twaggin and I. Me. I wouldn't repeat it."

"I would!"

"There! You see? No consideration for my feelings."

"What about MY feelings? You're not the only one who's read 'The Lysistrata', you know," said Jonty.

Then, worried about his pronunciation, he started experimenting with the stresses:

"LySlStrata. LysisTRAta. LYsistrata."

Sofia had now finished her toilet. She took a final look at herself in the mirror, turning before it like a mannequin, and walked to the bedroom door.

"Come on! Finish putting your suit on. We shall be late, at this rate."

"Late. Rate," muttered Jonty.

"What?"

"I do wish people wouldn't rhyme things. Even the beer's wearing off," moaned Jonty. "I don't mind people rhyming things if I've had enough beer. I can even read John Betjeman, then."

"Come on!" she said.

"I'm coming! Maybe you'd prefer my flies open?" he asked indignantly, still fastening up his trousers.

They walked in silence across Parker's Pieces to the main road. The orange sodium street lamps shone through the leaves of the lime trees, changing them to a strange colour which Jonty could not find words for.

"I don't think morticians are the same shape as me!" he said, to break the silence, jiggling his shoulders. "It's tight under the arms and the gonads."

Sofia did not reply. Jonty glanced at her. She was looking straight ahead. Her silhouette was clear against the lights.

'They aren't the same shape as you, either!' he thought. 'Not unless there are women undertakers. Taker-unders. Takers-under. I think I'd prefer a woman to take me under. And then take me over. Right bloody now! Death and buggeration to the Owenses!'

Near Addington Hospital they were hailed by a man who was trying to put something in a parking meter; but they didn't stop.

"Got any change?" he shouted. "It needs a sixpence—English money."

Jonty automatically put his hands in the pockets of his borrowed suit before he remembered.

"Not a bean," he shouted back.

"A new penny will do! They're nearly the same size."

"What – as beans?" shouted Jonty.

The man turned away and continued with his agitated attempts to push something into the parking meter.

Jonty could hear him audibly muttering to himself: "Bastard thing! Appointment's at seven. Metri-bloody-cation, my arse!"

There wasn't far to go now. They were just passing the Wren Chapel of his College: through the Porter's Lodge gates, into Old Court, under the arch of the brick wall into the Thomas Grey garden, and – Oh, hell! Jonty had forgotten that there was no access to the Master's Lodge from this end.

They would have to walk right round to the short gravel drive at the front of the house.

"Sorry!" said Jonty. "I don't have a key to this gate! I forgot you couldn't climb the wall in that dress."

She sniffed disdainfully, and walked off quickly in front of him. She was still in a miff.

The Master's Lodge was surrounded by a very large garden which was itself surrounded by a very wall-like wall. Jonty knew that it was high and the garden planted with many tree-like, shrub-like and flower-like berberis, which, at this hour, stood as an assortment of shadows surrounded by shadow, like liquorice sweeties in a box.

Over the wall was the Court that held the rockery, the succulents and the frustrated ambitions of Neweyland, which were – dozens of windows ablaze with light and in defiance of the Dean's residential policies – being relentlessly irradiated.

But within the Master's garden wall, obscurity held its sway – except for a weak, globular, white lamp on a long curved metal arm above the square stone doorway.

Was it symbolic of the Owenses' marriage? Jonty wondered.

A misshapen circle of light fell onto a flagstone in front of the doorway and climbed lopsidedly up the steps of a small porch into the vestibule.

Sofia walked up the steps and knocked on the vestibule door.

"You know what's needed here, don't you?" asked Jonty loudly.

"What?"

"A pair of huge china pomeranians whose eyes light up when you press their—"

"—Shut up! Leave your vulgarity outside for tonight."

"Me! Vulgar? I was only going to say – when you press their RSPCA money-boxes! Lady Owens is fond of pets, you know, as well as antiques. Sir Leslie was a bargain. Pure pedigree!"

The door was opened by a young servant girl wearing a white lace cap, apron and a dark blue middy. She smiled at them. An elderly kitten, with sparse short fur, a scraggy neck and ears that were too long, purred against her shapely ankle, stringy tale up, stubbled back convex, displaying its breeding.

As they entered, Jonty pinched the girl's cheek.

"Fancy! A real tweeny!" he said.

"It's not!" the girl said, surprised. "It's a Cornish Rex!"

"What is?" asked Sofia, taking off her cape.

"The kitty! He said it was a—"

"—Oh, I see! I'm not sure I like it. Looks unnatural! Why do they call it that?"

"Dunno!" said the girl.

"That's its name!" said Jonty, bending down to stroke the kitten so that he could covertly study the girl's legs, while Sofia prettied herself up in front of a full-length hall mirror. Under his hand, the kitten was arching its back even higher, leaning heavily against the tweeny's ankles and looking at Jonty sideways.

"I can now see quite clearly," said Jonty "that it's actually a cross between a Cornish Pasty and Rex Harrison. Hence, its name. Of course, the breeder should have called it a Pasty Harrison; more appropriate. But he didn't think of that!"

While he had been petting the kitten and talking, Jonty had carefully summed-up the girl's legs. They were nice, very nice. He let his eyes rise as far as the calves at the skirt's hem, then, baulked, looked up at her.

She was smiling down at him, as if she knew a thing or two. He stood up and gazed into her eyes.

"Later!" he said, gently, "Later! I don't like to be rushed!"

The girl did not reply, but looked levelly back with an expression that revealed nothing.

Sofia had turned abruptly away from her mirror at his words and was now staring purposefully at him with tightly compressed lips.

'That's one in the eye for the Lysistrata!' thought Jonty.

The tweeny beckoned them to follow her down the stubby hallway to a heavy oaken door with square panels.

How was it that they managed to look squarer than most of the other square panels he had seen? Had four and half pints of Greene and King's best affected his eyesight? Was sexual deprivation taking its toll?

The tweeny's hand was on the doorknob.

'Now for it!' he thought, and took a big breath.

17

Jonty's first impression was that they'd stepped into a long low brown shoebox, full of people.

The room smelt of leather, Sir Leslie's cheroots, Sir Leslie's sherry and Sir Leslie. Before he had time to look about him and find out who was there, a tall, rather pretty woman, in an Oriental-type dress, approached them. She had very white prognathous teeth. She also smelled of Sir Leslie's deodorant.

"So glad you could come, Arnold!" said Lady Owens.

At variance with University custom and as a counterpoise to Sir Leslie's habit of calling undergraduates "Er – er – er ," she made a point of addressing them by their Christian names.

"I don't believe we've met?" said Lady Owens, smiling at Sofia.

Before introducing them, Jonty paused minimally to correct his initial impression: the scent he thought had belonged to Sir Leslie clearly hadn't. Near at hand, it was patent that Lady Owens favoured a peculiarly masculine brand of talcum powder. Or had she run out just before the party and borrowed some of her husband's?

"Lady Owens, Sofia. Sofia, Lady Owens."

"How do you do?"

"How do you do? What a lovely dress, my dear!"

Lady Owens took Sofia by an elbow and propelled her gently towards one of the several little groups of people standing about the room between the small square tables, each of which held a folded blue board, pencils, pads, and a plastic sandwich bag of Scrabble cubes.

Squarely, before one of the groups in a corner of the room, stood Sir Leslie, broad as he was long, bow-tied, suited, decantered, like a problem you couldn't see your way round. As he poured, he enunciated his clichés, very loudly and clearly.

And wasn't that Bristlebrush Toeless, the Professor of Psychology, in that group near the window?

From yet another group, Twaggin spotted Jonty standing in the doorway, and waved at him with his sherry glass, so that his near neighbour, a fair-haired youth, jumped backwards in alarm, brushing furiously at his lapels. Twaggin turned and gave the youth a quick flash of his beard in apology, who ignored him.

Jonty waved back and began counting the guests – twenty – and himself made twenty one – and, oh yes! the Owenses – twenty four in all.

That meant six simultaneous bloody games!

He could only hope to find his way into a group that was congenial. Where was Sofia? Ah, there! Lady Owens was introducing her to a group with – Oh, God! – Redshins in it. Per chance, Sofia's dress would prove fatal to him and he'd collapse in the middle of putting together a twenty-four-point word?

In addition, there were three undergraduates he knew vaguely and a girl in red he didn't know at all but would attempt to know as soon as possible. To one side of him, Jonty caught some more of Sir Leslie's bleatings:

"Yes! But you must look at the logistics of the thing. The way I see it is—"

Jonty closed his ears and groaned. Even if it hadn't been common knowledge that he was President of the Cherry Hinton Verse Speaking

148

Group, it was impossible to miss the fact that Sir Leslie believed in Speech Training as one of the humane and liberal arts necessary to modern civilization. Certainly, without it, Sir Leslie would have been a lesser man. Now that he'd got as far as "logistics", it wouldn't be long before he found opportunities for baahing out his beautifully modulated renditions of phrases such as: "In this day and age…" and "The drive towards de-escalation…" and "It's in the pipeline…" and "If you can't stand the heat of the cooking, get out of the kitchen." Et Cetera.

Perhaps he should just try to be sociable and ask Sir Leslie if he'd ever tried a rendering of "The Boy Stood on the Burning Deck" (obscene version)? Jonty was trying to make up his mind about this, when Lady Owens returned.

"You know everybody, of course, Arnold?"

She was propelling him towards Sofia's group: that might provide a chance in the course of the evening for spiking Redshins' guns, or whatever it was he happened to expose. And Jonty was willing to offer favourable odds on what THAT would be.

"Well, everyone but—," said Jonty, indicating the girl he had noticed a short while before.

"I'm so sorry! Lena, Arnold. Arnold, Lena."

"Hallo!"

"Hallo!"

She gave Jonty a nice smile, who was very glad to accept it. He smiled broadly at her in return. She wore a red velvet evening dress, with a black scarf. The dress fitted her beautifully. Sofia watched Jonty regarding the key locations with approval.

Before anyone was embarrassed, he managed to take his eyes away from Lena to greet the other members of the group, but purposely left a nod of acknowledgment to Redshins until last, who looked bleakly back at Jonty from a point some miles behind his pale blue eyes.

Jonty was struck again at how scrawny his body was and how big and ugly his head was, which, upon first seeing him, had conveyed to Jonty with great force the idea that Redshins's composition hadn't been properly thought out. The bits were there all right, but they didn't seem to be in the right proportions and relations to each other. Even if

149

you took his face alone, you could see it was just a rough prototype, a mock-up for an improved model – a Redshins Mark II, or whatever.

Redshins moved his icy blue eyes away from Jonty and settled them on Jonty's wife, and they nearly crossed themselves trying to squeeze into her cleavage. Redshins was running true to form: Jonty wondered where HIS wife was. He hadn't spotted her yet. Perhaps he'd left her at home in Grantchester, baking Oldee Worldee scones?

Suddenly, one of the undergraduates called Brown, who considered himself to be an earnest disciple of Kingmaker's, re-attached himself to Redshins, who was clearly irritated by the move. Brown said, fervently:

"To get back to Mrs Beeton's Cookery Book: surely, you can find the religious sanction for the Philosophical Radicals in Mrs Beeton, can't you?"

Redshins's demeanour cooled a few more degrees, and he responded, arcticly: "Well, I suppose we HAVE Mrs Beeton! But I don't read her, you know."

Then, with a little more warmth, he muttered: "I wonder what happened to MR Beeton?"

Brown did not answer the question, and Jonty was halfway through his own reply when someone put an empty sherry glass into his hand.

"I think he took a job as second cook, somewhere – " (the sherry glass appeared), " – when all the grace went out of his wife's puddings."

Redshins laughed aloud. Brown stared at Jonty as if he'd just been invited to pop into Sir Leslie's berberis bushes with him. Jonty shrugged and smiled. Brown did not return the smile, but looked with perplexity across at Sofia, who was blithely talking to another of the group.

Redshins took the opportunity of letting his eyes rework the vee-shape from Sofia's pectorals down to her navel and up to her pectorals again.

'Funny!' thought Jonty, 'his mind doesn't seem to be situated so far behind his eyes, this time.'

Brown was still gazing at Sofia with perplexity: HIS mind was clearly at a bench mark of *naiveté* well before the letter 'vee' in his sexual alphabet, so his chances against Redshins in the Scrabble competition were almost nil.

'He probably gets stuck at the letter "I",' thought Jonty.

He was just about to ease himself away from the Brown-Redshins nexus and insinuate himself into a conversation with Lena, when Sir Leslie surged in and began to pour sherry into Jonty's glass from his decanter.

"Oh, thank you, sir!" said Jonty, in surprise.

"Hello! It's – Er – Er – , isn't it? Glad you could come."

Quite un-embarrassed, secure in the knowledge that what and whom he knew were sufficient unto the day thereof, Sir Leslie turned to Lena, and said: "A little more, my dear? That's right. Let me introduce you to – Er – Er—"

'—our Twenty-Four-Hour-a-Day Air Freshener!' thought Jonty, sipping his sherry.

Sir Leslie, pouring, inclined himself over Lena's glass.

Jonty was presented with the top of his bald pate and its two bright thick silver hairs brushed straight back, one each side, along its centre.

Jonty straightened his back, firmed his shoulders, and craftily measured himself against Sir Leslie. Vertically, they were about the same height. Horizontally, Sir Leslie was a good deal taller.

He finished his pouring and went away, enunciating beautifully, holding his decanter out in front of him at shoulder level: a voluble balloon on a stick. Jonty turned towards Lena and tested out his opening gambit:

"Tell me, Lena, should Birmingham become a centre of rural beauty or be preserved for purposes of Industrial Archaeology?"

Lena ignored this and said unhurriedly: "I'm New College. What are you?"

Jonty told her.

She had a husky, coaxing voice. "I'm doing Modern Languages. What do you do?"

Jonty told her.

"I'm very fond of Scrabble. Aren't you?"

Jonty told her.

"Oh, well!" she said, *"I* think Sir Leslie and Lady Owens are absolute dears! It must be an awful lot of trouble for them, a party of this size. And it's the third or fourth this term. Don't you think?"

Jonty closed his eyes and counted up to ten – very slowly. When he opened them, Lena was watching him with great intentness out of her gold-flecked orbs.

Jonty took a breath, and conveyed to her his views on the Owenses' parties as quickly and politely as he could.

She looked at him steadily, quite still, as empty as a blank cartridge.

'It really was a pity! A superb chassis and no brain – as if somebody had mounted a water-pistol on a ceremonial gun-carriage and drawn it out in full public view along the Royal Mile! You just can't believe it.'

But Jonty knew he HAD to believe it, because, Oh dear! life was, sadly, full of very leaky water-pistols left open to public gaze on magnificent carriages!

Not long afterwards, Jonty excused himself from Lena and made a tour of the room, leaving Sofia, Redshins and the girl in red, together.

Sofia had led him to believe that the Owenses would provide fodder, but there was no sign of it and his stomach was beginning to feel like a replacement for Mr Jarrold's.

A waiter was weaving in and out of the groups with a trayful of politely-filled sherry glasses; Jonty managed to subtract two as he passed by him.

"This is for a friend," said Jonty, holding one aloft.

The waiter looked at it, sceptically.

When the waiter had gone, Jonty drank them both off and then positioned himself on one side of a group whose glasses Sir Leslie was mending from the decanter, and got them both filled again. Sir Lesie had reached the point where, provided he was allowed to go on articulating without interruption and with great elegance, he was no longer aware of who was at the end of an arm holding a glass. Sir Leslie, enunciating rapturously, went on to the next group.

For the time being, Jonty decided to stay where he was, listening to the raw-boned, long-faced, heavy-jawed undergraduate who was trying to look like W.H. Auden, and succeeding, even down to the lick of thick hair over the forehead.

"It was a terrible story," he was saying. "Edward Thomas went to Oxford, you know. During the Blue China period—"

"—Is that where he met Eleanor?" someone interrupted.

"Oh, no!" replied the Auden clone quickly. "That was much later. During his Tin Mug period. A great improvement on Oxford."

The man sawed his elbow in the air when he spoke. Did Wystan Hugh do that?

"But still heartrending. A life of real Grub Street."

Standing to one side of the group, a waiter appeared with a silver dish full of what, to Jonty, looked like lightly browned twigs. As he proffered it, the understudy's sawing elbow jolted the bowl into the waiter's diaphragm. The man, clearly and loudly, said "Ouf!" and lost his grip on the vessel, which clanged as it dropped and deposited a neat pile of shiny twigs on the glossy oak floor. Jonty was surprised because he had thought it was only in comics that characters said that.

Auden's stand-in glanced round limply, saw what he had done, turned back to his anxious audience and went on talking blithely about Edward Thomas. It was a pretty cool performance! The real Auden could not have done better.

Meanwhile, the waiter had gone and returned with a dustpan and brush and was about to gather up the edible twigs for the rubbish bin. Jonty, who was famished, had to prevent himself from pushing the man aside and scraping them all into the pockets of his borrowed suit and going into the garden to eat them.

'How long are the Owenses going to allow us to stand around ninnering and yaffling about Edward Thomas and Mrs Beeton? Where is the grub? Is Mrs Beeton, by any chance, preparing it in the kitchens? Are they going to play a recording of Edward Thomas reading "Adlestrop" while we eat it? Why don't they start their bloody festival of Scrabble?'

18

Even having to put up with fifteen minutes silence while everybody waited for Sir Leslie to come up with a three-letter word to earn a shattering score of two or three was better than having to endure the polite gittering around him, wasn't it?

Jonty left the Auden coterie and walked across to Twaggin's group.

Twaggin could usually be relied on to antagonise or disgust the company he was with, and Jonty felt the need to be entertained. But, on this occasion, Twaggin was silent, standing with arms folded, staring morosely at Lady Owens, who was rhapsodizing about her passion for collecting doorknobs.

"Of course, I favour the lovely glass ones, with those darling intricate whirling patterns inside. Most beautiful! You can find the initials of the maker inside, you know! Like paper weights. They were very proud of their work. And no wonder..."

Her prognathous teeth flashed tirelessly.

"...When you get your first one—"

'—Just heat and serve,' thought Jonty, tiredly.

She went on glittering and scintillating like one of her own doorknobs.

'That's funny! I haven't noticed any.' Jonty turned and looked at the heavy oak door. 'Yes, there it is, right enough!'

A huge coloured crystal-glass doorknob: shaped like the top half of a cottage loaf, with the navel where it should be. He could have held it in both hands – almost. Jonty worked his way round to Twaggin and whispered in his ear.

"I shall go mad! Not even frankfurters on a stick. My stomach is swearing in Urdu. Where do they keep the sherry?"

Twaggin whispered out of the side of his beard: "It's incredible! She's already recited the complete inventory of furnishings for their house in the Stockbroker Belt of Bucks AND the extent of the acreage, but we've had only ONE bloody sherry!"

Jonty groaned. Lady Owens's eyes flickered, looked into his for a moment, recovered and talked on.

Jonty leaned towards Twaggin's ear, in a whispered voice-over. "Twenty four across and twenty four down. Rich as Creosote, mean as Scrooge. Five letters."

He paused: "Where' s Soapy?"

"She's coming later. I know the answer," Twaggin whispered back.

Jonty winked, detached himself from Twaggin and drifted across to a group that was getting sherry from a waiter.

Too late, he realized that Sir Leslie was in it, as well as the water-pistol, Lena!

Sir Leslie had given up dispensing sherry, but not, alas! his platitudinous orotundities, which, thank heavens! Lena was absorbing, with her gold-flecked eyes wide open – although she made politely weak attempts to interrupt his faultless elocution from sentence to sentence.

Jonty consoled himself by a swift grab at the waiter's tray, swallowing the sherry Ginger-ale-style, and taking another before the waiter had a chance to pull it out of range.

"Of course, I quite realize that young people at this moment in time want to get down to the grass roots of – "

"—Oh, please, Sir Leslie, don't—!" said Lena.

"—of – of the – er – social problems of the time. But what you don't see is that we're light years away from—"

"—Oh, please, Sir Leslie —!" replied Lena.

"—from – er – the fully democratic society, or, as many prefer to call it, the anarchistic society. However, with so many ideas in the pipeline, we're in—"

"—Oh, please, Sir —!" Her interruption was ignored.

"—in for social upheavals of some magnitude. In fact, a night of the long knives is—"

"—Oh, please —!"

"—almost inevitable, and I fear I shall live to see the collapse of civilized values. From which you, my dear, won't find yourself immune."

'O – oo – oh!' Lena gave a shuddering orgiastic sigh.

She could go no further: Sir Leslie had driven her back point by point against one of the small Scrabble tables and it was at that moment Jonty realized with gleefully obscene pleasure why the dialogue had sounded so familiar to him!

Should he tell Lena the joke afterwards?

Lady Owens's frequencies were suddenly heard above the hubbub in the room.

"Come along, people! Are we all ready for the tourney? That's right! Sit down. Anywhere. Anywhere at all."

Jonty had doubts that Lady Owens seriously meant what she had said. But if she did, it was Jonty's intention to sniff out the larder and sit in it, or, rather, lie full length in it, on the first shelf, and eat his way steadily upward through the other shelves, even if they were quite bare and made of solid teak.

The last two sherries had turned his stomach into a vacuum and made him drunker.

People were drifting in ones and twos to chairs at the Scrabble tables. Jonty loitered near one of Lady Owens's display cabinets, which was full of horse-brasses, hoping her arithmetic was poor. But it wasn't.

When everyone was seated, there were still two vacant seats: one at Lady Owens's table itself, and one at a table in the centre of the room, where Sofia, Redshins and Sir Leslie were sitting.

'What pure bastard luck! Heads I lose, tails I lose.'

Sighing resignedly, Jonty walked rather uncertainly towards the table in the centre. Lady Owens hallooed at him from her seat:

"Oh, Arnold, we can't have that!"

Startled by her cry, Jonty faltered, and looked down furtively to see if his fly had come unzipped.

'No! Seems all right!' He continued his uncertain trek to the centre of the room. 'What is it we can't have, then? Have I got a hole in the seat of my hired trousers? Are my—?'

She hallooed again:

"Mr Redshins! Over here, over here!"

Unwillingly, Redshins rose; involuntarily, his eyes dived with Sofia's vee. His expression fell, too, but leavened almost at once when Lady Owens hallooed yet a third time.

"And Sofia!"

Lady Owens at last left her seat, shuffled a few people about from table to table, announced that she was finally satisfied and returned to her own group.

This left Jonty sitting in the centre with Sir Leslie, Lena, the Auden substitute and an enormous sense of futility.

Desperately, he looked about him. Redshins's prototypical face was fitting itself with a smirk of satisfaction as he found himself seated opposite to Sofia at another table.

Twaggin, from a position near a mullioned window, stared at him dolefully, as if considering the current political situation in Cyprus. Jonty lolled back slightly in his chair, let his eyes roll upward, and tried to look like Saint Sebastian with arrows sticking in him. Judging by Twaggin's response, he was successful.

"Ready – er – er?"

Sir Leslie was holding out the plastic bag of letters and smiling indulgently at him over his red spotted bow-tie. As Jonty recovered himself and reached towards the bag, he felt an immense hankering to tug at Sir Leslie's neckware to find out if it was on elastic, although he knew with a profound conviction that Sir Leslie's bow-ties would at least be of the genuine tie-up variety, however execrable they might be in other ways.

"Thank you," said Jonty.

Sir Leslie passed the letters around the table to the others.

Jonty busied himself arranging his seven on the little wooden rack and tried to locate the flunkeys with the sherry; but both the sherry and the waiters seemed to have been guilefully withdrawn. A few lucky individuals had glasses still unfinished beside them.

Och! what prospects drear! Jonty's stomach, as empty as his sherry glass, in sympathy with his thoughts, moved another inch or two towards his shoes.

"Letters all set up – er – er?" asked Sir Leslie.

"Yes. Oh, no! Sorry! Nearly. There!"

He looked up at Lena; she was watching Sir Leslie positioning his letters with a soft little smile playing, like the innocent it was, around her lips. Auden, like the innocent he wasn't, frowned at his row, moved his mouth, and nodded his head rhythmically.

'Searching for rhymes?'

"Me to start then, I believe," said Sir Leslie.

He put an A on the green cloth. Jonty had drawn a Q.

Sir Leslie's pink face got pinker with concentration and began to clash rather badly with the spots on his tie.

Jonty began to muse on the problem of how to get hold of some food and some more booze.

Maybe he could find a stale lard sandwich or a damp charcoal biscuit in the kitchen? Where WAS the kitchen? What would be the strategic time to go?

Meanwhile, Sir Leslie, after a series of "Ums!" and "Ahs!" that went on for some time and progressed geometrically in decibels, sorted out three letters.

'Here it comes!' thought Jonty, 'After a record series of pains in the Labour Ward, another shattering set of triplets has been delivered!'

Sir Leslie placed a J and then an O very deliberately in the centre of the board.

'What on earth – ?

'I do believe the old bugger's going to spell my name!'

Jonty was assailed by an inexplicable panic at the manoeuvre and was just about to remind them all in the high-pitched squeak of H.G Wells – which seemed peculiarly suited to the occasion – of the rules of the game, when Sir Leslie added a letter B to the other two.

"Eight and one makes nine," he enunciated faultlessly, "And three – thirteen! Will you keep the score, my dear?"

"Twelve," said Auden.

"What? Oh,yes! Sorry!"

"That's a very good start, Sir Leslie!" said Lena.

Jonty looked gloomily down at his own little rack of letters. His impression, at first glance, was of a long row of O's and some D's, B's and J's.

'But how can that be? I'm allowed only seven! Seven! Bang goes my plan! Can't turn Sir Leslie's prodigy into BLOOODY GOOOD JOBB with only seven letters, can I?'

He looked miserably again at his chances.

'I'm good for a score of at least two!'

It wasn't long before Auden romped ahead, leading the field by several lengths, during which time, Jonty had managed to form his seven into the impressive grouping of SSODDIT.

At the moment, he was trying to get the arrangement to conform more exactly to the way he would pronounce it and decided it would be more exact and kinaesthetically pleasing spaced out as: SSODD IT. A pity they didn't supply exclamation marks! That's just what he felt was needed to complete the pattern.

The room was quiet, very full of bent heads and the sound of steady breathing.

A few moments ago, Sir Leslie had startled the peace of the company by lighting up one of his cheroots, and he was now adding to the pollution problem with gusts of smoke that nearly equalled in size those emitted by the Dean, and easily surpassed them in vileness.

On his empty stomach, Jonty felt nauseous, but he had to endure it for the present. He would just have to wait for an opportunity to escape.

After Sir Leslie's scratching and shuffling had ended, the annihilating near-silence took over again; but Jonty could see that a bludgeon of boredom had gone up and down the room clobbering here and there one or two chosen victims beside himself.

Twaggin was leaning at angle of forty-five degrees in his chair, almost asleep. Brown was comatose. But Auden, Lena, Redshins, the Owenses and few of their acolytes were vividly, soundlessly awake.

Finally, Jonty could bear it no longer. He shuffled his bottom and rocked slightly, as if in some pain, and hoped that it conveyed the idea that he needed urgently to make water, and might well do it under the Scrabble table, unless!—.

Lena flashed him a quick Sunday-morning face that said clearly: "How COULD you?"

Auden ignored him and went on biting his nails.

Sir Leslie looked fleetingly at him, inhaled and exhaled a few times in response, as if sending signals of disapproval, Indian style, and then nodded to his cheroot, giving it permission at last to go out.

Jonty was quick to take his cue. He said "Excuse me!", stood up, and got out while the going was good. He went through the nearest door.

Outside, in a corridor, he breathed a huge sigh of relief.

19

The tweeny who had let them into the Master's Lodge came up the corridor towards him.

"I think you've got the nicest legs in Cambridge," said Jonty. "But, for God's sake, find me a drink! Or a shot of LSD. Or a copy of *The Daily Express*. After an hour in the Scrabble Chamber, I'm craving for decadence!"

"What a funny man!" she giggled.

"No, honest! Can you get me a drink?"

"Ooooh! I don't know. It's not allowed. I could get the sack."

"Sack will do!" said Jonty. "I'll drink anything."

She looked blankly at him, and a little aghast.

"All right! I can see you're unacquainted with the Fat Man of Gads Hill."

"No, I don't know that pub!"

"Just tell me where it is, and – ," Jonty started in exasperation to say.

She was looking about her furtively and, seeing no-one but the two of them, she nodded towards a doorway leading off the corridor.

"—There's a cupboard in there," she sniffed, and walked off quickly before anything further could ensue.

Jonty watched with pleasure her shapely rump as she returned in the direction from which she had come, probably from the kitchens.

Then, he opened the door she had indicated. It led into another small passageway, with another door at the end.

It was really no more than a deep and roomy cupboard, dimly lighted from above.

He entered and closed himself inside.

Most of the space was taken up with a huge old sideboard, against one wall. On top were several decanters, half-full of sherry, and three or four bowls of the twiggy snacks. He stuffed a handful of them into his mouth and munched with relief. Then, taking fistfuls, he padded out the pockets of his hired suit. Afterwards filling up one of the decanters from the others to its heavy cut-glass stopper, the twigs crackled and rustled as he moved. He grabbed the decanter that was now full of sherry and, making sure that no-one was about, he crossed the corridor outside into a small hallway and climbed the thickly carpeted stairs.

Their treads did not creak once.

At the top, he found himself on a long lighted landing covered with a runner that had a stiff one-inch pile and a quarter-inch felt underneath it. It was like walking on compressed whispers, honey-coloured. He strolled backwards and forwards on it for a while, enjoying its luxury and munching twigs.

On one side of the landing were windows with brocaded curtains and gold tassells that presumably overlooked the garden of the Lodge. On the windowsills stood a lot of snarfia in pots, which had little aluminium markers with pencilled names on them stuck upright in the soil beside the stems.

On the other side of the landing were a number of closed doors, all of which had glass knobs with the same kind of purity, brilliance and intricacy of pattern as the one he had seen downstairs. A little touch of Lady Owens in the night!

They were large, about the size of good Jaffa oranges, easy to get a grip on.

He grasped one that was full of whirling electric blues and ethereal greens and elusive rose colours on a plain white-painted door halfway along the landing, and turned it carefully.

He peered inside. He was in luck! He entered, closed the door, pushed home the bolt, leaned against it, and sighed.

"Done it!"

After putting down the lavatory flap and its frilly cover and sitting on it, he took a good long pull at the sherry. It was smooth, like polish, and sourish, like vinegar – not at all like that served earlier to the Scrabble players

Perhaps the kitchen maids kept their cleaning fluids, secretly, in the decanters on that sideboard and, inadvertently, somebody had mixed them?

But it stopped the churning in his stomach very effectively – by dissolving it and turning it into a hole, which he then tried to counteract by swallowing down more handfuls of twigs.

The effect of these was quite different. His pupils felt to be getting bigger and smaller, like f-stops on a camera whose metering had gone wrong; and, most interesting of all, each eye did it at different rates.

Luckily, his ears were still stationary; but he didn't like the sensation that hovered in their vicinity, which told him that soon they would begin to fizz and afterwards begin to whirl like catherine wheels.

"Christ!"

Then, as he watched, unbelievingly, the Lady Owens doorknob on the inside began to go through an aggressive territorial display. It puffed itself up and got smaller, again and again. He expected it soon to start hissing, as if it were some kind of African toad, its domain threatened by his decanter.

He took another urgent pull at the sherry.

Surprisingly, this eased the situation: the doorknob squatted down and remained silent. He felt very relieved at this turn of events, as visual alcoholic effects were acceptable, but audible ones weren't, especially in Cambridge.

However, just to be on the safe side, he kept his eyes closed while he finished off two pocketfuls of twigs as noisily as he could to disguise any other possible sound effects.

When at last he opened them, his pupils seemed to have settled down to a fairly normal performance and no noises came out of the doorknob.

Looking about him, things appeared approximately familiar. Those were surely sprays – weren't they – and bottles – and dispensers – and packets and tubes on – what was it? – a glass shelf? Yes, surely!

'So, up to about two feet visibility, I'm working! What's that, yonder, that flat vertical thing? Is it a...? It IS a wall! And – a wash hand basin. It's under the mirror   But I won't look in the mirror in case it's empty!'

He decided to open another pocket of twigs, instead. The crunching and snapping sounds were reassuring and, as he ate, his stomach began to feel less like a hole in the road and more like a mainline sewer.

'If I keep eating, will this roaring waterfalley-feeling stop?'

He looked about him again to see if anything had changed.

Most things were what they had pretended to be a few moments ago but they were now waving about and bending a bit, as if seen through a heat haze.

'If it doesn't stop,' he thought desperately, 'I'll climb into the lavatory pan, pull down the cover and gurgle away on the flood.'

Filtering slowly into his consciousness, came heavy flat thumping sounds hurrying along the landing. Somebody stopped at the door and rattling began. He waited for it to subside, but its urgency increased.

"You'll have to get out at the next station," called Jonty in his best imitation of the Dean, hoping he wasn't the one who had stopped outside and tried the knob.

A foot banged against the door, followed by a surprised little grunt. After that, an impatient sound.

"There's a nice clean one at Six-Mile Bottom!" he called out.

The rattling stopped, to be followed by muttered expletives which faded and grew and faded, like a faulty Tanoi system, making his ears ring.

Then the heavy clumping walk went up the landing. Jonty hoped with great fervour that it was Redshins, full as a gooseberry.

What on earth WAS this stuff made of that he was drinking?

He sniffed at the decanter with great concentration, but couldn't make up his mind for quite some time. In the end, he decided that it must be cleaning sherry – guaranteed to give hardened users a high gloss finish on their tonsils and tiny frayed holes in the weave of their stomach linings.

That is, if they ever got past the beginners' no-tonsils-no-stomach stage, which semed doubtful. He poured it into the lavatory pan. It ran over the porcelain, oilily, leaving a light oaken sheen on it, and drawing a thin film of light-oak across the surface of the water. It was fascinating!

Somewhere in the background, there were vague opening and shutting noises, and relieved flat thumpings going away.

He flushed the pan. It didn't make much difference to its colour, but it gave it a pleasantly grained effect.

'Wonder what it's done to my stomach-lining?' he thought, woefully. 'Stained it the colour of a fireman's sweatband for the rest of my life, I bet!'

He looked about for some cleaning powder, but couldn't find any.

However, there was a long-handled plastic brush with short white bristles, like those worn by the Professor of Psychology, but otherwise healthy. He tried it, and it worked after a fashion – like the Professor of Psychology. The pleasant oak-grained pattern on the pan had gone and, in its place, was a frenetic wire-mesh effect on an unsavoury background – like one of the case histories Toeless recounted endlessly at cocktail parties. He might even be recounting one this very minute between games...

What else could Jonty use?

He turned and peered at the glass shelf under the mirror, making himself accidentally aware that there WAS a face in it, after all, but who it belonged to was another matter. THIS face was drunk and belonged to some weedy four-eyed nyaff with a full moustache who could be ignored with impunity.

Jonty picked up an outsized tin of talcum powder, oval-shaped, with a brown tweed pattern printed all over it. He sniffed at it, gingerly. It had the same masculine smell he thought he had detected on Lady Owens, earlier. He sprinkled the powder liberally into the pan, which gave it a prissy, powdered mien, but which was to be preferred to the neurotic brushed-mud look he'd produced a moment ago.

He straightened up. Alas, too quickly!

Sluice-gates in his stomach opened up once more and his eyeballs felt as if they were wandering aimlessly around the inner surfaces of his skull.

Desperate, he stretched out his arms and pressed at the walls on each side of him. Surely, that would stop them leaning in and out so much? Had he somehow wandered into an Edgar Alan Poe story when he opened that white door?

He shut his eyes. He clenched his fists. He closed his mind.

But, in an unlocatable place, something inside him sensed that he had become a pupil in a mad eye, dilating and un-dilating, pulsating to some mystical and, in the end, annihilating rhythm. What could he do?

He tried breathing in and out, deep and long.

This stabilized him somewhat, stopped the relentless pulsations and returned his eyeballs to their sockets.

He did it again. Again, it worked.

Various unidentifiable organs seemed to have settled back into hollows and spaces that belonged to them.

What about the outside world? Could he risk opening his eyes, his fists, his mind?

Guardedly, he relaxed.

Yes, the walls stood still, the lavatory pan was immobile, the door was fixed!

Thank heavens! The worst seemed to be over.

He breathed again, but this time normally, and with relief.

20

He looked longingly at the door.

It was only a few steps away. How, at the same time, could it be a long way off?

But it had to be reached.

Yes, it WAS possible to put one foot in front of the other, after all! He felt that it was a miracle he had reached it without falling over.

He grasped the Jaffa-sized knob, turned it and pulled gently. The door did not open. He pulled harder. It didn't budge.

Had Redshins crept back soundlessly, and was he hanging on to it now from the other side?

Jonty grasped the knob with both hands, placed both feet together on the bottom of the door, and leaned backwards, letting his arms take his weight, like a steeplejack held by his belt halfway up a factory chimney. Nothing happened. He jerked his bottom, hard, feeling the tug on his shoulders. Not a fraction of movement.

He let go of the knob, backed off, and tried creeping up slowly to take it by surprise. The door stayed shut.

He yanked and pulled and twisted and coaxed it. He even stood up very straight, frowning, and said "Open Sesame!" at it. But still nothing happened.

Jonty was getting crosser and crosser. He shelled it with obscenities. He blasted it with profanities. All to no avail!

Here he was, locked for ever and ever in Lady Owens's WC with a drunken nyaff and a moustache, a brush that looked like the Professor of Psychology, a tarted-up john, an indecent tin of male talcum powder, and an empty decanter of sherry-flavoured furniture cleaner. A likely set of companions for eternity, they were!

He decided to launch a final assault on the enemy's position. He puffed out his chest, pointed his arm forward like a cavalry sword, and cried: "Platoon, charge!"

This time, he made an impression. The doorknob came off in his hands.

He found himself sitting on the floor, with the heavy glass knob swirling its colours in his lap, together with the tin of talcum powder, which had emptied itself in a white fragrant mound onto his left thigh. The door was a little ajar.

Why, oh why, hadn't he remembered? The door opened outwards, INTO the landing! Worse and worse!

As he got to his feet, a shower of scented chalkdust poured onto the floor.

Swearing, he took toilet paper and brushed it up as best he could, afterwards putting it down the pan and flushing it away. It left a large white daisy on his hired trousers. He tried sponging it off, but that made it look as if he'd been trying to mix a quantity of ceiling plaster on the inside of his thigh.

What was he to do now?

He couldn't go back to the Scrabble Party looking as if he'd tried to do that, could he? God knows what kind of a pervert Sir Leslie would think he was, not to mention the horror of Lady Owens when she saw him!

And what was he to do with her bloody doorknob? Where could he put it?

Yes, that was the right question to ask, all right! If you ask the right questions, you're halfway to getting the answers, aren't you?

Miserably, he looked about him; miserably, he put the top back on the empty talcum tin and replaced it on the shelf, but hidden behind a jar of cleansing cream.

No answers came; and in great chagrin, he sat down on the seat of the loo, knowing that he could not stay there for the rest of the evening.

What the hell WAS he to do?

He would just have to climb out of a window and never be heard of again; just become a number, a punch-card, on the files of the Bureau of Missing Persons; a memory; a forgotten anguish; a pursing of the lips in Lady Owens's conversation, an angry stammer in Sir Leslie's; an outsider; a stealer of doorknobs in hired suiting; an inadmissible episode, unfitted to be counted among the reminiscences of the Reverend F.A. Newey; a nobody; a desecrator of toilets; a failed BA (Cantab).

No! It was too horrible to contemplate. He just couldn't face it. Being a failed one of them was unthinkable! He would just have to find some other answer.

That was all very well. But what? Just bloody what?

Perhaps he should strut back into the full scrimmage of Scrabble players, sideways, so as to display his thigh better for Sir Leslie, tossing the doorknob from hand to hand nonchalantly for Lady Owens, while humming the Marsellaise, and simply brazen the whole thing out?

Isn't that what Twaggin would do? He would. But then – he'd got a Greek Orthodox beard, and that made all the difference. Doing it without one of them wouldn't be easy.

Jonty made a snap decision: there wasn't any point in hanging about in a jakes.

That was for sure!

The landing was empty, except for the massed disapproval of Lady Owens's potted snarfia ranged on the windowsills.

The loo door wouldn't stay shut. He made a little wedge of toilet paper and jammed it underneath. Why hadn't he had the foresight to bring a padlock to the Scrabble Party with him?

He walked down the corridor and opened another door.

He found himself in a medium-sized bedroom lit dimly by a streetlamp shining through a window. A single bed, two chests of drawers and a long fitted wardrobe lined the walls. There were no snarfia, berberis, or horsebrasses around. On a wall, a blown-up photograph of immense proportions, featuring a South African-born actor impersonating Sherlock Holmes, gazed down at him from below a Highland deer-stalker and above an Inverness cape – much too warmly dressed for Hollywood. A neat red set of Conan Doyle's detective stories mulled over unspeakable crimes on a little shelf above the single bed.

SIR LESLIE'S ROOM, no other!

Jonty went back and locked the door on the inside, which was when he discovered that he was still clutching the large glass doorknob.

So he unlocked the door, crept out onto the landing, selected a sturdy-looking snarfium in a good strong pot, and made one or two attempts to lift it bodily out of its vessel.

The plant resisted.

Jonty went back into the bedroom. Luckily, there was a paper-knife on top of a chest. He returned to the pot and carved it around the perimeter of the soil, as if coring an apple.

He tried again. This time, the soil and root system came up in one chunk on the end of the plant. Delicately, he crumbled some of the soil away from the bottom into his palm and put it into a pocket with the twig crumbs; then, he settled the doorknob in the bottom of the pot and replaced the plant on top of it. It leaned a bit, so he straightened it up and made sure the stem was in the centre of the pot, remembering to press it firmly down and to replace the aluminium name tag beside it.

If it were properly watered, it could grow a family of little doorknobs, couldn't it?

Cross a snarfium with a glass knob and what do you get? Multi-coloured glass leaves!

No! Green glass balls!

Wrong! Answer: a prolonged halloo from Lady Owens.

Relieved to be rid of the doorknob, Jonty went back into the bedroom.

In the long wardrobe, he found several pairs of dark trousers that nearly matched those of his hired charcoal suit. And they had legs of almost the same length as Jonty's, which was a stroke of luck, as he had never taken the trouble to assess Sir Leslie's legs.

He removed his hired own and put on a pair of Sir Leslie's.

Standing there in the Holy of Holies, the realization suddenly hit him of exactly how different Sir Leslie was from him. They fitted him as snugly as a small waiting-room; there was space enough for two (even three) other people inside, provided they all had very thin calves and ankles for negotiating the high rate of taper from waistband to turnups.

Jonty tried folding over the waistband in front.

No; that was out of the question. Apart from pinching certain of his vital organs when he moved, it looked deliberately eccentric.

He tried again, folding the surplus at the back. That was just as bad: it felt as if his buttocks had been fastened together with carpenter's glue, and then clamped together to dry.

Furthermore, something under the crotch seemed to be trying to castrate him, and that surely had to be Sir Leslie's trousers as well, because alcohol had never had that effect on him before.

'Still, from those decanters, I suppose I can't be sure!'

He knew that he still FELT drunk, which must point to the fact that he WAS drunk, mustn't it?

He'd have to take the matter up for discussion with Smitty, sometime.

But the eyeball-wandering and stomach-storming effects had worn off, so he guessed he wasn't AS drunk.

However, when he discovered that he'd managed, without realizing what he was doing, to fasten Sir Leslie's braces to Sir Leslie's fly buttons, so that he couldn't straighten up, he knew he was still PRETTY drunk. Why didn't the old pachyderm wear zips like everybody else? Were his fumblings of such an order that he routinely zipped up his pubics as well?

No; he couldn't be THAT inept, could he?

More likely to be that Sir Leslie's tailor had never heard of zips, and hence Sir Leslie himself had never heard of them. Or perhaps he regarded them as gadgets only worn by sex-fiends, hippies and revolutionaries?

By trial and error, Jonty eventually found that the best solution was to fold the waistband so that it bunched at both hips. This reduced the quantity of cloth sticking out in one spot and made it easier to disguise its enormous girth.

He'd also come across a couple of fairly large safety pins in one of the drawers with which to fasten down the two wodges of cloth at his sides.

Of course, it meant he couldn't use the pockets, but what the hell, Archie, what the hell?

He was lucky to have any trousers at all. If the worst had come to the worst, he could have found himself going back to the Scrabble Party in jacket and underpants, trouserless.

Anyway, the only thing he had to put in the pockets was a pair of plasterer's breeches, and he couldn't pass those off as small change, could he? No, he couldn't.

Nor could he assign them to the same fate as Lady Owens's doorknob. There wasn't a snarfium or a pot big enough.

Leave them under Sir Leslie's underwear in one of his drawers?

Risky! Lady Owens probably made him change his lingerie too often.

Hide them in a lampbowl, like the dipso in Charles Jackson's 'The Lost Weekend'?

No; the tweeny regularly switched on and off.

Burn them in the wash hand basin and flush away the ash? What about the smoke, the smell and clogging up the plughole?

Besides he'd have to pay for them if he didn't return them to the hirers.

Of course! Why hadn't he thought of it before? He should have put Sir Leslie's on OVER his own!

Too late. Oh God! There was only one thing to do now.

He opened a window and peered out: he was overlooking a gravel drive at the side of the Lodge.

He rolled the trousers up as tightly as he could and dropped them out.

As he was closing the window, he thought he could hear the grit complaining under somebody's feet, but he wasn't sure. It could have been a residual sherry effect.

It was time for more deep breathing! He straightened up, inhaled heavily, balanced his head, and prepared to go downstairs.

Now, could he manage to look as if he had suffered for years from chronic internal difficulties, had fought and won, sit down with composure and stun Sir Leslie with a word like TINTINNABULATIONS, while secretly wearing a pair of the Master's trousers?

Of course! He wasn't a Godley for nothing, whatever the appearances to the contrary.

When he was halfway down the stairs, a door opened and he heard voices.

It was at that moment Jonty remembered he had left the empty sherry decanter in the WC.

He rushed back, retrieved it and shut himself in Sir Leslie's bedroom. In panic, he stashed the decanter in the Master's sock drawer and himself under the bed.

The voices got louder as they climbed the stairs: a group of three or four people were coming up to the landing.

What on earth for? Had Lady Owens organized an orgy? Surely she couldn't have a communal longdrop secreted away on a mezzanine floor; or a jacuzzi?

A voice that sounded very much like the Professor of Psychology's remarked that one of the plants seemed to be drooping rather badly. Afterwards, the sounds got muffled and indistinct and Jonty heard them go into a room and shut the door.

That had been a close one!

Jonty whipped out onto the landing.

Quite right! As Toeless had said, the snarfium plant looked terrible. It drooped like one of the Dean's most fervent ideas, flaccid and dry, and it had shrunk.

Jonty took out the doorknob from underneath the soil, replaced the plant, gave it a drink of water from the bathroom and put it back on its windowsill, praying it would revive.

Then he rushed into the Master's bedroom and dropped Lady Owens's doorknob out of the window after his trousers and just managed to reach the bottom of the stairs before the flushings and door-openings began on the landing.

The Owens's Scrabble Party was turning into a nightmare.

Jonty stood outside the oaken door, listening to the chatter of the Scrabble players inside the room. He had only a moment or two before the group from upstairs came down to where he was standing.

His heart was thumping with trepidation, and indications of his earlier symptoms began to return. His ears buzzed. His eyes were playing tricks again. His stomach felt queasy. He really shouldn't have poured that cleaning fluid on top of four and a half pints of Greene and King's best bitter, should he?

But there was no help for it now.

He put a hand tentatively on to Lady Owens's cherished glass sphere, took a big breath, and – suddenly, taking him by surprise, something solid and heavy and soft bumped against his shins.

He looked down, fearful that he was hallucinating again. But no! It was real: a larger and older version of the sparsely haired kitten he had seen earlier was rubbing itself ecstatically against his legs. This one's ears were serrated by old and forgotten battles. Jonty bent down to stroke the cat. Its head had bumps and welts all over it. He felt as if he was stroking a piece of coconut matting with eczema.

"You randy old Tom!" he said, admiringly.

Then, Jonty felt the sitting-room door inexplicably pressing itself against his forehead.

It was beginning, very slowly, to inch open. The sound of voices was starting to expand, cone-shaped, like a huge megaphone.

He felt himself slowly, floatingly, toppling over and over and, just for a moment, he glimpsed, very clearly indeed, the texture of the Owens's damson-coloured floor carpet before – finally – he saw nothing at all.

21

"Coming in! In that state!"

"Please don't go on, Sofia! Just get me a treble Alka-Seltzer and a chaser of Bi-carb, there's a good girl."

"Knocking the Scrabble board off the table, and – Oh! it was the most embarrassing moment of my life."

"Shhh! Not so loud! You'll fracture my malleus!"

"It's too much! I can't – "

"—You can! Anyway, they looked at my sentence! They cheated! Ooooh, this head! Somebody changed it into SID DOTS. It isn't fair!"

"Just when are you going to grow up?"

"Grow up? I don't even know if I'm going to get up – ever again! Bring me something to swallow, will you? Go on, be a sweetie!"

"Oh, you! You – well, YOU, that's all! You're TOO MUCH!"

Jonty's reaction was to close his eyes.

He vanished.

Somehow, somewhere, somebody began to shake him and he felt himself coming back bit by bit, like the Cheshire Cat. A voice was calling to him, getting nearer. Was it the Red Queen? What was she saying?

"Sit up and drink this!" said Sofia.

"I don't want to sit up. I don't want to drink it. I don't want to get smaller! SSODD IT! I want to go back where—"

"—Don't be childish! Drink it up! I've brought your Alka Seltzer."

"Have you got something to slow down the flow of my blood?! Something to – Oh, dear!"

Jonty's eyes were open; but if he could actually see what he thought he could see, things were more serious than he'd imagined. He'd have to take it slowly.

He closed his eyes, counted up to twenty, and then opened them again, apprehensively. What had been there before was still there now, and it was still doing the same thing.

He closed his eyes very tight and very quick and whispered: "Sofia!"

Hearing his subdued tone, she answered sympathetically:

"What do you want now?"

"Do me a favour! Tell me what you've got in that glass in your hand."

"Oh, for God's sake, what – !"

"—No! Don't shout! My head's fallen into two equal halves. Be kind to me! Take a good look at it, and tell me what you see – exactly."

"Oh, dear!"

She sighed deeply. "Just a glass of Alka Seltzer! What do you think it is?"

"I don't know! What's it doing?"

"Doing? How'd'you mean – doing? Just being a glass of Alka Seltzer, I suppose."

"No! I mean – fizzing! It isn't fizzing."

"Should it?"

"Of course it should!"

"Oh! It isn't, is it?"

"Well, what IS it doing?"

"It's just there!" said Sofia. "Inside the glass."

"I mean the capsule! What's it doing?"

"Well, you know what it's doing, silly! It's floating on the water."

Jonty gave an immense sigh of relief.

"You can see it, too! Thank God! I thought for a minute – Oh, Sofia, you darling!... It should go to the bottom and start sending bubbles up like mad. What the advertisements call effervescing."

"Oh, should it?"

"You mean, you don't know!"

"Why should I? I never even heard of Alka Seltzer until I met you."

"Incredible! I cut my back teeth on these things."

"My family was teetotal!"

"That explains a lot!"

"I'll have to throw it away," said Sofia, holding the glass in front of her shortsighted eyes and gazing into it with puzzlement. "It must be bad!"

She left the bedroom and went into the kitchen.

Jonty leaned back painstakingly onto the pillow. He sighed in thanksgiving. He had had a reprieve: he wasn't mad after all! Wearing a hangover you could wrap several times round your head was a mere gnatbite after what he had thought was happening to him a moment ago.

Nevertheless, the fear that Sir Leslie's cleaning sherry had partly dissolved his stomach, the muscles of his eyes and a million or two of his brain cells, causing him to see solid objects afloat like Alf's button, would have administered a severe enough shock to anybody's system.

"But I'm going to be all right," he said to himself.

And then, despite the awfulness in his head and the unspeakableness in his mouth and the uncooperativness of his innards generally, his usual concern for accuracy in such matters forced him to mutter:

"Or as near as I'll ever get to it."

Sofia returned with another full glass.

"I've opened a new tube."

"Good."

It was better with his eyes shut.

"Arnold," called Sofia, gently.

"What?"

"It's doing it again!"

"Can't be!" he said, keeping his eyes firmly closed. "It has to be fizzing!"

"Well, it isn't. Look!"

"Not likely!" he said. "You must have filled the glass with heavy water."

"I got it from the tap in the kitchen," said Sofia.

"Then Hacking Cough has had the plumbing secretly connected to the Cavendish Laboratory! We're on their heavy water supply! What other possible explanation can there be?"

"I don't know! I don't think she did that! Anyway, what difference would that make? Open your eyes and look!"

"Something's making a difference, isn't it?" asked Jonty, keeping his eyes shut. "Look at the alternatives! Either, there's something wrong with the water; or with the Alka Seltzer. But this is the second tube you've opened. Unlikely to be that! So – we're both mad! And Sir Leslie's sherry is the culprit. What else is there?"

Sofia made no reply, but she pushed the capsule down under the water with her finger. It ascended to the surface with exactly the same alacrity and confidence as before, bobbing slightly.

"Look what it does, Arnold."

When Jonty remained with his eyes closed, she shouted at him in exasperation: "LOOK!"

Jonty opened one eye and Sofia repeated the manoeuvre.

"See!"

"Here, let me have a go!" said Jonty, opening both eyes.

He pushed the capsule down. It ascended to the surface with exactly the same alacrity and confidence as before, and commenced bobbing.

He lifted it out and examined it. Then he began to laugh, but stopped at once and started to groan instead.

"Oooh! It hurts! You know what you've done, don't you?"

"What I'VE done! Well, I like that! All – "

"—No, listen, lovey! Where's the tube?"

"Here."

She took the glass container from the pocket of her dressing gown and handed it to him. He removed the floating capsule from the glass of water and dropped another into it. Immediately, the fresh one sank and began to bubble furiously.

"See!"

"Oh, Arnold, it works! What – "

"—There's a polystyrene dummy on top! That's what you put in!"

"A dummy! What for?"

"Keeps 'em dry, I suppose."

She also began to laugh. "I'm sorry! I thought – ! Oh, Arnold – "

"Not half as sorry as me! I was afraid you'd have to bring in some burly men with white coats, and send me to join my old man!"

"Don't be silly! I wouldn't!"

"I shall be able to go to Kingmaker's tutorial, after all."

He groaned and clutched his head. "Little as I feel like it, now!"

"When?"

"Eleven! Still got a couple of hours to recover. Ooo—er! I'll never play Scrabble again. It's totally corrupting!"

"Don't remind me! You were disgusting. How are we going to get Sir Leslie's trousers back to him?"

"Doesn't bear thinking about! All I want now is to sleep."

"And that decanter you left in his sock drawer? And that hired suit?"

"I don't know! Oh dear, dear, dear! It seems all I forgot was to scrawl OUT OF ORDER all over her loo with her own lipstick and sign it."

"Yes, that's about right!"

"You're a great comfort, you are! Why don't you just tell the Dean I died in the night?"

"He wouldn't believe me!" She paused, considering it "Would he?"

"All right! I'll give you the evidence. I'm going to do it now. Goodbye!"

And, so saying, Jonty pulled the bedclothes over his head, putting a stop to their conversation. He heard Sofia's bare feet pattering away to do whatever it was she was going to do.

He lay flat and tried to relax. He attempted to do it from the feet upwards, consciously and deliberately, the way he had been told to in the books he had read on Yoga. First, the big toe of his right foot, and then the other toes in turn, down to the pinkie.

Meeting with reasonable success there, he began on his left foot. His plan was to move gradually upwards: calf muscles, quadriceps, biceps femoris, et cetera, et cetera, until he reached his erector spinae, trapezius, and the muscles in his neck whose names he could never remember.

He wasn't doing too badly with his muscles, but with his thoughts he seemed to be powerless. They raced on and on, hithering-and-thithering as they wished, producing a nightmarish paella of the previous night's events spiced with random dashes of desperation and anxiety, and his headache refused to go away.

The theory was that when you had completely relaxed you would fall into a dreamless sleep. So much for the theory!

Physically, he was as flaccid as over-boiled cabbage; mentally, he was a set of bizarre and unappetising concoctions, a caravanserai of domestic and exotic sequences in technicolour, between blank spaces that had no commercials.

'Oh, Mother of mine, Dear Mother,' he wrote in the blanks,

> 'I must apologise for leaving it so long without dropping you a line and doing it only if I'm drunk. But I think I'm about to be sent down for violating one of Lady Owens's doorknobs and a pair of Sir Leslie's cast-offs.'

He paused, trying to ignore another feverish sequence.

'How're things up there? Dad is still in the Bin, following out the pools and doing his systems. I don't really know how he makes out for getting hold of his "lotion", as he calls it. I'll find out if you're interested. Being a student and reading lots of books and meeting crowds of people is all right, especially if they're like Twaggin, or even like Kingmaker, but when they're like Dewey and Redshins it's anything but all right. I'm recuperating from the Owenses' passion for Scrabble at the minute as well as the biggest hangover so far, and if I had to make a choice I'd choose spontaneous combustion, like that character in 'Bleak House'. Still, the beer's good here, and I met a chap called Smitty who knows exactly what to do with it and where to get it... Just hang on a minute while this little lot goes by!'

Jonty pressed both hands to his head in an effort to slow down the pictures.

'I'm back! Of course, if eventually I graduate and you are able to feel proud of me, as you always wanted – still, mustn't think of that just yet, while I'm still in the wood. Not that I know what things are all FOR; they haven't taught us that bit yet, and you didn't have a chance to get round to it – as I know you would have, in your own good time. But, I've got a lot of patience, really, like you. No! What worries me most is Sofia. Don't misunderstand! The sex is marvellous. It's the not-sex that isn't. And I've no doubt she loves me, as I love her. But, somehow – it's hard to explain – I can't reach her. We seem only to touch with outstretched arms and at the end of our fingertips? Do you know what I mean? The worst is – she doesn't seem to know we're like that. Oh, yes, we can hug and kiss and touch – in THAT way – but it isn't THE way. At least, this is how it feels to me. Am I off the track? Is this the way it was with you and Dad; or have we missed the turning somewhere? Not that there's even any sex, lately; she's Lysistrat-ered me, put herself in purdah, gone taboo. Says I don't acknowledge our marriage. Could she be right? Mary, Mother of mine, please tell me that she isn't!

'Wish me luck. In everything. If you have any bright ideas, let me know. I've got none of any kind. Next time I write, I'll promise to be sober.

'Please guide me home!

'Take care.

'Your ever loving son, Arnold.'

Having managed to complete his letter, in spite of the repeated interruptions from his body and his mind, he felt soothed and, soon, he was fast asleep.

An hour and a half later, Sofia went in to wake him.

"It's time for Kingmaker's tutorial," she said.

"It can't be!" he grumbled, coming up out of the darkest of depths and yawning and gulping in air. "It's only halfpast Doomsday!"

How he went through all the operations required to reach Kingmaker's rooms—washing, dressing, drinking tea, cycling, entering, sitting down, etcetera—he did not know; he had no recollection of them. Something had done them for him.

Nevertheless, he came to a slight degree of self-awareness while actually hearing Kingmaker's nasal tones and glottal stops in Kingmaker's own rooms.

Extraordinary!

Perhaps his reading of Yoga had at last borne fruit and he'd arrived somehow by levitation and astral translation? Was there a body back in Mrs Cough's bed, sleeping peacefully, and answering to the name of Arnold Jonty? He must remember to ask Sofia.

"...The great act in examinations," Kingmaker was saying, "is to bring in – relevantly – all that you are able. It's an opportunity for exhibitionism! But I stress again, RELEVANT exhibitionism. That's it!..."

Kingmaker was giving good advice. It was one of the last tutorials he would hold before Finals and Jonty was really trying to listen.

But apart from the fact that his head felt like a plastic bag full of stale washing-up water, Kingmaker was wearing odd socks and Jonty just couldn't stop trying to work out if Kingmaker had got them on inside out as well. He had encountered both socks before, but never in their own pair. It was only a matter of trying to decide which was the outside weave and which was the inside weave; nonetheless, it was far from easy.

"...The whole situation is artificial, of course," Kingmaker was continuing. "It's an act of highbrow robbery, you might say, and you, the victims, must stand, or rather sit, and deliver against the clock..."

Then, there was Sofia.

She had gone all frigid on him lately, and his performance at the Owenses last night would almost certainly aggravate the frigidity and how was he to get Sir Leslie's breeches back to Sir Leslie and the doorknob back to its loo and what did Kingmaker think he was up to in having such large strong hands when he was such a weak little man and in having the left one bigger than the right and why was he spreading his fingers out like that? Was he about to perform some kind of juggling act? If so, he'd have to change his spiel because it didn't fit!

"...If there's a question on Blake in the Eighteenth Century paper, my advice to you is – avoid it! Blake has become one of the heavy industries of modern times, especially at Girton. They've got a Research Fellowship in Blake, you know. It's been occupied for years by—"

Jonty looked round Kingmaker's room for the umpteenth time. Anything less like Neweyland was difficult to imagine.

Jonty reckoned that, apart from the large Georgian window looking out onto the large open courtyard of the College, he had seen rooms like this one under granite stairwells in the tenements of the Gorbals.

The flaking walls held several sepia-tinted photographs of Matthew Arnold, who, Kingmaker had once said: "...looks like a noble Victorian sheep."

Letting Arnold do that on those walls was bad enough, in itself; but add to it Kingmaker's pitiful attempts at furnishings and the experience began to verge on the outlandish; especially as, on the white painted mantelpiece – which was naked of anything else –

reposed one of the smallest and baldest busts of William Shakespeare Jonty had ever set eyes on; in white alabaster, too.

On the wall above the bust was an oblong of lighter colour – it could scarcely be called a stain – where one of the Arnold studies had weathered and fallen to pieces in its frame. The demise was fairly recent: in Jonty's first year, the Great Man had still been extant.

"...All undergraduates now have got a better understanding of poetry than had the prominent historian, G.M. Young, who said: 'I say a poem scans when you can hum it to a simple tune.' No, I didn't make it up! That kind of answer today will get you a solid third – if not a special!..."

Kingmaker's rooms were in some ways comforting: behold the obvious affinity they established with Sofia's housekeeping!

For example, Kingmaker had stuffed the knee-well of his writing desk full of old yellow-covered copies of Philosophy and stacks of greaseproof lecture notes so that he couldn't sit at it. Was it Freudian?

Musing on the matter set up an ache of regret in him, and he realized once more that he was both fond and not fond of Sofia.

She seemed to have this two-pronged effect on him: at times, she could knot the lining of his stomach into a spun-out wad of haggis so that he got belligerent with sexual desire; while, at other times, she could turn his libido into a retractable organ of great delicacy, like the fragile horns of a snail.

What a complicated ballsup it all was, this learning to live with people!

Why couldn't we have a radar built in, to tell us who to avoid and who to seek out? Why was it necessary to make mistakes? Why couldn't Creation have put into us a learning device that was foolproof and didn't make wrong choices? Was there something philosophically impossible about the idea?

What a mixture of the attractive and offensive Kingmaker was! Although operating on utterly distinct levels, that was another similarity between Kingmaker and Sofia.

At the moment, he was being engaging:

"All the Provincial places ought to shut down, I think. Don't quote me on that! I know this is a bit of a digression but – look at what they produce."

He mentioned a young and very successful novelist.

"Of course, he's a genius, you know! Somebody told him!"

Kingmaker paused and made a little intake of breath under his sloping front teeth.

"...He's got all the temperament of a ballerina. 'Oh, I couldn't possibly!'... They finish at the white-tile places thinking they know something. Well, they'd be quite harmless as garage hands... But that's not the worst. They've started inbreeding! You know the sort of thing – a Professor marrying his pupil. There's many a good man ended that way. Oh, the women are much worse! Look at – "

He mentioned a prominent literary female of the London set.

"How did she get there? Literary editor of that socio-political journal...? Well, I mean! She WAS married to that pseudo-intellectual – Michael – er – likes mountains –what's his name? She knows a lot about climbing, you know. I mean Alpinism, not the other sort. Though she knows a lot about that, too!..."

Today, Kingmaker had decided to put on one of his calculatedly offensive acts. Of course, the undergraduates loved it. But, apart from his cattiness, it was his brilliance of intellect that won him his disciples.

Jonty looked round at the score, or so, of faces smirking slyly at each other, while Kingmaker backbit happily.

Most of them sat on the grey-carpeted floor, balancing their notepads on knees, thighs or anywhere convenient. About six of their number were squashed up together on Kingmaker's ancient, carrot-coloured sofa on one side of the room. In front of the empty fireplace.

He had two armchairs to match: they were made of the same kind of tent canvas as the sofa, but with soil-stains left on them. Kingmaker always sat in the worst one himself, leaving the other armchair for whomsoever might fancy it. Presently, it was Jonty. Long tufts of grey straw poked through the arms and seat of Kingmaker's throne.

'Does your tired old suite embarrass you?'

Not Kingmaker, that's for sure. He was quite at home surrounded by rubbish, as was Sofia. Every trace of the extreme nervousness he showed at his lectures had gone. Here, he was among his devotees.

Kingmaker held up one hand, in a characteristic gesture, spreading his fingers, rigid and wide apart.

"...In writing Criticism, you can only remind people of what they know already. After all, they have read the work. That's the business of Criticism. It's also the art of sitting examinations. You make people more sharply aware of things. They know them vaguely. Your job, as Critic, is to make your point in a way that is directly relevant to your purpose. You are not concerned with logical definition, with philosophy..."

'It's all right for you,' thought Jonty, 'lolling in that chair, talking about definitions, wearing gear like old dusters thrown over a clothes horse – shirt (open to the navel), waistcoat of leather (buttoned up to the clavicle), thick grey flannel trousers (stiff as gumboots), cord jacket (fading and fraying over your rump) – you've got your degrees! What about me? How'm I going to retrieve the trousers of that hired suit? How'm I going to put back that doorknob, and decanter? How about Sir Leslie? How'm I going to pass my Finals? That's not easy, you know!'

"...Then, there are all the obvious things: read the paper through first, thoroughly..."

'And what about winning Sofia over when she's dead-set on not being won over? And why don't you stop looking like a small brown gnome, with aquiline ears and – Oh, God I feel lousy!'

"...So all I can do now is to wish you luck! Goodbye and good...!"

The realisation that he had had all the help he was going to get from Kingmaker (or from anybody else, before the Finals that were close now) revved up the symptoms of his hangover and he felt again the surge of the washing-up water; it was beginning to slosh again round his eyesockets and to spill into his ear-wells.

What could he do? He was drowning...! How was he going to manage to swim out to Sofia?

How?

22

After Kingmaker's tutorial, Jonty had gone back to the flat to try to study for a while, given up, and then persevered in making his way to the famous Copper Kettle in the centre of Cambridge to wait for Twaggin.

It had been an arduous journey, but he had finally got there and he was now on his third cup of coffee, had a table to himself, and was feeling better.

But the coffee wasn't really good enough to make King's College Chapel look any better, was it?

Hardly anything would be good enough for that!

He had spent the last half hour watching the tourists and visitors pass by outside the window of the coffee shop, surprisingly few of whom seemed to wear the healthy, active, pink lobes of yesteryear.

What did they mean by disporting these grey hulks as if they didn't know they'd got them on, watching but not listening? Were they all wax-logged, or deafened by pop groups?

Jonty took another sip of coffee. It had done its job, but it never tasted as good as it seemed in Westerns with Kirk Douglas, no matter how he felt.

Perhaps you had to have the right ingredients: stew it for hours on a hot stove in a rusty pot, wear high-heeled boots, hate fences, suffer a consuming nostalgia for the Old West, and only then would it taste like real cawfy and not like something you trod on round the branding fire?

Yes; Ruskin had been right about that chapel, hadn't he? As he had nearly said, it did look as if it had rolled onto its back and stuck them in the air.

But the question was: WHO had got the trousers and the doorknob?

Who had taken them? Why hadn't they been there after the party? Had Sir Leslie found the decanter in his sock-drawer yet?

Had lady Owens reported him to the University Proctors, the Dean or the University Senate, or only one of them?

DID THEYKNOW WHO IT WAS THAT HAD CASTRATED LADY OWENS'S LAVATORY DOOR?

Jonty was miserable.

'Ruskin must have felt like I'm feeling now when he wrote that description of King's College. But is it accurate?

'For example, how many udders has a sow got? Two rows of them! Yes, that's all right. But how many in each row? And what brings Ruskin knowing about sow's tits when he lived with his mother all his life and married only once and that was a failure? Like mine.

'This coffee WAS made from a fresh cowpat!'

One of Kingmaker's comments on Ruskin came back to him, put out in his usual adenoidal pontiff's manner while scratching the hairs on his chest between the buttons of his leather waistcoat:

"Poor Ruskin didn't have a chance! His mother went up to Oxford with him. She sat on him! Very heavily. It was hardly his fault he married the wrong one. I suppose everybody would have been the wrong one, as a matter of fact."

There must have been more to Ruskin than met the eye and what met the eye was bad enough – almost as bad as King's College Chapel over there – which would have looked nothing without that superb chestnut tree growing in front of it.

That gave it its flavour, the little screw of salt in the bag of crisps, the little touch of Harry in the night.

Where's the little screw of salt in my marriage?

Why can't I touch something in the night?

I shall begin feeling full-time like Ruskin, if this goes on.

Every bedtime, Sofia acts as if she's practising to take religious orders – and in that bed, in that bedroom, with that mirror.

What's so terrible about refusing to acknowledge your own wife, for Christ's sake? In PUBLIC?

I'm only too ready to acknowledge her in private, with everything I can lay my hands on, and a lot more that's too big to hold, as well.

I can marry the wrong wife better than anybody else – without needing my mother to sit on me in Cambridge. That's one better than Ruskin!

'What's so terrible about knocking over a Scrabble table that somebody called Sir Leslie is sitting at?

'It wasn't even as if HE knew I was wearing his trousers, was it? Could I help poking my elbow in Redshins's eye?

'Who said I broke it up? I didn't know the party was going to break up just after Soapy arrived, did I? How'd you know that wasn't Lady Owens's intention all the time?

'How did I know it would come off in my hands?

'Why does Kingmaker ALWAYS wear odd socks?

'How the hell do I know who took the trousers out of the berberis beds?

'Why was Redshins trying to curl up in your navel all evening?

'How did I know you can make ceiling plaster from Lady Owens's talcum powder?

'Why did you enjoy Redshins trying to do that?

'Is there going to be a question on the hammer beams of Ely Cathedral in the Tragedy Paper?

'I couldn't go home carrying one of Sir Leslie's decanters in my hand, could I? He might have noticed. Well, he might! How do I know what was really in it? I'm just telling you what it looked like and why shouldn't I be vulgar? I like being vulgar.

'Does Kingmaker really know what's in the exam papers or have they kept them locked away from him again?

'And if Redshins doesn't give me a First in the Elizabethan Paper after what he said to you, wouldn't you stuff the Nonesuch Donne up his backside, if you were me?

'I can't help it if you don't think it was talcum powder, can I? How can I show you the doorknob and hired trousers, if they aren't there any more? What do you THINK it was?

'You don't call that reasonable, do you?

'Take me for some kind of pervert, or something? How do *I* know where they've gone?

'Oh, my God! You don't think SHE let me do it to her, do you?

'I wasn't out long enough, was I? It wasn't that long, was it?

'All right, it was!

'I know I'd have liked to, but just don't be silly! What makes you think she'd let me because she's a tweeny?

'Has Sir Leslie informed the Dean?

'And that I would have, because I'm me?

'Why does Kingmaker write his notes on greaseproof paper?

'Where's Twaggin? Why is that bloody Makarios so bloody late?

'Who said I think her legs are better than yours?

'Oh, Christ, yes! If you must know, I did it to her in the fluff under Sir Leslie's bed – just to be kinky – and she made me so randy I couldn't help pulling off Lady Owens's doorknob and throwing it into the driveway after pouring talcum powder and cleaning sherry on my hired suit; then we had a knee-shaker, standing up inside Sir Leslie's wardrobe, and while I was kissing her all up and down her throbbing thighs and calf muscles and feeling dizzy with the smell of pussy, I put

Sir Leslie's trousers on by mistake after throwing mine into the berberis bushes and then I came back into the Scrabble Party and knocked over Sir Leslie's four-letter words and how the hell am I supposed to revise for the Tripos and sodding deathwatch beetles when you keep asking all these sodding questions?'

Jonty put his head in his hands and groaned.

Instead of coming from a Kingmaker tutorial, he felt as if he'd been to a three-week session of the Spanish Inquisition where he had had to take the part of both Victim and Prosecutor just after he had attended the Annual Conference of the Tory Party at Blackpool as a delegate of the P.L.O.

Perhaps he should risk another of the fresh cow pat coffee they sold here to get rid of the feeling?

He got to his feet and shuffled across to the counter, where he gave his order, grumbling again at the price and the smell of the branding irons.

One of the assistants watched him dubiously, and turned and whispered into her friend's ear, who was doing something to a milkshake. Then they both turned to look at him.

He went back to his table with his coffee.

They kept looking at him at intervals, and whispering, until Twaggin came in and sat down at the table with Jonty, when both girls started to giggle.

"What would you do if girls kept looking at you?" asked Jonty.

"Look at THEM!" said Twaggin. "And then I'd – "

"—I mean, as if I'd put a pinch of snuff in my coffee?"

"Girls always look at me like that. Then they giggle."

"But it's all right for you! With a beard like that you could easily put snuff in your coffee. I couldn't."

"It's an odd thing! I've noticed that a number of my friends suffer from illusions of grandeur. Yours is rather different. It's an illusion that you're clean-shaven – except for that wisp on your top lip – clean-minded and sane. Are you, or are you not, maintaining that you are incapable of putting snuff in your coffee?"

"In this coffee, I am!"

"What, capable or incapable?"

"Capable."

"There you are then," said Twaggin. "Q.E.D."

Jonty told him what it tasted like.

"The quality of the coffee is immaterial," said Twaggin. "It's one's propensity for evil that counts. Besides, it can't taste worse than a decanter full of vinegar, can it?"

Jonty was startled.

"How on earth did you know about that?"

"Natural powers of perspicacity. Anybody who walks three times round a Scrabble table before pushing it on the floor must either be indulging in rituals of a magical nature, or just plain drunk. My money's on the latter. Anyway, I happened to be conversing with one of Sir Leslie's waiters a moment ago in the Market Square. Very interesting! He says somebody drank half a decanter of vinegar and stole a full one with sherry in it."

"It wasn't full!"

"I *thought* it was you! Where's the decanter?"

Jonty told Twaggin all about the episode.

"I didn't know it was vinegar, but I knew it tasted like something for cleaning Lady Owens's horse brasses. I was thirsty. I was hungry. I was being forced to play Scrabble. What other extenuating circumstances do you want?"

"And why did you pull her doorknob off?" asked Twaggin.

"Oh, my God! Is that bruited all over the University, too? When are the Proctors going to frogmarch me down to the dungeons? Where are they – under the University Press?"

Twaggin said nothing.

"I just don't see how you or anybody else could know about the—. I don't even know where the bloody thing is myself!"

"Don't fret yourself, my boy! Only Soapy and I know about this."

"Soapy and you! How does Soapy know?"

"That's easy! As you are aware, she came late to the Scrabble Party."

"I know, I know! And..."

"She found a pair of trousers with nobody in them and a doorknob without a door."

At this point, Twaggin leaned across the small round table towards Jonty and said, in a baritone stage whisper: "IN SIR LESLIE'S FLOWER BEDS!"

The two assistants giggled audibly. Jonty looked apprehensively over his shoulder.

"What took her into the flower beds?"

"She was entering the driveway, when she saw a pair of trousers come hurtling from a bedroom window. She almost decided to ignore them. But she didn't see how it could be intentional, and she didn't see how it could be a mistake. So she searched around until she found them."

"Good thinking!" said Jonty. "She didn't – ?"

"—Of course not!" said Twaggin, anticipating his question. "But it wasn't long before a doorknob followed the breeches. She put the doorknob into a pocket and the nether garment inside her topcoat. Nobody saw."

"My thankfulness is terrific, as Hurree Jamset Ram Singh used to say. Tell Soapy!"

"I think she knows! She used to read *The Magnet*," replied Twaggin ponderously.

"Oh, did she?" asked Jonty with great scorn.

Twaggin was enjoying himself immensely. He began, in a very leisurely fashion, to take something out of his overalls pocket (his dress for the day) and held it up before Jonty's astonished eyes.

"Is this it?" asked Twaggin loudly.

"Put it away, you fool!" squeaked Jonty. "Do you want me carted off on the tumbrils? It's valuable!"

"My beard obscures all! I know it's valuable."

"You wouldn't believe it, Twaggers, I thought at the time I heard somebody scratching around in that driveway.'

"Lucky it was our dear Soapy, eh? If it hadn't – "

"—I know! But there wasn't time to be careful. I wish I was dead!"

"That could be arranged. Don't ring us, we'll ring you!"

"It's all right for you! How am I going to get Sir Leslie's breeches back in his wardrobe and Lady Owens's doorknob back to the john?"

"You could fall off a punt and drown in the Cam."

"Be serious!"

"My! You are shook up, aren't you? All right! Why not send him an anonymous parcel?"

"Won't work! He doesn't know his pants are missing, yet. Wouldn't a parcel make things worse? I mean, they must know about the doorknob, mustn't they, but—?"

"—Doorknobs, not doorknob."

"What? Don't be silly! It was only one."

"Two!"

Twaggin pulled another object from another pocket and showed him two doorknobs, concealing them with his beard. The new one was a lovely specimen of deep blacks and vermilions and yellows swirling splendidly into their own crystal centres. Jonty could see that much.

"Now, look here! That wasn't me. I ought to know how many bloody doorknobs I—"

"—Don't get shirty. It was me!"

"You? Oh, my Saviour! Now, we're in it. Or, to be more accurate, I'm in it!"

"It just came off in my hand, as the bishop said to the actress. It was an emergency. I tested one and it was locked. Some fool said, try Six Mile Bottom. I had to do something pretty—"

—The sounds of the heavy flat footsteps played back in his mind, full as a goosegog, outside his john!

He'd hoped it was Redshins. Reinforcements had been at hand, and he'd sent them galloping on to the next station!

Oh, the ironies of drinking cleaning fluids in water closets!

He might have guessed it was Twaggin. Who else walked on two unshod pancakes?

"You hadn't already been in the one I was in, had you?" asked Jonty suspiciously.

The number of doorknobs that man must have violated in his time was probably countless!

"Are you casting aspersions on my continence?"

"I just thought... Anyhow, what happened?"

"A natural enough mistake, in the circumstances. I was about to leave and tried to open the door; but some fool of a carpenter had screwed it on the wrong way round and – whoops! There it was!"

Jonty groaned.

He was doing a lot of that this morning. Perhaps his diet was deficient in something vital?

"At breakfast, the happiest sounds come from a baby fed on..."

What with Sofia's breakfasts and College lunches, what else can you expect?

The answer is obvious: weak, sickly, groaning infants.

'Maybe a course of sterilized baby foods in fifty-seven varieties will help matters? But it'll just be my luck to need the fifty-eighth.

'Certainly, SOME drastic remedy is needed.

'Perhaps I should send a telegram to Redshins: THE GAME'S UP REDSHINS WE ALL KNOW YOUR WIFE SELLS AFTERNOON TEAS IN GRANTCHESTER.

'It won't help the Owens situation. But it will help the Redshins situation and, in some obscure way, that will help the Owens situation. Maybe we can manage to throw suspicion for the whole fiasco on to Redshins? Let him curl up in his own wife's cleavage, if she's got one, and—'

"—So I just had to hide the bloody thing away for a while," Twaggin was booming out, for everyone to hear. "And smuggle it out at the end of the party. Hence, the overwhelming accumulation of fertilizer we appear to be in!"

The assistants were now giggling wildly.

"Some of which we're drinking in this coffee," called Jonty loudly.

Their giggling stopped at once, and they turned back to their hissing machines.

Jonty offered to buy Twaggin a cup. He refused.

"Wise man!" said Jonty.

"But I'll have tea," said Twaggin.

They bought it and, after Twaggin had suitably subdued the assistants by examining them minutely with folded arms and bristling beard, they went back to their table to discuss the pros and cons of the matter.

Very soon, they had concluded that there weren't any pros, and decided that they had better wait for one to turn up before doing anything at all.

So Jonty took the chance of telling Twaggin how badly things were going between him and Sofia. When he had finished Twaggin announced deeply:

"I don't believe in marriage."

"Yes; that follows! It fully explains why you are married."

Jonty had been waiting for an opportunity to mention this matter to Twaggin, ever since he had filled Jonty's bath with broken beer bottles.

"No! Soapy believes in it, though."

"And that was the only way you could get her to – ?"

"—Not at all! We'd been having that for a long time. But I wanted HER. Marriage was the only way I could keep her. So, we married."

"Very convincing! Hence, your incurable sniffing after Sofia, I suppose?"

"You make it sound so canine!"

"Isn't it?" asked Jonty.

"Not at all! That's just to show her," Twaggin replied, blandly.

"Sofia?"

"No. Soapy."

"Show her what?"

"That even though we're married, I'm still single!"

"Very subtle!"

"Soapy has the same freedom."

"But she doesn't WANT the same freedom, does she?" said Jonty.

"Too bad!" replied Twaggin. "That's one of the consequences of the movement for Women's Lib. That's what *I'm* like! That's what *you're* like! Most men are like us! They want equality with US. We don't want equality with THEM. They can't have it both ways."

"Sounds like a good recipe for indissolubility!"

"It does put a certain strain on things. THAT, I will admit!"

"Why do you keep it a secret?"

"What? My marriage?... Well, that's easy! It puts women off if they know one is—"

"—Not these days, it doesn't! Equal privileges! Equal promiscuity!"

"Ah! But the perverse thing about me is that I'm not attracted to women who don't mind sleeping around. It's the faithful ones I go for. There's no thrill in depraving depravity! Depraving virtue is what turns me on! Curious, isn't it?"

"Why?"

"Why what?" asked Twaggin.

"Why innocence? You want to—!"

"—God knows! Touch of the de Sades, I suppose. Bloody diabolical, but there it is!"

"You want to deprave virtue because it is THERE!"

"No! Because it is VIRTUE in theory! But I'm fairly pure in practice. From choice, I might add."

"Why?" asked Jonty. " If not from conviction!"

"Don't know! It seems to take such an amount of time, if you go in for it on any scale. And if you don't do a lot of it, it doesn't really seem worth bothering with, does it? Perhaps it's a case of the voice of lions and the acts of hares, as the Bard pointed out somewhere?"

"Won't hold water! You hide marriage because you want to corrupt innocence. But you don't bother to corrupt it, because you haven't got the energy! So why hide it, in the first place?"

"It's the principle of the thing!"

"Not up to the Twaggin mark at all!"

"It does sound pretty thin, doesn't it?" agreed Twaggin.

'I'm slim,' thought Jonty. 'You're thin. That's skinny!'

Twaggin drew in a deep breath, regretful that his argument and his pose had not stood up under scrutiny; but he was perfectly good-tempered about it.

"They're open!" he said. "What about having one?"

"Each?" asked Jonty.

"Each!" replied Twaggin, with a booming chortle.

'Happiness is the shape of a brown dumpy,' thought Jonty.

That was the idea! He could work more conscientiously on his Spring drinking programme, couldn't he? It wouldn't help the Sofia situation, but it would help the Jonty situation. Practice was important!

Perhaps you lost the capacity for getting drunk as you got older, as well as for having sex?

Anyway, he couldn't take the risk, and he was in a position to do something about one of them, if not about the other.

He'd better grasp the opportunity with both hands – in a large glass noggin.

"Let's go, my friend!" said Jonty.

23

Jonty was three parts in the wind once again, but he believed he was more skilful when he was tipsy.

He was making a noise like a 250cc motorcycle on the Wall of Death. Monster responded nicely, taking the corner of Dust Road with finesse.

A large man wearing a line of unbroken hair for eyebrows and carrying a medical bag leapt backwards with great athleticism onto the kerbstones, just in time.

It was clear that he saw no skill at all in Jonty's performance.

"You silly young bastard! I'll report you to the Proctors. Don't you see there's a surgery, here?"

In reply, Jonty waved happily to him.

The argument that Twaggin and he had just staged in the pub with another of the Cambridge groups had exhilarated him: he felt as if he had just been waited on by Redshins, University Lecturer in Pornographic Poetry, wearing a short frilly apron, in his wife's tea-garden.

When Jonty reached the gate of One Dust Road, the doctor, luckily for Jonty, had gone and Monster went quietly to his stable in Mrs Cough's nude hedge under the window.

Last night, during the period of the Scrabble party, this group had been singing Elizabethan madrigals under the Bridge of Sighs while standing up in punts – no mean feat – and, today, they were filling the bar with noisy self-approval. Their disturbance and cockiness had angered Twaggin, so he had chosen to insult the one member of the group who wore a beard: it was a spit deep and stiff enough to screw a handle on.

Jonty suspected that Twaggin was more offended by the man's style of hairiness than he was by his boisterous manners and had decided, in view of his size, to pluck him by his madrigals rather than by his beard.

"Singing part-songs is hardly a suitable activity for men," boomed Twaggin truculently. "Anyway, it is inferior to water-polo as a sport."

Spadebeard, who appeared to sing castrato, trilled a high response:

"That's absolutely philistine rubbish!"

Twaggin, basso profondo, went on to say that water-polo was not only a healthier activity, it sounded better, and that he, personally, was acquainted with at least a dozen players who had perfect pitch, which accounted for the fact that they could throw a goal from fifteen yards out, and how many madrigal singers did Spadebeard know who could even swim?

These comments seemed to confuse them a good deal, and later the arguments got even harder to follow, but everybody enjoyed it – with the possible exception of Spadebeard – who, when Twaggin and Jonty left, sat sullenly dribbling into his beer.

As Jonty climbed the stairs, he remembered the scene with great relish.

He went straight to Mrs Cough's sofa and lay down on it: he needed a brief respite for things to settle down a bit and become steady again. It felt very much, he imagined, like lying on Mrs Cough, who wore metal-ribbed corsets and bulged in unexpected places; so, as soon as he could, he sat up and blinked carefully at the room.

He was aware that the usual balance of the habitat – a blend of Coughist decay and Sofian disorder – was subtly different; but he couldn't quite place how.

Drawers that were half-shut before were still half-open now, and they appeared to be full of what they were always full of: hairpins, glue, body-stockings, tubes of ivory white, stamps, wizened oranges, cotton-reels, tubes of yellow ochre, letters from Alexis, two plaster bas-relief wall-ducks which had kept flying for ever and ever in the direction of Parker's Pieces until Jonty had taken them down, and tubes of cobalt blue for painting portraits of soup with.

The tired twin straw armchairs seemed to be the same: they still yawned hugely, promising a repose they could not provide, littered with cups, *Weekend Mails*, bras, saucers, briefs, plates, pairs of trews, and glossies like *Vanity* and *Housewife*.

The coalscuttle held its usual pile of beer-bottles – waiting to be collected by Twaggin and incarcerated in his large plaid bag.

The holiday posters put on the walls by Sofia still shone blandly out, continuing to announce sunny places in Spain and Jamaica and cheap rail travel between mythical sun-drenched places in an imaginary Britain, as well as advertising mystery tours by coach round a Black Country that had been suitably washed, bleached and neatly ironed by the artists.

In fact, normality reigned everywhere.

So, why did the place seem to be different? Was it simply another case of things seeming to be different when they were really the same? Or, of seeming to seem the same when they were really different?

Maybe, lately, under the pressure of Finals, he had let the actuality-watching slip a little? Perhaps he should step it up a bit?

You never knew when existence would get up and start winging away.

That was a consequence of mixing with mass-produced decoys like Newey, Redshins, and the Owenses: it led you to expect stasis; it blunted you; you couldn't see what was what.

Another good thing that beer did was to make your eyesight dimmer and your sense of reality keener, wasn't it?

By the way, where was Sofia?

Why wasn't she busy painting one of the innumerable varieties of tinned food they had on the market, and wearing her mules and her tie-and-dye sweatshirt? Had she gone shopping for new models?

Then, he spotted what had been disturbing him: her easel, stool and palette had gone from their places in the middle of the room.

That was it! It was the space that had nothing in it (except the bald carpet with dandruff) which had made him uneasy.

In Sofia's world, space was not for putting things into orbit in, but for cluttering things up in, and she was very good at doing it on account of the practice she had had. Emptiness of a radical kind like this was a serious matter!

Where had they gone and where was she?

First, Jonty went to look in the kitchen, which usually he entered of necessity only, for breakfast and suchlike, and, at other times, only in dire emergencies: the Coughist-and-Sofian compounds were particularly powerful in there.

Second, he visited the bedroom. The crater in the mattress wasn't even smoking and there were no signs of life on its arid slopes.

Third, he returned to the sitting-room.

Had she pinned a note to the mantelpiece? No! Nothing except the mindless Toby Jug smiling endlessly at its head full of pencils and knitting needles, and standing beside it two derelict bottles of nail varnish, and a plastic dustpan warped by the heat, and an old mug thirsty for nescaff, and the bare patches of Mrs Cough's shelf – all mordant with dust. Otherwise, the mantelpiece was empty.

Not knowing what to do next, Jonty had returned to the Cough-shaped sofa and was preparing to go to sleep, when Sofia unexpectedly turned up.

"Oh, you're back, are you?" asked Jonty.

"I don't know! If it's me you're talking to – yes, I'm back. If you're talking to someone else, I'm not!" replied Sofia, testily.

"What do you mean by that cryptic remark?"

"Don't you know?"

Some impulse was warning Jonty not to follow that line of enquiry directly, just at present. He decided to step up his Sofia-watching, instead.

Apart from a very sullen expression, she was wearing a mini dress, sandals, and apparently nothing else. But she had always had the ability to look as if she wasn't wearing any underclothes. Jonty liked it. It was one of the first things he had observed about her. While many females showed ridges of elastic over thighs, hips and waists, or rucks, knots, wads and lumps at other assorted sites, Sofia looked invariably smooth all over.

Jonty didn't know how she achieved this effect, but he found it sexy and it seemed to promise things – some precisely, some vaguely. Many of the promises had been kept and a few hadn't, and that was also sexy. There was no doubt that what he liked about Sofia he liked a lot.

"You're looking very luscious today, he said, quoting from a current West End hit," said Jonty.

"And you look as if you've drunk too much again, she said, quoting from another!" Sofia retorted.

"It's not nice not to be nice when somebody's trying to be nice," said Jonty, determined to like her looking sexy and determined to let her know he liked it.

"Maybe somebody's trying to be too nice too late," said Sofia.

"Me? I'm always nice to you!" replied Jonty.

Sofia looked down her nose.

"Well, nearly always. And you can't be TOO nice! Can you? Does that make sense?"

"Yes! Why not?"

She was belligerent.

"Well," said Jonty, trying to smooth her down with reasonable tones, "if I like someone, I like that person to be nice to me, and I don't mind HOW nice she – he – "

He stopped, aware he'd made a mess of his sentence structure, and then restarted quickly.

"They can't be TOO nice. It's only if you don't much like someone that you don't want that person to be nice to you," he said, this time carefully avoiding the grammatical pitfall. "Isn't it?"

"Who's arguing?" replied Sofia, airily.

"Ah, like that, is it? That's not a nice reply!"

"Who said it was?" she asked truculently.

This question, for some reason, made him conscious that he was lying on the Cough-shaped sofa without enjoying it; so he sat up and looked at Sofia lounging on the litter in one of the armchairs, showing off most of what she had to show in a shape that was very unlike Mrs Cough's, decidedly aware that he was enjoying it.

He wondered whether it was quite decent to like, as much as he did, the nice bits that she had, when he disliked the not-so-nice bits equally as much, if not more.

This was a question he often came back to, especially of late: if he liked the nice bits ENOUGH, could he learn to like the nasty bits SUFFICIENTLY?

And, furthermore, if this was what loving somebody required, it was sodding complicated, wasn't it?

"Look!" said Jonty, suddenly, "Why don't you just tell me what's the matter – what the matter is, and let's get it over with?"

He was as much annoyed with himself for fluffing another construction as he was with Sofia for baiting him. He must be more squiffed than he felt.

"You see! That's what's so bloody infuriating about you! You think people's feelings are to be 'got over'. Well, they aren't! Some feelings can't be got over. They're just there – whether you like them or not – and a fat lot of good talking about them will do!"

"You know, if you keep going on in this un-nice way, I shall stop thinking you're half as sexy as you really are."

"That's another thing! You've got a one-track mind and it always runs into the same siding, doesn't it?" asked Sofia, witheringly.

"Siding! Sex is main line express stuff, not goods-yard milarkey."

He grinned wickedly.

"Of course, I don't mind doing a bit of shunting, now and again!"

"And there was I, the first time I met you, thinking you were so intellectual!"

"Who? Me? When? It's a lie!"

"Yes, you! When we were with Crehan in The Woodman spouting all that guff about poetry."

"Oh, that! Don't let that throw you! It was a sort of mating dance. I wanted you. Anyway, you watch your language – calling me intellectual. That's libellous, you know! No, that's wrong. I mean, slanderous! To be called one of them – and by your own wife – hurts!"

"Just a mating display?" repeated Sofia, tight-lipped.

"What do you mean – just? I went to a lot of trouble to put that on. I was trying to show you I wanted you. Nothing wrong with that, is there?"

"No, of course not! But why don't you try to put something on now? Why don't you show me you want me, now?"

"I do! I'm always doing that. But you banished me, like a monk, and not just for Lent, neither. I suspect you've been putting bromide in my tea! That's why my brain overheats when I'm trying to think up new mating dances and I've just been telling you how—!"

"—Not like that! You're always ready to show me you want me like THAT! I mean, in other ways. As if you're fond of me. As if you LIKE me. And I mean – fond of ME and not only my equipment. As if – I – "

"—Oh Christ! This is all too metaphysical for me! How do you expect me to separate what you ARE from what you look like? What you are IS what you look like, among other things – isn't it? If you hadn't looked like what you do look like, I wouldn't even want to know what you are, would I? Oh, Jay Aitch See! You're making me sound like Redshins explicating a sonnet by John Donne. Or, rather, John Donne explicating a sonnet by Redshins. How can I ever forgive you for that? It was all this stuff on the outside," said Jonty, indicating her body with a wave of his hand, "that attracted me in the first place!"

"I know that, Stupid! But you don't have to concentrate on that alone and forget the inside, do you?"

"I see! Love you for yourself alone and not for your yellow hair!"

"What?"

"I've often wondered if that bloody myopic Irishman knew what he was talking about when he wrote that! Is all this metaphysical foreplay what you and Twaggin indulged in while you were fondling his beard in our bed? Soapy said you might have!"

" No, it isn't! And I wasn't fondling his beard! But – well – he did mention Santa – Santa – what's his name?"

"Claus!" supplied Jonty. "What were you fondling?"

"Fool! And I didn't – ," said Sofia, somewhat mollified by Jonty's flash of jealousy.

"—Yana!" said Jonty, recovering himself smartly, and trying to get back to his placatory role.

"Yes, that was it! Santayana. George Santayana."

"It's indecent! Quoting American philosophers in my bed! 'Furtive unchastity, under me own roof!' I'll punch Twaggin's head!"

"At least, HE talks to me in a nice way, as if I matter, as if he CARES about me!"

"As if he likes the way you feel, you feel? And I don't, I suppose?" said Jonty, not able to keep up the tone of conciliation.

"Pig! You never TALK to me at all, never mind in Twaggin's way!"

Jonty was silent because he knew this was true. He rarely discussed anything with Sofia.

Oh, yes! He TOLD her about things – about Redshins, the Reverend F.E.N., the Owenses, and the rest. But that was like talking about the development of silent films in Russia: it was remote from life, a bit of social history. Whereas, Twaggin, clearly, had been able to put his finger on something in Sofia that, up till now, he hadn't been able to touch himself, even by accident.

Perhaps, it WAS his own fault?

Hadn't he come to believe that she hadn't got it anywhere he could reach, this intrinsic place, where what he was would fit?

Perhaps he should do some tentative scouting around and hope to come across the site? Were there any maps? Where was his compass? Was it sensitive enough?

"What, are you saying nothing? Most of the time, you grumble about the way I keep house, my paintings, the way I make tea, and things like that!"

"Well, we ARE married, aren't we? Even if we aren't living together. We can't spend our days living past each other, can we? You know how I hate poking about in a rag-and-bone yard! And you spend days on end painting and neglecting—!"

"—I'm not neglecting anything! I never promised to keep your house spick and span. I told you I was a slob before we married! Living in a mess..." she swept her arm along the air, "doesn't worry me a teeny-weeny bit! So there it is!"

"It certainly is!" said Jonty.

"Why don't you ever ask me about my paintings? What I'm trying to do? What I'm aiming at? My philosophy of art?"

Jonty believed that he had very cogent reasons for not doing that; but it certainly wouldn't help matters to tell her what they were right now.

He took refuge in an evasion. "I don't understand that kind of modern art."

"Well, you could try, couldn't you?"

"You're driving a hard bargain, ma'am."

"See what I mean?"

Jonty saw.

"I'm sorry!" he said.

"Good heavens!"

Sofia sat up straight on the bulging straw armchair.

"Well, that's a change!" she said, in astonishment. "You've never apologised before, have you?"

"Anyway – where IS your painting?"

"At the station."

"Station! What –?"

"—And my suitcase. I'm going to Birmingham for a while. On the 4.30 this afternoon. Alexis is getting married tomorrow."

"Deserting me, are you, just before Finals? What about my –?"

"—Here! What time is it? I shall have to fly. 'Bye, 'bye! I'll write."

She stood up, smoothed down her mini, and was halfway to the door before he had managed to stutter: "G-give Alexis my best wishes, eh?"

But she'd gone before Jonty could ask when she was coming back and why she was taking her easel to a wedding.

24

Three weeks had passed. Jonty had received no word from Sofia about Alexis's wedding, or about herself; but he was feeling pretty good, nonetheless. Finals had finished last week, and he had congratulated himself several times on managing to be present for every one of the sessions and for completing the papers.

Of course, with Sofia away, he had gone back to rooming in College, and so far this morning, he had succeeded in eating a breakfast of fried bread and egg-joke before Mrs Stickett had arrived – and before she had performed another of her monologues on undergraduate morals and the rigours of bed-making.

However, she had contrived to challenge him on the state of his frying pan. "What've you cooked in that pan, then, young man?"

"My breakfast!"

"Yes, I see you've 'ad a negg! What did you use? Tonette Boot Polish?"

"Not at all! But the secret of cooking egg-joke is never to wash the pan. That colour is the trick of the trade!"

"It must come out all brown!"

"It does! That's why it's called egg-joke."

She had given a monumental sniff, which told Jonty far more adequately than any words exactly what she thought of his culinary arcana, so he had decided to make himself scarce during her chores and take a hot bath.

So far, he had spent an hour and a half soaking in one of the College tubs: only four people had sworn and hammered at the door, which, he felt, wasn't at all bad, really.

Most of the time he had spent in working out curses that he could intone under his breath in the presence of the Reverend F.E.N for not setting a single question in the Tragedy Paper on the feeding habits of Deathwatch Beetles; or on the processes of preferment in the Anglican Church; or on the gardening hints to be gleaned from Gray's 'Elegy Written in a Country Churchyard.'

The F.E.N hadn't even worked anything of the kind into the papers on the Eighteenth Century Background. It was quite disbuggerous!

Of course, the Reverend FEN could have been forgiven if he hadn't spent so much time and energy giving out the strongest possible signals that his tuition had the virtues, at least, of relevance.

Couldn't one expect, therefore, that his *modus operandi* and tutorial content had some relation to the forthcoming examinations? Not so!

He had fooled everybody.

He had consistently avoided any serious approach to the curriculum, and had he not, bumblingly, put his wares on the educational market in the same format he had brought to perfection somewhere about the year of the General Strike?

The answer to the question was a resounding Yes!

But Jonty felt a reluctant admiration, all the same, for the religious personage in question. It was surely an achievement of a kind? Didn't it show an unwavering singleness of purpose to be only taken up with the things that mattered to him alone?

Yes, to both questions.

How had it come about, then, that he had managed to get himself put in charge of the moral welfare of others, particularly of junior members of the University of Cambridge?

Had he hired a theatrical costume, dressed himself up in it and got himself the job of Dean on the strength of the disguise? Wasn't it a consequence of his cloth, surely: people were conditioned to believe that religious dress equalled morality and responsibility?

Jonty had come to believe that they were unrelated. That they SHOULD be related, was a horse of a different colour, as they say.

What did the Dean know of moral purpose, altruism, the greatest good of the greatest number, and the rest of the syllabus on the English Moralists?

Jonty was doubtful if the Reverend Newey could have passed the paper even if he'd been given the wink on the questions beforehand.

He even found difficulty in enunciating some of the names of the authors that Jonty had had to read – as, for example, Bolingbroke, whose name he pronounced phonetically, whether from ignorance of English usage or dislike of Deistical doctrines was anybody's guess.

Any acquaintance Newey had with the concerns of the English Moralists must be of a theoretical and nodding kind; quite unlike the terms of familiarity he was on with Incompetence, Gardening, Egotism and Ambition.

How many generations of undergraduate resentments had been brought to luxuriant inflorescence by the green fingers of the Reverend Newey would never be known.

Nonetheless, Jonty couldn't help liking the old idiot. He didn't intend to create such consequences.

Undeliberate bastardy just happened to be a function of his life, a fact of his behaviour. Like the spikes on his succulents; he was one of the 'unintentional idiots' so cherished by V.I. Lenin.

The Dean couldn't help the colour of his fingers, could he?

No!

Jonty had come to realize that it was the deliberate kind of bastardy that had to be fought, and especially those who exploited it.

Having worked the Newey-conundrum out to his own satisfaction, Jonty climbed from the bath, dried himself, dressed, returned his towel and toiletries to his room, and then strolled down to the Porters' Lodge to see if he had got a letter from Sofia.

The curly-haired Pickwick-faced young porter handed him, with his customary obscenity, two letters. "Both in a plain cover, mate! Same firm as mine, I expect. Try 'em for size, first!"

"I will! Can't get 'em big enough, usually," said Jonty, who always went along with him.

"Like bloody windsocks, are they?"

The porter exploded into laughter. "My problem exactly! Don't do anything I wouldn't do!" he shouted, as Jonty walked away with his letters.

Jonty could see by the handwriting that one of them was from his father. He put it into a pocket, until later.

The other he didn't like the look of. It merely addressed him by name, with no stamp and no domicile. Probably official! Although there was no crest on the envelope, so it wasn't from the Admin proper.

He examined the calligraphy with care: it appeared to have been written by a clapped-out literate wasp dragging its pointed sodden rump across the envelope.

Only Newey had a fountain pen and a hand and a mind that wrote like that; but the ink had changed to Royal Blue from Royal Black.

Had the cost of his tobacco gone up again?

As Jonty read it, the ends of his stomach began to twist in opposite directions, as if Mrs Stickett had wrung it out like a pillowcase on washing day.

The young porter, who had observed him open and read the letter, put his head out of his office door and called out loudly: "Gotcha at last, 'ave they? Nickin' College cutlery again, is it?"

Jonty felt white round the gills, but he manfully held up two obscene fingers at the young man before walking slowly towards the rooms of the Dean. By the time he arrived, he had recovered some of his *sang froid*. The Reverend Newey was at home and, surprisingly, answered to his knock at once.

As usual, he was standing in a huge pall of smoke, almost obscured, like a factory stack before the enforcement of the Clean Air Act. He was holding up to the light a small plant with a lot of spikes in a tiny pot, examining it closely.

"Ah, come in, Jonty, come in! Doesn't look too good, does it?" asked the Dean, taking his Petersen out of his mouth and pointing to the plant with the stem of it.

Jonty peered at the plant with distaste. Apart from its offensively dark-green greenness, it looked to Jonty as all right as it ever would.

"I'm not much good on berberis, I'm afraid, sir!" he said.

"What? Berberis?…"

"Or Snarfia," added Jonty.

"Oh! Yes, I see! Well, look at that?"

The Dean stabbed at the plant with his pipe.

"It's mould! See it?"

Jonty observed a little patch of something that, up until the present moment, he had thought only afflicted goldfish when they floated sideways in bowls.

"Mmmm!" he commiserated, non-commitally.

Had the Dean been over-feeding the ant eggs?

"Maybe it's had too much water, eh, Jonty? A succulent like this should – I must keep it under observation and – er – er—."

"—Observe it?" offered Jonty.

"—Er – see how it turns out," concluded the Dean.

"That's what I meant," said Jonty.

"I'm sure you did, Jonty, I'm sure you did!" replied the Dean absent-mindedly.

He was looking for a suitable place to put the plant down in.

He seemed to be quite unaware of where he had got it from, and blithely passed over its empty drip-dish that looked accusingly up at him from his coffee table. He eventually placed it at the most convenient corner of his desk, and turned to Jonty, peering blandly at him from behind and around his Petersen.

"Yes, Jonty?" he asked, smoke popping from his mouth.

"I believe you wished to see me, sir," replied Jonty.

Newey removed the large, curving Petersen from between his teeth, incredulously: "I did?"

Jonty, with a heavy shuddering but suppressed sigh, held out the note that had summoned him.

"You sent this, sir!"

Newey stared at Jonty's hand for a long time, quite bitterly.

'Is he going to comment enviously on the unaccustomed cleanliness of my fist? Or is he getting himself ready to deny all knowledge of it?' Jonty was thinking, when the Dean said quickly:

"Oh, yes! There WAS something. Sit down a moment, Jonty."

He indicated the sofa in front of the coffee table. Jonty sat down. The Dean remained standing.

"I'm sure it's nothing to worry about, Jonty, but the Master – has been rather –"

'—So his guess had been right, after all!'

"—rather disturbed about – er – certain incidents that took place in the Lodge – er – some weeks ago. He is interviewing those who attended his – er – party, on that evening. He has reached your name, Jonty!"

At this point, the Dean looked away, moved round his desk, sat down in his swivel chair, leaned back, pressed his neck further down into his dog-collar, and shook his head.

'Started with it, you mean!' thought Jonty, and wondered what awful calamity was about to drop on him from a dizzy height.

"No!" said the Dean, continuing to shake his head. "He is not going to make it a matter of College discipline. So it is out of my hands. You see, Jonty, he expressly wishes to avoid that!"

"Oh, yes?" gasped Jonty weakly, feeling that he couldn't bear to hear another word of the Dean's calculated vaguenesses. "What—?"

"—That is why he wishes to talk to you personally and privately, Jonty. Normally, of course..."

The pause was agonising. Newey leaned forward over an upturned hand, removed his Petersen from his mouth, tapped out the bowl of it into his palm and gazed at the little mound of white ash there.

'If that's what he does, no wonder he thinks my hands are so clean!'

The Dean eventually emptied the handful of cinders into an ashtray and buffed the palm on the thigh of his broadcloth trousers before rubbing both palms together.

'Grubby old bugger!'

The complexity of the whole operation seemed to have made him forget what he was about to say, and he looked vaguely round the room at his plants, before his eye fell again, with a slight start, on Jonty sitting stolidly on the sofa.

Had he expected him to have gone away by now?

"Normally, what, sir?" asked Jonty, in irritation.

"I beg your pardon, Jonty?"

"You were saying, 'Normally, of course.' But you didn't finish."

"Oh, I see!" he said vaguely, and paused again.

Then, quickly, he shot out at Jonty:

"Could you manage three o'clock, this afternoon, at the Lodge? The Master is a very busy man, you know!"

"Yes, certainly!" said Jonty, as if he were looking forward to it.

"Splendid! Well, that's settled, then," said the Dean, commencing to re-pack his Petersen with fresh tobacco.

'Nothing splendid about it, you old junky!'

Jonty realized, with some consternation, that the Dean's subpoena had badly upset his composure and that he hadn't even managed to summon up the presence of mind to employ a single one of his silent curses newly-fashioned in the bath for special chanting in the presence of the Dean himself.

A resounding victory to the meddling cleric in question, that was!

"Goodbye, Jonty."

"Goodbye, sir."

Jonty got up and walked across to the heavy panelled door.

As he was closing it behind him, he saw the Reverend Newey gazing dolefully at the patch of fishmould on his little spikey berberis, with an expression that proclaimed he was once again commiserating with himself on the bloodiness of the situations that recurringly confronted him in life, and wondering how he could work a cactaceous theme and imagery into his next sermon.

'Good luck! Let me know which Sunday you have it scheduled for, and I'll pin up a warning in the Screens!'

Outside, in the passageway, Jonty's first impulse was to buy a single ticket to John O'Groats, and, as soon as he had arrived there, look up the sailing dates for Scandinavia. Or had the execrable board of British Rail discontinued the line as unprofitable?

'Anyway,' he thought miserably, 'I haven't got the money.'

After considering several other courses of action in descending order of cowardice, he decided that discretion was the better part of valour and that he'd have to persevere until the guillotine was ready to fall.

'If you stick it out, they always chop it off,' he lamented. 'But you can't NOT stick it out, can't you – can you – can't you?'

He kept repeating the two question tags to himself, aloud, as he went along, trying to determine which was the correct one.

25

He found himself walking mechanically along the Cam.

The air was friendly, the sky puffy with the little white clouds usually seen only in children's primers, the birds affable, the river normally murky with a decided absence of punts on it.

So Jonty made up his mind to ramble along its banks and, when the time came for his sentence, to go into the Lodge with his lungs full of fresh air

He might be in dire need of a lot of bright red haemoglobin when Sir Leslie had finished with him!

Jonty hadn't got much recollection of how the aeons between his interview with the Dean and the time of his scheduled encounter had passed, but he presented his knuckles to the vestibule of the Lodge at precisely one minute to three, according to the University Library clock.

The tweeny with the nice legs opened the door and giggled when she saw him, and giggled again when she was showing him into Sir Leslie's study.

Jonty didn't giggle at either opportunity, but simply looked at her miserably, not even having a sufficient head of steam to mention her legs.

"Please wait here! I'll tell Sir Leslie you've arrived," she said, and giggled once more, this time behind her hand, showing a nice sensitivity to the occasion.

Jonty looked about him.

The atmospherics of the Master's study were quite unlike those generated by Newey's pot-plants, teak, mahogany, balkan tobacco and nineteenth-century armoury.

Somehow, the light in Sir Leslie's study seemed to have been filtered through a bad attack of indigestion so that the scattering of colour-harmonies moved only a few notes away from the dominant of bile-green.

The floor carpet was a smooth one-toned pool of it. The leather chairs were frog-coloured; the heavy drapes were dyed in the tints of cheese-mould; and the wallpaper had been specially chosen by Lady Owens to tone in with the hue of the steamed spinach Sir Leslie was so fond of.

Everything was a flatulent variation in the basic key of the burp.

Even the surprisingly few books that the Master had on shelves in a solid glass-fronted dresser looked woefully indigestible.

First, Newey's fishmould; now, this!

Jonty felt in his pockets for a stray milk of magnesia tablet, but he was out of luck.

What a bloody awful day! And it had started so well!

Jonty decided he could risk putting his briefcase down, at least, while awaiting the entrance of the executioner.

He leaned it against the leg of a large table that had a number of very expensive atlases opened out on it, showing the cartography of the same countries in different historical periods.

Was Sir Leslie planning a safari; a coachtrip; or something more ambitious, like a time trip to Persepolis?

Twaggin had told Jonty that the Master was some kind of a scientist, and quite eminent in his field.

At the end of the table, stood two glass-topped display stands: one was full of pieces of rock with neat little hand-printed labels in front, and the other of dead butterflies, also labelled.

Had he shot them all himself on one of his safaris?

Jonty wandered over to the mantelpiece and looked at the display of photographs above it. Every one seemed to be an example of Holmesiana, especially the central study that looked you straight in the eyes: the South African actor that Sir Leslie had in his bedroom?

One and the same!

And there was another of him in profile, accentuating the hawk-like structure of his nose, the beakiness of his chin.

Was that Sherlock Holmes's deerstalker, in close-up? A lovely bit of cloth, it looked. And this in middle close-up? So Sherlock Holmes liked his pipes curlier than Newey's, did he? Interesting!

And there, in the middle-distance was one, he supposed, depicting the great detective's violin.

He peered at it: was that a bead of the sleuth's sweat on the chin-rest, or a defect in the print?

And here was a panoramic view of somebody's study, giving sharp focus to things like magnifying glasses and microscopes, as well as tobacco jars; and a blunt-looking syringe, not so well focussed.

His Baker Street den?

And who was that? Doctor Watson? Sir Arthur Conan Doyle? A relative of the Owenses? It was difficult to tell. He should have labelled them like the specimens in the cases.

Jonty stood back and surveyed the room again. It certainly had Sir Leslie's stamp on it, but it wasn't easy to see which field of science he was eminent in, or even if he was eminent in any.

Nonetheless, Jonty felt he was beginning to form some idea of what kind of a scientist the Master was; he would just need more time to sort out a few polite formulas to describe it.

After all, he only had Twaggin's word for the eminence bit.

If he had had to make a guess, Jonty would have said that Sir Leslie fancied himself first as an amateur sleuth, and second as a geologist or a lepidopterist.

Such a choice would explain why the Master was indulging in this bit of private grilling of Jonty, wouldn't it?

It would!

Jonty hoped that Sir Leslie didn't possess X-ray eyes, like characters in the comics he'd read as a boy! He'd be able to see what he had in his briefcase!

But when he recalled the appearance of them, he knew the odds were against it; because apart from their eyes being closer together than usual, they had the slightly yellowish tinge of a certain kind of boiled sweet not famed for its tele-sightedness.

"Ah! You are here, I see!"

Jonty was aroused from his musings by Sir Leslie's greeting. He hadn't heard him come in. He felt as if he had been caught muttering aloud to himself and started guiltily.

"Good afternoon, Sir Leslie."

"Godley, isn't it?"

'Oh, my Gawd! He actually knows my name! Things are worse than I thought.'

"Yes! That's right!" said Arnold Jonathan Godley aloud, with as much aplomb as he could muster.

"Interested in Sherlock Holmes, are you?"

"Well, only as a – "

"—Ah! Pity! Well, sit down," said Sir Leslie, waving him into one of the frog-coloured leather armchairs.

The Master himself took the other one. They faced each across the bile-coloured carpet.

"You are Arnold Jonty, aren't you?"

Did he think he'd sent an impostor in his place?

"Er – yes," said Jonty, hesitantly, as full of trepidation as Sir Leslie was of composure, who, now, in silence, seemed to be contemplating the birch trees through the window behind Jonty's chair.

Sir Leslie was even more spherical than Jonty remembered.

He was sporting the same bow tie he wore for the Scrabble Party, but had added a thick jacket, made out of woven strands of corned-beef, with little globules of fat hanging about on it, and a well-pressed pair of spam-coloured trousers.

Did this mode of dress assist, by sympathetic magic, the peristaltic action of Sir Leslie's stomach? Or simply blend in with the generally digestive decor of his study?

Whatever the reason, his couture did very little for his complexion, which was inflamed and painful-looking, like a steadily ripening pimple.

'Make-up so natural, you can barely see it?'

Even the skin on his hands seemed to be involved in the overall plan.

'Times when you hate being a man?'

Perhaps it was all due to that polishing sherry he was so fond of?

Jonty regretted that he had no indigestion tablet to offer him. He might appreciate one and it might make him think of Jonty's transgressions in a kindlier spirit.

"Good, good!" said Sir Leslie, eventually. "I've heard a lot about you – from Mr Newey."

'Is that so? I'll stuff every briar pipe he owns into his chapel organ! Together with his cacti! All Things Bright and Beautiful, my eye! May fish-rot blight every leaf in his rockery! May – '

Jonty's silent flow of curses was moving inevitably towards its flood, when Sir Leslie added: "—He tells me your work is often quite brilliant, Jonty."

Jonty stopped in midflow. He was dazed.

"I beg your pardon, Sir Leslie?"

"Don't be surprised, Jonty! Mr Newey is a most perceptive man, and he takes great delight in singing the praises of his students, you know. Why, very often—."

'—No, I didn't know! I've never heard the bugger sing. Or even chant. Mutter, yes! Often. Has he, by some chance, been holding out on me? Praising ME! Incredible!'

The blow that this comment of the Master's had given Jonty turned him deaf, and he heard neither the details nor names of the undergraduates that Newey had spoken up for.

But some kind of permeation had taken place, for he was slowly realizing that, if what Sir Leslie had told him was accurate, the Dean was in for some radical re-assessing from him and Twaggin.

The Master droned on about an apparently unrelated collection of topics and people; slowly, in delicately graduated shifts, he edged himself towards his purpose, and into a position from which he could simultaneously flatter and educate Jonty.

Or was he softening him up for the big chop?

Whatever Jonty was in for, he could only sit where he was and listen.

Sir Leslie was in full spate.

What could be more worthy of effort than the opportunity to develop one's intellectual, moral and artistic capacities in an atmosphere redolent with scholarship, glorious with history, and shining with the beauty of King's College Chapel?

What was more compelling than the pursuit of the true, the good and the beautiful?

In this violent and bloody arena of a world, the places were indeed few, and getting fewer day by day, where free mind could meet free mind, where the liberal virtues could be practised, where the unselfish impulses could be indulged without danger, and where civilized behaviour was not considered a mere affectation.

Was this not so?

He was quite sure that a man of Jonty's qualities and sensibilities could not help but agree. One had to strive to keep in one's heart the tolerance to view the foibles of others – their failings, their sillinesses, and their incompetencies – with charity and love, no matter how hard it may be.

And, yes, that brought to mind something scarcely worth a mention; but as he happened to be dilating on matters in general, perhaps he could be forgiven for running the risk of boring Jonty with it?

Indeed, he would rather value Jonty's opinion, if he could bring himself to consider, for a moment, the somewhat trivial items he was about to adumbrate?

At this point in his peroration, Sir Leslie eyed Jonty, diagnostically.

If Jonty had been more in charge of himself, he would have resisted the urge to reply at all.

As it was, he found himself nodding and imitating the register of Sir Leslie's discourse.

Certainly, there was a great deal, a very great deal in what Sir Leslie had said. These things were valuable and must be preserved, like the jewels they were; and one could add other gems such as honesty and sincerity, which brought a lessening of hypocrisy and a refusal to speak to the Redmen of the Plains with forked tongues.

Sir Leslie seemed to like that image, giving a half-smile at it, so Jonty was induced to add a further touch or two.

Yes; there was a lot in what Queen Victoria, Rhodes of Africa, Kipling of India, and Kitchener of Khartoum had said, also.

However, one had to –

'—Just how long is this sodding pantomime going on for?'

Jonty paused to regain his *sang froid* and Sir Leslie took advantage of it to add a few further gems that seemed to have more point to them than those he had enthused about so far.

Regrettably, such things were to be expected – certain individuals always felt compelled to destroy what was strange to them and what they didn't understand – both Lady Owens and himself had suffered from such individuals before – why, even a few weeks ago, some individual or individuals had...!

What could have prompted these persons unknown to have acted in such a savage fashion, and furthermore —?

If there was a knuckle to this conversation, Jonty felt that Sir Leslie was getting too near to it for comfort.

Had the Master considered the possibility that these were not the depredations of savages but unfortunate accidents that had happened to intelligent persons?

No, that hadn't occurred to him; but was it not a very odd kind of accident that made it happen twice on the same night?

Yes, that did seem strange; but was it beyond the bounds of possibility that not only had it happened twice, but to different individuals?

No; that had not occurred to him either, but he would give it very careful consideration.

Yet, in the circumstances, how could the complete disappearance of two identical objects be explained in that manner?

It certainly sounded silly; but it was a well-attested fact that people did very outlandish things when they got into a panic, and –

Well, that certainly *could* be an explanation and both Lady Owens and himself would reconsider the matter in the light of the comments that had been put to him – and after a most interesting discussion, perhaps a cup of tea would not be found unwelcome, eh, what?

Sir Leslie got up; yes, that was the right expression, not rose, but got up.

Jonty wondered: Had the Master got up and gone out of the study – instead of ringing the little silver bell that stood beside his chair to summon the tweeny – to allow time for Jonty's guilt to spread its slow poisons throughout his bloodstream?

Jonty had known he was going to need that haemoglobin; but was it going to last?

How long was the Master going to stay out? Was this some sort of Holmesian device for uncovering the crime?

Would he return only when Jonty had begun to swell and turn a bad colour, thereby revealing the culprit?

As long as the interview had gone on, Jonty had the nasty feeling that it had been got over a little too quickly for Sir Leslie to feel that all the proper decencies had been preserved and all the admonitions made.

Had he now gone to fetch the Sword of Execution, or the Proctors, or Lady Owens?

Jonty looked at his briefcase leaning against the table leg, and groaned.

Oh, why had he packed it with the pair of indescribable trousers and two severed doorknobs?

Just what had he imagined he was going to be able to do with them? – nip out, hang up the breeches in Sir Leslie's wardrobe and re-attach the doorknobs to Lady Owens's johns?

When? How?

The study was probably under surveillance at this very minute!

Maybe he should hang the doorknobs round his waist on a piece of string and put the trousers on over them? He could always make out that he'd got an unbelievably large scrotum, if any remarks were passed

Were castrati still sought after by the Choirmaster of King's College Chapel?

Did it matter if you had the operation after your voice had broken? Was there a life after death?

At that point, Sir Leslie unexpectedly returned, with the tweeny carrying tea on a tray.

Jonty thought he could detect a subtle change in Sir Leslie's mien and wondered if things were about to enter a new phase.

What would he say if Sir Leslie should gently enquire about the contents of his briefcase?

The Master seemed a trifle more decisive than before, as if he'd taken on a role he liked.

What was he cooking up? Was the difference in his face simply due to tension, or had he really learned to lessen the space between his eyeballs? Was he also studying Yoga? Was there poison in the tea?

While Sir Leslie regally re-positioned the orb of himself on his frog-leather throne, Jonty, feeling like a subject condemned to a life-sentence in the palace dungeons, watched the servant, as if she were the last tweeny he would ever see, pour out the tea, and then cross the study and close the door behind her.

She really had the most marvellous legs!

The door was the colour of cabbage that had been boiled for a week.

Sir Leslie was sipping his pap-coloured tea and igniting one of his light-tan cheroots.

So it wasn't poisoned, after all! 'Maybe in the sugar.'

"I don't take it, thank you!"

"As you wish."

'That's stopped his little game!'

"My wife thinks I should speak more plainly to you, Jonty, than I have up to now. As I place great confidence in my wife's judgement in such matters—"

'Entirely misplaced! I thought I caught a familiar whiff of that luxury bath preparation for women who care.'

Jonty was afraid that his worst premonitions were about to be confirmed.

Had Lady Owens's opinion prevailed against that of the Dean? Was Newey's story about him being brilliant entirely apocryphal and only some of Sir Leslie's soft soap, after all?

The Master began speaking slowly, in simple words, with distinct pauses. Had she managed to convince her husband that Jonty's mental age was really about seven, despite a precocious gift for imitation?

See, Jonty, see. Here is a door. It has a doorknob. This is another door. It has a doorknob, also. The doors are Daddy's. But the doorknobs are Mummy's. Mummy likes her doorknobs very much. The doorknobs have gone. Where have they gone? Mummy thinks some naughty boys pulled them off. Daddy does not like boys who pull off their Mummy's doorknobs. Daddy wants to pull off something from the naughty boys. But see, Jonty, see. Daddy will not hurt Jonty. Daddy is kind. Mummy is kind. Mummy and Daddy only want the doorknobs back. They want them safe and sound. Mummy and Daddy know it was a joke, a naughty joke, but a joke all the same. Daddy will be kind. He will not pull anything off the little boys. Now, come Jonty, come. Be a good boy. Tell Daddy whodunnit. Shake hands. No smacks. Cross your heart and hope to die? Barley? Pax? Cave? Look. Daddy has his fingers crossed.

WHO DONE IT, JONTY?

Sir Leslie's lofty condescensions had made Jonty so angry that he found himself hunched over his tea sucking up rapid and noisy mouthfuls of the tepid liquid without lifting the cup from the saucer. Not only did this seem relevant to the situation but, as well as quenching his inexplicable thirst, it gave him psychological relief.

'He thinks he can get it out of me like that, does he? He thinks me and Twaggin dunnit, does he? He wants me to clipe, does he? He thinks I'm on Janet and John Book One, does he?'

Jonty continued ferociously to suck up mouthfuls of the tea.

The Master was pulling at his earlobes, nervously watching him.

"Sir Leslie, your interpretation," said Jonty, having at last, with deadly control, finished his tea, "may well be the right one."

'Two can play at that game, mate.'

"And I wish I could help you. But—"

Jonty looked at his briefcase, bulging serenely with the bulk of Sir Leslie's trousers and Lady Owens's doorknobs, leaning against the leg of the table. It gave him great satisfaction to see it there.

He HADN'T mentioned them, had he? He had INTENDED to mention them when he came, hadn't he? He WASN'T going to mention them, was he?

"—it's difficult to see of what assistance I can be to you, other than to say, if ever I come face to face with the culprits, I will certainly convey your sentiments to them."

"I would be glad of that, Jonty. Yes, certainly."

'Is he trying to encourage his lobes to grow to shoulder length? Doesn't he know that ears are the only members of the human anatomy that keep growing throughout the natural life of the organism?'

'What kind of a scientist is he?

'I'm glad I shan't be around when he retires. It's going to be an embarrassment to know an unscientific knight with ears like a Doberman Pincher's lolloping about on corned-beef shoulder pads.'

The negotiations, having been reduced to deadlock, Sir Leslie muttered excuses about pressing engagements, and showed Jonty out *prontissimo.*

However, before Jonty could leave the gravel of the driveway, Sir Leslie called after him, and flourished a letter.

"Oh, Jonty! Please be good enough to convey this letter to the Dean. It contains a ridiculous notice about – er – aubergine cutlery, to which Lady Owens's signature was appended. A forgery, of course! It has rather distressed her, I'm afraid. I suppose you don't happen to have heard who might have penned this ridiculous composition, Jonty?... I see... Yes, I'd be most glad. Goodbye, Jonty. Goodbye."

Jonty realized that Sir Leslie had been fully aware from the beginning to whom exactly he had been talking; and that, now, he could not lose or destroy the envelope for Newey without supplying the proof that Sir Leslie was looking for.

Stalemate!

26

It had taken Jonty nearly twenty-four hours to recover from his interviews with the Dean and the Master; but sitting in the bar of The Locomotive at lunchtime the following day, Jonty had begun to bounce back. The mere recounting to Twaggin all that had transpired had consoled him enormously, and the beer had helped nicely to complete the healing process.

"Is 'sherry party' one word like 'paperback'?" asked Jonty.

"Is 'paper-back' one word?" asked Twaggin.

"Yes."

"What're you doing?"

"Composing a telegram."

"What for?"

"To send."

"Who to?"

"Sir Leslie Owens."

"Holy Moses! You must be mad. He's only a quarter of a mile from where we are sitting! Why don't you go and see him if it's urgent?"

"It isn't and I don't want to!"

"Phone him, then."

"Worse!"

"Why not write him a letter?"

"He'd recognise the handwriting."

"Oh, I see! You don't want him to know who it's from?'

"No! I mean, yes! That is, I want him to know who it's from, but not to know it's from me. See?"

"No."

"It's too complicated to explain. We'll be going down tomorrow and I shall send it from Bletchley."

"Why Bletchley?"

"Partly because the name is horrible enough to harmonize with this telegram; and partly because it'll suggest to Sir Leslie that the sender isn't in Cambridge."

"Suggest! Won't it be clear that he isn't?"

"Not to Sir Leslie!"

"Let's see."

Twaggin took the paper out of Jonty's hand without waiting, and read it:

EVERYONE LIKES SCRABBLE. WIFE'S KNOBS DELIGHTFUL. I STOLE THEM AND RUINED SHERRY PARTY. I APLOGISE.

"A confession! You should live so long, you disgusting apostate. A betrayal! A retreat!"

"Not the way I read it!" said Jonty.

"How do you read it?" asked Twaggin.

Jonty read it aloud to him.

"*Merde!* Of course! *I* should have seen that: for questions, you write statements. For apologies, a mis-spelt query! For confessions,

231

innuendo and chutzpah. Well, yes! That does put a different complexion on it."

"I learnt it from you."

"Well, thanks for the compliment!"

"He made me as guilty as hell yesterday! So, on the one hand, I feel some sort of gesture is needed. But, on the other, I feel there isn't. With this," said Jonty, shaking the draft telegram in the air, "I get it both ways."

"But you might as well send a letter. You can't send a telegram without a name. It loses its point."

"I thought about that. Look!"

Jonty printed carefully a name underneath the message: REDSHINS.

"I suppose," said Twaggin, doubtfully.

"I shall send back the trousers from Bletchley by registered post, too. That should wrap things up, nicely!"

"Supposing the Master contacts Redshins?"

"He usually goes mountaineering in the vacs!"

"He still won't believe Redshins sent it," said Twaggin, emphatically shaking his beard. "There are no mountains in Bletchley."

"Well, it won't matter! He'll have his trousers back, and he still won't know who it was, will he?" replied Jonty patiently.

"But he doesn't know they've gone! Better just to keep them."

"They're no use to me. You have them."

"No fear!"

"There you are! Sir Leslie might as well have the benefit of them; he bought them."

"True, true! It's the knobs they want. What're you going to do about them?"

"I only stole one."

"All right! What are WE going to do?"

"That's the question I keep coming back to. My best instinct is to get it across that Redshins was behind all this."

"We could parcel them up as well and go and have some crumpets in the letch's teagarden."

"What good would that do?"

"Then we could secrete them in Redshin's study, couldn't we?"

"Hey, that's not a bad idea! But, wait a minute! Wouldn't he just report them as found, eventually?"

"Probably! But would the old boy believe him – everything pointing to Redshins's guilt? I'm told Sir Leslie's not very keen on his unsavoury hobbies!"

"Have another! Let's get properly tanked up and think about it."

"Thanks, I will!"

Jonty sat in the third class carriage going over these thoughts as the local train swayed and clattered its toddling pace towards Bletchley, musing on the events of his last few days in Cambridge and on sundry other matters. He recollected the conversation in the pub with amusement and relish. Even when being with Twaggin seemed anything but a pleasure, it was actually a pleasure. That was one of the contradictions about the man that Jonty had not yet fully worked out.

And being with Sofia was, in some ways, similar. Why hadn't he heard anything from her since she had departed for Alexis's wedding?

Perhaps she had decided to commit bigamy and they'd both married Crehan, turning him into a trigamist as well? Were they living in a happily trigamous *menage a trois?*

Would they welcome and invite him in when he arrived in Birmingham to form a merry quadigamous *menage a quatre?*

When did a *menage* turn into a *kibbutz?* How big could a *kibbutz* get before it exploded?

Jonty's spell of enforced chastity was taking its toll.

On Cambridge Station, before the locomotive had started to hiss and puff, he had watched the shapes of girls through summer frocks with great avidity, feeling restless, hungry and humble. He had sat still and willed them to come in.

But apart from his suitcase and a brown paper parcel, he had remained alone in the carriage.

Then he had pleaded with his eyes, but they had still ignored him. He had cried out with all the loneliness he could muster for a ripely breathing girl – any girl – to enter the carriage and fall into his arms. He had whispered at the top of his lungs for them; he had shouted with the loudness of feathers falling onto pillows for them; he had endlessly imagined their limbs spread on the luxuriant bed of his desires, compliant as kittens, as full of submission as houris; but no-one had come.

He had felt desperate. In due course, his desires had lost their lustre, their romance, their unreality; and even a kneeshaker, vertical in a stuffy broom cupboard with a tweeny he hardly knew had begun to seem attractive by the time the train had got under way.

As he recalled it, he felt disgusted with himself.

Was he turning into one of the mass of the indiscriminate? Was he going to be just another little dog, a perennial sniffer after the drug that steamed in every one of them?

Was he going to—?

Apart from which, his bladder was beginning to feel uncomfortable.

"Just like bloody British Rail," he grumbled to relieve his feelings, "to have a non-corridor train between Cambridge and Bletchley, and absolutely no chance to get out on the way!"

As the train inched its slow length along, he felt he couldn't hold out for any stretch of time. He looked out of the window at the slowly passing fields.

It shouldn't be much longer, but you could never tell. The stodgy outskirts of Bletchley hoved into view at least five minutes before; but then the train had started to squeal its way forward a millimetre at a time on nearly-locked wheels.

It was probably the train-driver's first trip, and maybe he wasn't sure of the way? In any case, it was fairly clear that he was very young and, until now, hadn't been on anything faster than a scooter.

At the present rate it was going to take the best part of a week to cover the last forty or fifty yards to the platform.

Jonty closed his eyes and held on to himself, manfully. His fancy was beginning to toy with desperate remedies when the locomotive shrieked its whistle, seemingly in fright, and the carriage shot upward for a time, as if just released from Cape Canaveral, hovered, then stopped dead. Jonty's buttocks slid on the seat: the train had finally arrived at the station.

Jonty threw open the carriage door, made a hard landing on his heels, and raced for a small brick structure at the end of the platform.

When he came out the train had gone.

He made for a smug-looking porter, lounging near the door of the Buffet. As Jonty approached, the porter backed into the doorway.

"My luggage was on that train! What does bloody British Rail think it's playing at?"

"They're running late, sir!" said the porter with great equanimity, and winked heavily.

"You mean, it should have arrived last Monday week? I know that. Everybody knows it. But what about my—?"

"—That's all right, sir! All safe and sound."

The porter opened the door of the Buffet, on which he had been resting, and announced grandly, by sweeping his arm outward and down with open palm, Jonty's case and parcel just inside the doorway. The man stayed in his posture, ostentatiously, smug as a churchwarden, waiting.

"Well, I'm dammed!" said Jonty.

"Yessir! It often 'appens 'ere, you know."

"Getting damned?"

"Sir?"

'No wonder he looks smug. An old sweat like him must make quite a nice little income on the side out of rash and incontinent travellers to Bletchley, the quaint little outpost of an Empire given away by the great Winston Churchill.'

The porter was watching Jonty's hand with the keenness of an eagle.

Was he, by any chance, an ex-remittance man?...

Jonty took his hand out of his pocket and let the porter see it clear and empty.

"Thanks very much!" said Jonty.

"That's all right, me old china!"

It was no longer "sir"!

The man lost his smile, turned away, and began walking off, sadly shaking his head, but not entirely without smugness.

Such was the rump of Empire!

Jonty picked up his belongings, deposited his suitcase in the Left Luggage bay and walked into the town to look for the Post Office. What more appropriate place to mail Sir Leslie's trousers from than one whose name was an anagram of 'Blotch, lewdly and retch'?

'Well, not quite an anagram! What's the term for a near-anagram?'

Twaggin would know.

A pity that the symbolism of the postmark would be lost to the sleuth of Cambridge.

His first words to Lady Owens, on opening the parcel and seeing his defunct trousers, would probably be a beautifully enunciated observation along the lines of: "Aggie! The middle button is missing from the fly."

As Jonty came out of the GPO, he felt an unimpeded jubilation rising inside him at the brainwave he had just had. Silent music soared to a crescendo in his head and his solo voice, together with his unfulfilled selves, sang, like a chorus in a pagan Magnificat, silently:

'Look at me, free, white and twenty-five in the sad, bad, wicked streets of Bletchley, praising all alone the young girls longing for consummation beside their phallus-shaped phones in the latest pastel shades; celebrating the women over forty who are the rich, the sensual, the promiscuous Madames who encourage the men who are status-conscious, overweight, and randy as ferrets, to never-endingly go on sniffing it out; while I myself, who sold Monster for a pint of best Mackewan's to a College Porter with obscene fingers yesterday, have just today posted a pair of trousers that would fit a Suffolk Punch to a nineteenth century specialist from Girton, bewitched by George Eliot; and who will become the proud owner of a degree of Bachelor of Arts

(Cantab); and who, maybe later on, will be famed in folklore as the brain that almost master-minded the Great Doorknob Scandal.

' "Ah, life is sweet brother! There is night and day, brother, both sweet things. Moreover, there is a wind on the heath, and if I could feel that, I would gladly live forever".'

"—Look where you're walking, mate! That's my Sunday corn you're assaulting!"

"I'm so sorry!" said Jonty.

"Not as sorry as I am!" said the man.

Jonty watched an elderly gent in a smart suit, with a drooping carnation in his buttonhole, a briefcase and a local accent, limping exaggeratedly away along the pavement.

'Could he ever have been as randy as a ferret,' Jonty wondered, 'even in his horniest dreams?'

Deeply, commiseratingly, he sighed.

Not even a glorious sense of jubilation could do anything for Bletchley, it seemed.

If George Borrow himself had just arrived from Spain, and come marching through the thoroughfares of the town selling his bibles, playing his fiddle, and instructing them on the niceties of Romany, the citizens would, it seemed, simply have pointed to the oval medallions they had screwed to their gateposts saying 'No hawkers, canvassers or peddlers', and have run him out of town as an illiterate vagrant.

Yesterday – the Grantchester Fiasco! Today – Bletchley!

Tomorrow – anybody's guess!

The world, it seemed, ran true to form, like British Rail.

Jonty wandered, allowing his built-in beer-detector to guide him to where he was always happy to go.

As he went, he pondered yet again the momentous observation that life always happened *in time*; it didn't occur all at once, like a photograph. It was more like a morbid symphony which necessarily entailed that only some sounds came together and that, mostly, the noises came one after the other.

But if the things of life, the events, the whatsits, whatever, had to be of the same order of damnableness, in sequence, why should they have to follow bumper to bumper, exuding thick clouds of toxic fumes and hooting?

That was not at all clear, was it?

And, furthermore, why should the drivers have to be people like Newey – no, we'll let Newey off in view of his recent information about him—.

Well! like Treblitt, Dummock, the Owenses, the leaders of political parties, the presidents of the United States, France, African countries, the international banks, the leaders of the USSR, and most of the opulent stockbroking crew who pushed up their blood-pressures daily commuting out of the poisoned centres and clogging up the routes for the poor bloody pedestrians?

Jonty felt that his metaphor had taken him away from what he really wished to say.

Nevertheless, he still felt he was onto SOMETHING – perhaps nearer to a question he had asked before somewhere, somewhen that went more like: why was life ALWAYS so much like itself?

Surely, it could be like something ELSE for a change? Well, what?

Good question.

Why not make it more like, for instance, a group of drunkards locked up in a brewery for an eternal weekend?

There would at least be the satisfaction of getting bloody good and tight. And, with luck, you might even die squiffed; or die FROM drink, if you wished.

Wasn't that as good as what went on for most of the time around and about this big whirling globe of ours?

Moderate tipplers would have the chance of becoming immoderate tipplers. If any natural teetotallers crept in by mistake, they'd learn to take a drop because of the social pressures to conform; or, if they preferred to die rather than drink, they could drown themselves in the vats.

'If life were like that,' thought Jonty, 'it would certainly be better than most of what I've seen up to now, and a lot better than this bit they call Bletchley.'

He found himself looking at a sign that announced The Robin Hood. Obviously, his detector was working well. The man on the board in Lincoln Green swung blithely in the breeze.

'Is he open yet?'

He was.

"A pint, please."

"Which tap?"

"The tap that makes you drunk."

"They all make you drunk, mate. Some are a bit quicker'n others, that's all!"

"Okay, that one!"

The barman took a bright glass tankard from a shelf behind him and held the mug below the tap, grasped the shiny-handled beer-pull and lowered it at his chosen speed. He had to pull it only once. He had gauged it exactly. He placed the beer, brimming on the counter.

"Here you are! Cheap at half the price."

Jonty sat down at a marble-topped, claw-footed, three-legged, round, Victorian table near a window.

He was the first morning customer.

The barman busied himself polishing the spotless counter with his bunched-up mutton-cloth duster.

Jonty took a large pull at his beer.

Ah, a lovely quaff! So here he was! And where was Twaggin now?

Jonty had forgotten to ask him if he was going back to his father's taxi business in London; but he guessed he wasn't. He'd just have to wait until the Archbishop let him know.

Good old Twaggin, one in a million!

He'd probably turn out to be a famous critic one day, a celebrity of some sort, Somebody. He was as mad as a hatter, but quite brilliant!

And Soapy! What would Twaggins's father think of her?

She was Twaggins's reinforcement, the nylon heel and toe to his hairy wool sock. They needed each other. They loved each other.

Jonty looked into his drink, speculatively.

And Sofia? Does she love me? Do I love her? Where does she fit? 'What am I? What does she have to fit to? An educated Dropout...?'

He decided to give up that line of inquiry. At the moment, it was too uncomfortable.

For now, it was better to go over the Grantchester Fiasco again, wasn't it, and see if they'd missed any more loopholes?

To console himself, he lifted his elbow once more.

'This beer is certainly a drop of the good! I think I'll have another.'

27

Jonty took the first sip of his second pint. It was cool and smooth and had the right amount of froth, just enough to let him know the beer was alive.

Jonty looked up at the barman, appreciatively.

"You keep it good," he said, holding up his tankard.

"Ah, we do that! Pipes and taps sluiced out once a week, reg'lar as clockwork."

"Here's to it!" said Jonty.

"Down the hatch, mate!" replied the barman, and returned to rubbing his taps.

'Ah, lovely! That really washes out the taste of Mrs Redshins's tea.'

Jonty's mind went back to the previous day, in her Grantchester tea garden.

The air had been as balm; the chestnuts had opened out their green brollies proudly; the tremor of the poplars' leaves had made the shadows tremble, Parkinson-like, on the tablecloths; and the garden had been full of the scent of snarfia.

Twaggin was pouring out more tea, and the day had seemed nearly flawless. Nearly.

"This tea is so weak," he boomed, "it's having a struggle to get out of the spout. How many cups in a quarter pound packet of tea, Jonty?"

"Don't know. Let's ask her."

"Not today! Too risky! We don't want to attract attention."

Considering that Twaggin, when he had reached for the milk, had already poured half a bowlful of sugar into one of his sneakers, the remark illustrated his incredible ability to detach himself from irrelevancies and to look at the bones of the matter before him.

"Today, we have to be as inconspicuous as Newey's mind. Watch for the right moment!" he said, in his loud bass voice. "In a few minutes, I'll have a shifty round the back, pretending to look for the jakes. You keep your eyes skinned, here. Watch that parcel! If I spot Redshins's study, we'll pop it in."

Twaggin's blue jeans, check shirt, white sneakers and indescribable beard swaggered round the corner of the cottage and disappeared.

Jonty sat humbly among the twittering gentility of Mrs Redshins's tea garden.

He was doing his best to look as if he wouldn't ever donate iron washers to the Dean's collection-box for the Restoration of Ely Cathedral; as if he wouldn't dream of pouring Sir Leslie's polishing sherry down the can; as if he wouldn't stuff ornamental doorknobs into pots of John Innes' Compost No 1; as if he wouldn't ever seduce tweenies inside built-in wardrobes; but to look as if all he wanted was to drink weak tea, endlessly, in Rupert Brooke's Grantchester.

Was his impersonation succeeding?

He looked about him.

Wide-brimmed hats, summer frocks, and animated discussions on fruit-bottling sat cheerily at the tables. Spectres with yellow hands, Colonial expressions, well-cut lightweight suits, and a consuming interest in the Stock Market reports, moved their lips and read under the trees. Tiny green aphids, exhausted from producing honey-dew, dropped steadily onto the puckered-up table cloths.

No; he was not being watched.

Gentility, for reasons best known to itself, ignored him and went on delicately nibbling at the Cake of the Week.

But Jonty would not have been surprised to see Rupert Brooke actually materialize and begin strolling about, orating on the pansies blooming all before his little room – except for a sneaking suspicion that it was the wrong time of the year for pansies, at least, for the naturally-grown kind.

Were there any here now, in the beds or at the tables?

Look at ill this berberis growing about, and growing so well! Look at all the twerples, twerpling in the trees, and doing that so well!

And look at all of THEM, oozing the civilized virtues, and doing it so badly! Yet they appeared to like doing what they did, and to like it very much.

Is there something wrong with me?

'Please, God, in the name of James Thurber, make me a normal healthy boy!'

A movement at the wicker-gate entrance to the tea garden caught his eye.

A man and a woman were coming in. She was very small, and very pregnant, with no eyebrows to speak of. He was very large, his stomach was very flat, and his eyebrows seemed to have been barbered to look like an unwaxed Kitchener moustache.

Oh, cripes!

Jonty felt something fall soundlessly into a deep dark well inside him.

That was the doctor from next door, and he was looking around for a suitable table in the shade.

Jonty held on tightly to Mrs Redshins's teapot to prevent himself scurrying away to hide in the thatch of her white-washed cottage.

No, dammit! Why should I feel like this? I haven't done anything to the doctor, have I?'

He released the teapot and put his hands nonchalantly on the cloth.

The movement drew the doctor's attention and his eye fell on Jonty. He scowled fiercely at him.

Clearly, he would have loved to drop-kick Jonty from the centre of the lawn right into Byron's pool, just for practice; or, maybe, try a place-kick for touch, out near the Gog-Magog Hills.

He made an involuntary step towards Jonty and stopped.

'I'll tell the Ref, if he does!' thought Jonty.

The doctor spotted a suitable place near the berberis hedge, at the other end of the garden, as far from Jonty as he could get. He settled his wife in her seat and went to the other side of the table where he lowered himself into his chair so that the breadth of his back and shoulders were arrestingly displayed to Jonty.

At that moment, Twaggin came strolling round the corner of the cottage.

Jonty heaved a sigh of relief: it was going to be harder to drop-kick two of them into Byron's Pool.

But Mrs Lovingood's reaction to Twaggin was quite different from his: her hands twitched convulsively on her stomach as she sighted him. She leaned across and began whispering to her husband in an agitated way and nodding her head towards Twaggin, who looked blithely about him; unaware of Mrs Lovingood's consternation, his short-sighted lenses dazzled themselves in the sun.

The doctor jerked his head over a massive shoulder, stared at Twaggin, and appeared to tremble slightly before turning back to his wife. He said something to her, and she visibly relaxed.

Twaggin, who had now reached the table, let his buttocks fall heavily onto the woven seat. The chair creaked.

"I think I've spotted his study. But it's all locked up. We shall have to think of something else."

Jonty nodded abstractedly.

Thank God Twaggin wasn't wearing his bearskin; or humping his bagful of empty beerbottles about with him. Or that bloody doctor would have stuffed both of them into the bag with the bottles.

Had Twaggin provoked him further, he might even have packed them, organ by organ, into the bottles themselves. He was looking wicked enough to do anything, Jonty felt.

He thought it best to warn Twaggin about the doctor and his wife. Twaggin was unperturbed.

"She's reputed to wear her raincoat in bed, you know!" he said.

"I believe you," said Jonty. "She's as neurotic as hell. She must be, to have married him! I don't fancy running any risks, with her about. She might deliver prematurely under the tablecloth and blame it all on us!"

"Don't worry!" said Twaggin, soothingly. "Mrs Redshins's tea is non-alcoholic. We're allowed to drink in here. We're over eighteen... You don't happen to have qualifications in midwifery, I suppose?" he added, musingly.

"Why don't we just send the knobs back with our compliments?" asked Jonty, suddenly, completely unnerved.

"Or, our compliments with knobs on!" replied Twaggin humorously.

"No, listen, man! I'm serious."

"Serious? You sound *distrait*. That would mean doing the decent thing, silly!"

"We could betray The Cause for once."

"Don't hustle me! It calls for a clear head. Let me think."

Twaggin put his head in his hand, like Rodin's Thinker, to show that he was working on the problem. But Jonty was rattled and couldn't be stopped.

"Why don't we own up? Sir Leslie said he'd overlook things. Oh, dear! After this, the Senate will never entertain those suggestions for a new exam paper I sent in."

"He expected you to do it there and then, idiot! You missed your chance. You made things worse by keeping mum. That proved you weren't a gentleman. It is allowed for gentlemen to assault doorknobs when drunk. It is NOT allowed for gentlemen to lie. Gentlemen own up when challenged!"

"Oh, Christ! And I thought he was just trying to get his wife's knobs back, not prove something as obvious as that. Me – a gentleman! How could he be deceived?... Newey lies all the time," added Jonty, scathingly.

"That's quite different!" said Twaggin, serenely. "Newey is a member of the true church. Clergymen are allowed to lie temporally in the interests of eternal truth. He wouldn't lie about doorknobs, would he?"

"He's always thinking up reasons for not taking his supervisions."

"That again is different. He has other duties. He regards it as a matter of correct priorities. Who knows? He might be right!"

"Anything Newey does is, by definition, wrong! That's part of the Consitution, isn't it?"

"Excuse me?"

'Oh, are we back to that, again?' he asked himself. "You've changed your tune a bit, haven't you?" said Jonty aloud, challengingly.

"I've come to the conclusion he's got more perception than I gave him credit for. As the College Officer responsible for the moral welfare of junior members under his wing, he complimented me on the stability of my behaviour this term, and on my academic performance at the University," said Twaggin, sniffily, mimicking the Dean's diction and variety of English.

"Everybody has his price, I suppose! What's mine?"

"In my opinion, there's only one thing we can do now," said Twaggin, ignoring the provocation.

"What's that?"

"Sell them!"

"But that's stealing! For gain! Punishable before the law! Technically—"

"—Technically, my Royal Jewish arse! What else is there to do? We just HAVE to unload them. Come on!"

Twaggin stood up suddenly and began to stalk off, following his beard, carrying the parcel in his hand, his De-jeaned backside waddling at its characteristic height. Jonty groaned.

'Archbishop Makarios on holiday! Where's he going?'

Jonty followed him miserably, weaving his way in and out of the Vicarage-type tables and clientele. They looked at him in surprise and distaste as he went by.

The doctor had made a special point of turning round to watch him when he had risen to follow Twaggin. Now, both he and his wife were talking quickly, alternatively peering at Jonty and at each other under lowered lids.

Jonty had no difficulty in imagining what they were saying.

He cursed them silently:

'May showers of aphids drown themselves in your milk jug! May honeydew lie as thick as porridge on your toasted scones! May—. Where the hell is Twaggin?'

Jonty had now escaped the accusing eyes of the Lovingoods by rounding the corner of the cottage.

He saw Twaggin ahead of him, trundling – short-thighed, dignified – towards another white-washed cottage with a thick new thatch yellow as butter, and a wide primrose-coloured door that leaned open on an oblong of darkness.

Twaggin went in. So Twaggin and darkness were firm friends, eh? He had had the same feeling about Twaggin before.

Jonty followed him in. It was like walking into a drawer full of thick woollen socks.

Jonty stopped, sniffed, and waited for his sight to come back.

As he became accustomed to the gloom, a whole clutter of strange objects put themselves together before his eyes.

It was as if someone had taken a section of the Reverend Newey's study and pushed it up against a corner of Lady Leslie's mantelpiece, and then had crammed them all together into Mrs Cough's sitting-room.

African spears stuck out of Staffordshire pots that stood on Chippendale tables beside overweight armchairs in front of unsigned lavatory bowls behind Chinese screens above bevies of flowered Victorian guzunders.

A small wooden hand-painted notice, also anonymous, skulked behind a feather boa muttering the word 'Antiques' to itself, ashamedly.

An animal with fur on, whose taxonomy was doubtful, bared its teeth at an oval mirror on a stand, whose posture was uncertain.

The only reason for putting these *objets d'art* cheek by jowl that Jonty could discover was – they had all been used, and used a lot, and were trying to keep quiet about it.

Twaggin was undoing his parcel on a small table with slim and elegant legs, talking *sotto voce* to an undersized bald man in a dark lounge suit and red slippers that had slits cut over the toes.

The shopowner kept moving his feet about gingerly, while keeping them flat on the floor, as if they might come loose at the ankles if he lifted them up.

He also kept nodding his head and saying: "Yersh, I shee."

He seemed to have as little confidence in his teeth as he did in his feet.

When Twaggin had finished giving him his spiel, Baldie said:

"Yersh, but you Musht really she that (Shuffle, shuffle) things like theshe here are very mush (Shuffle, shuffle) a minority interesht and won't fetch mush (Shuffle, shuffle) on the open market."

"I understand. But surely you have—"

"—To be honesht, there'sh only one cushtomer in theshe partsh (Shuffle) who comesh reg'lar, (Shuffle) looking for knobsh of thish kind (Shuffle, shuffle). A Lady Shomebody from the Univershity. (Shuffle). And I don't think she wantsh any more just now." (Shuffle, shuffle, shuffle).

Twaggin gave a startled Bela Lugosi-type look at Jonty.

Jonty returned it, with good measure, *a la Boris Karloff.*

"Well," said Twaggin, "perhaps I should try elsewhere. I don't want to—"

"—Not sho fasht, young man. (Shuffle, shuffle, shuffle). I'll jusht look in my book. There'sh probably shomebody who wantsh a—"

Shuffle-shuffle-shuffety-shuff-shoo—shoo!

The old man disappeared into a back room, quite nippily, considering that neither foot moved a fraction above the floor.

"That doesn't sound very promising," said Jonty. "We don't want her buying back her own doorknobs. Let's go before he comes back!"

"No! See what he comes up with first. We don't HAVE to sell them, do we?"

"S'pose not! We could always tie them to house-bricks and drown them in the Cam," Jonty said, miserably. "But knowing Lady Owens, she's probably taught them to swim."

"Another possibility is shaping itself in my—"

Before Twaggin could specify the locality of its shaping and go on to outline what it precisely was that was forming, something dark and audible and hunched came through the doorframe, like a huge flying tackle.

It skidded to a halt in the small space left in the middle of the room, reared upright and began peering blindly about, and growling.

Jonty knew what it was, but what was it looking for?

Its den, maybe; or a newly-delivered litter of rugby balls?

While Jonty was weighing up his chances of leaping inside the unsigned lavatory bowl and firmly pulling down its wooden lid, Twaggin, he noticed, had lowered himself silently behind a headstone.

Dr Lovingood's eyes had still not accustomed themselves to the gloom of the shop.

Twaggin peered over the top of his headstone at Jonty. His expression asked clearly: "What does he want?"

Jonty peered back, trying to convey the message: "Bring out the coffin, let the mourners come."

Then, a roar, like Cambridge's first fifteen showering in a handbowl, filled the little shop. The doctor's sight had adjusted itself.

"So what are you horrible pair up to now? Hey?" came the roar. "Come on! Get where I can see you. Don't cringe about like lice. Been giving the Chinese Burn to the old man, have you? Hey? Filling his eardrums up with ink-pellets, hey?"

He roared with laughter at his own wit.

"Caught you in the middle of your little operation, have I?"

Shuffety-shuffety-shuffety-shuff! The old man was hurrying back into his shop.

"What on earth ish the matter, here? Oh! It'sh you, Dr Lovingood. I wondered what—. But I don't think we've got anything to interesht you, at the moment, doctor. (Shuffety). Let me shee! Club badgesh and mashcotsh, isn't it?"

"That's all right, Mr Cheeshe – er – Cheesewright. I came in after these two specimens," said the doctor, indicating Twagggin and Jonty with a twitch of an arm.

"I shee, I shee," intoned Mr Cheesewright.

"They walked out of the tea garden without paying, and Mrs Redshins is a friend of my wife's," said the doctor, as if that explained everything.

"Did they now? Hmmm! That wash very naughty, washn't it, very naughty indeed!"

"We didn't mean—. We just forgot. We would have gone back," offered Twaggin, tentatively.

"Are you doing business with this shower?" roared the doctor with great belligerence.

"I'm not sure, doctor. It'sh poshible they may have shomething I…"

"—Take my advice! Don't!... Come on, you two. Move! Mrs Redshins is standing by her till, and there's a pleece cottage up the road if you've got any disinclinations to fork out."

He took a step towards them, and they meekly moved towards the door.

"Ta-ta for now, Mr Cheeswright! Remember what I told you about these – these—."

Words failed him. He followed Twaggin and Jonty out of the gloom of the shop, through the door, and into the sunlight.

He was a man completely without doubts

28

Jonty shuddered as he recollected the humiliation that had been heaped on them by Dr Lovingood. He took a gulp of his Bletchley beer and flushed its astringency round his tongue and the roof of his mouth.

The local breweries certainly used a lot of hops. Nice!

So much nicer than the genteel weakness of Mrs Redshins's tea, the cloying sweetness of Grantchester and the ghost of Rupert Brooke.

'He liked the honey; why can't I? Does it point to my natural depravity? Or to the sentimental elements in his verse?'

But the biggest dissonance, in every sense, had been the rugby-playing medic.

'How does HE fit into such rampant gentility?'

"A very nashty moment that wash, very nashty," said Jonty aloud to his empty jar.

"Eh?" asked the barman, looking up from the Pink 'Un, the semaphore of the twitching tic-tac men in his eyes and the thunder of hooves in his ears.

"What's your fancy?"

"Another big pint, please."

"The favourite, eh?"

"You bet," said Jonty, entering into the spirit of the thing.

"What? Each way, double or treble, mate?"

"Any way."

"That'll cost you ten," said the barman. "Cheers!"

Jonty put his money on the counter beside the brimming tankard and made for the door.

"Mind the water-jump, just inside," said the barman. "We're waiting for the plumber."

And he went back to weighing up the odds.

Jonty returned, picked up his pint, squinted at it with appreciation, and said: "Here's to Newey!"

"What's his handicap, mate?"

"Spavined in the head."

"What's that?"

"Take too long to tell."

"It's your money," replied the barman amiably, and lifted up his paper.

He kept clicking his tongue at the losers, as if urging them to greater efforts.

Jonty went back to his table.

Thinking over the field, he had to admit that Newey, outsider that he was, had come up first in the Grantchester Stakes.

After Twaggin and Jonty had been dribbled and pushed back to Mrs Redshins by the incensed medic, and forced to pay her bill – "A genuine oversight, madam," said Twaggin. "Accepted," said Mrs R. Compelled to make an over-generous contribution to the little white box for Sick Animals, Jonty had informed Twaggin firmly that he was finished with smuggling illicit doorknobs and that he was now ready to surrender the contraband to the proper authorities.

"Failure of nerve!" scoffed Twaggin.

"Failure of bullshit!" replied Jonty. "Things get worse every step we take. Thicker and more evil-smelling. I'm backing my hunch. It might come up!"

"Announcing the 'No-idea Idea'. Taaa-raaa!"

Twaggin made a noise like the opening of a fanfare on a trumpet.

Arguing the point, they passed out of Mrs Redshins's wicker-gate and into the main street of the village. As they walked and bickered, they did not notice a big-headed, scrawny little man approaching them in the opposite direction.

"Good afternoon, Jonty, Twaggin! Out for an afternoon stroll?"

He stood in front of them, smaller than life.

They both looked at him without speaking.

It was a bad moment for Dr Redshins to materialize. He represented THEM: the owners of crafted doorknobs and marquee-sized trousers; the setters of piddling, nit-picking examination questions; the scribblers and signers of exeats; the appointers of Proctors; the bestowers of Special Degrees and sentences of rustication; cherishers-of and lookers-at other people's wives; the self-appointed purveyors of Civilized Values.

'Why doesn't he get himself stuffed,' thought Jonty, 'and exhibited on a wooden base in Mr Cheesewright's shop?'

Redshins seemed jumpy and kept glancing anxiously up and down the street.

Jonty's and Twaggin's silence didn't help him one little bit.

"How's Sofia, Jonty?" he asked nervously.

He glanced over his shoulder, in the direction from whence he had come.

'Does he think she's hiding somewhere?' thought Jonty.

"Don't know, Dr Redshins," he said, realizing that he found the alliterative d's disturbing, and resolved not to do it again. "Haven't heard. She's on safari, with paintbrush and soup tin – in the darkest jungles of Birmingham," said Jonty.

"Oh?" Redshins looked puzzled.

"She's attending a native wedding," added Twaggin, no longer able to remain silent.

"One of her friends."

"Oh, I see!"

He laughed aloud.

Jonty reminded himself to try describing it, when he got the chance. It would be worth it.

"Give her my best wishes, Jonty."

Jonty was wondering how to reply to that when Twaggin suddenly boomed: "We've just been run out of your wife's tea garden, Dr Redshins."

Then Jonty remembered: 'Redshins doesn't know we know! Good old Twaggin! Exactly the right reply.'

Redshins's mock-up of a face fell, making it look even more as if its designer had lost interest halfway through its composition.

Then he collected himself, smiled, and said in relief: "Oh, so you know about the teashop? I hope you don't mean it literally – 'run out'."

'Look here, Redshins! We don't want any more of your piddling exegesis of texts. All we—"

"—Yes, absolutely literally," said Twaggin. "We forgot to pay the bill and this white version of Cassius Clay dragged us back, made us pay up, and then ran us out."

"Who is that?"

"He didn't actually start shouting 'I'm the greatest!' He's more of a tight-head forward. But, I agree, that was the basic assumption," said Jonty.

"Whoa!" said Redshins. "Why don't you chaps slow down and tell me, bit by bit?"

Twaggin looked at Jonty. Jonty looked at Twaggin. Redshins looked at both of them.

"Shall we take the scholar-man into our confidence?" asked Twaggin.

"Well," said Jonty, "I suppose any change in the situation is bound to be an improvement. Why not?"

"Why not, indeed!" added Redshins.

So they told him – with all the frills. Redshins enjoyed every minute of it.

"It sounds deliciously incredible," he said.

For Jonty, the most incredible thing of all was that Redshins actually guffawed at their inventory of woes – which he did by drawing his breath inwards, instead of letting it out while he laughed, like normal people. It was more of a bray than a laugh: Jonty had heard the introductory bars of the 'Donkey's Serenade' sung like that one year by a pierrot on the sands at Rhyll. Before the singer got to the climactic breathing-out part, Jonty, with the spindrift in his hair, had left.

Now, confessing to Redshins, with the odour of hot toasted scones drifting over the hedge, he felt the same impulse again.

But Twaggin was enjoying himself immensely. He was adding his Mersey-tunnel boom to Redshins's Rhyll-bray, and causing a grey-haired woman in a white apron to open her mulberry-coloured front door in order to stare at them with puritanical lips pressed tightly together, and then to go in, and then to shut her door very firmly indeed. For Grantchester, perhaps it could even have been called a bang? A moment later, Jonty heard the sound of bolts being drawn.

Oblivious, Redshins brayed on and Twaggin continued to boom.

The white lace curtains of her cottage windows twitched open, her white face re-appeared and disappeared, and then the curtains were drawn firmly across the mulberry windows. She had no doubts that the trio represented a danger to all her verities.

"Holy Willie!" said Redshins. "I've often wanted to do something indecent to those doorknobs of the Owenses. But I've never had the nerve!"

Jonty was staggered. Was he going to be proved wrong again?

Was Redshins on the point of turning out to be 'a good chap'? Was he going to do a Newey on him?

"I'll do what I can to help," said Redshins.

First Newey, now Redshins!

What was happening to the Natural Order of Things?

What did Redshins mean by masquerading as one of them and giving the impression that he was even more one of them than one of them, when he wasn't?

"Refresh my memory! Sir Leslie's College is—" He mentioned a name.

"That's it!" said Twaggin.

"Better still!" replied Redshins, with satisfaction. "The Reverend Newey is your Dean. We're related, you know. Second cousins! Quite a useful coincidence."

Holy Moses!

It wasn't just a coincidence: it was a startling new concept to Jonty.

Newey related!

The idea might look all right on paper, but it sounded pretty far-fetched in practice. Newey – with a flesh-and-blood family! It belonged to the Theatre of the Absurd, like Twaggin's appearance.

"We've had clerics in the family for years! Not always a covenience. But – I'll try to have a word with him about it – about all this."

"Well, that's great!" said Twaggin. "Dr Redshins, we owe you."

"Don't mention it," said Redshins.

What an extraordinary world!

Newey with his bottle-shaped ideas, full of some colourless holy afflatus, actually related to Redshins with his phallus-shaped ideas, full of bawdy emendations and sexual footnotes to the religious verse of the seventeenth century!

Scions of the same generic tree!

Was it possible that the same hand that had messed up Redshins's face was actually helping Newey every day to mess up filling his pipe?

What fearful hand or eye could frame THEIR awful symmetry?

The possibilities of this line of thought were shattering.

Why, before he knew it, Jonty might even find that he had something in common with Sir Leslie and Lady Owens!

'I'll have to get a grip on myself. You never know where a thing like this might lead. Unhealthy thoughts grow into crippled acts! Before I know it, I could be living in a play by Samuel Becket. Might end up in the Bin with my Dad! I could even become respectable, if not respected!'

"Do you think that the Dean will help?" asked Jonty, dubiously.

"I think so. He's a kind man and, strangely enough, very understanding."

'You can say that again,' thought Jonty. 'If he understands having you as a cousin, he must be!'

"After all," Redshins went on, "it could have happened to anyone, couldn't it? Me, for instance! Anybody can pull a door the wrong way, while under the influence of the Master's polishing sherry, can't he?"

He gave another of his implosive guffaws.

Jonty didn't feel how, in all conscience, he could explain to Redshins how it nearly HAD happened to him.

If Twaggin had found his study door unlocked, well – just imagine! They'd have been saying: "Dr Redshins, it couldn't have happened to a nicer chap!"

But his good chappery wouldn't have extended as far as charitably accepting that, would it?

Certainly not.

Nevertheless, the whole situation called for a radical reassessment; especially of the shape of the ears of the man himself. There was more to his meatus than met the eye!

"Oh, by the way!" said Redshins, and stopped to look at them, inquiringly.

"Yes?" inquired Twaggin. "Can we be of assistance? One good turn..."

"It's possible—,"said Redshins, taking an envelope from the inside pocket of his jacket.

Jonty became aware, for no reason he could pin down, that his stomach had been tugged downwards a fraction.

"—That you might be able to return the favour and throw some light on this," he said, holding the envelope in front of him.

Twaggin looked at it short-sightedly.

"What is it?" he asked.

Jonty thought he knew.

"It's a letter," said Redshins, being deliberately slow and obvious. "From a publisher. Addressed to me. As University Lecturer in Pornographic Poetry. They want to—"

"—As what?" shrieked Twaggin, and followed it up with his Mersey Tunnel boom. "We don't have such a thing."

'That's what you think!' thought Jonty. *'Ecco Homo!'*

Jonty kept very quiet while Redshins continued.

"That is not the only misapprehension this publisher is under. Not only does he think that I have written to him on behalf of Mr Newey, but he appears not to know, also, which College I belong to! Furthermore, he seems to think I want to publish an anthology of dog poetry! It's very puzzling. I imagine it must be—"

At this point, the penny dropped. Twaggin stared accusingly at Jonty.

"It must be some kind of a jape," Redshins finished lamely.

"It is!" boomed Twaggin. "You've got to tell him, Jonty. You owe it to the man! Go on, then!"

Jonty told him. Redshins listened without a smile.

Afterwards, he said: "So you think I'm obsessed with sex, do you, Jonty? Well, I suppose one could, one could! I base my literary interpretations on Freudian theory, you see? But if so, you must blame Dr Freud, as well."

"I know! I do!" said Jonty

"Oh!"

"Along with that inbred, adulterous group of Viennese who Freud based his findings on! Hence, his own obsessions."

"I see! I see! Well, you're nothing if not consistent, eh, Jonty?

"I'm sorry for this – this –," said Jonty lamely, indicating the letter in Redshins's hand.

"Oh, don't apologise, old chap! No harm done! If I forgive you, you can forgive me."

"For what?" asked Jonty.

"For being obsessed with sex and being attracted to Sofia, of course!"

"Oh, I see!"

'So he knows how I feel about that, does he?'

"Yes, of course!" said Jonty.

"Good! So we're all friends, again," said Redshins. "Look! I'll see what I can do about the doorknob debacle. Give them to me. Thanks!.. Now, you two, I'll just wish you good results for your Finals, and all the best for the future."

He offered his hand to them and they shook it solemnly in turn.

Jonty felt unsettled by the shape that events had taken.

"You know where to find me, if you're ever up here again," he called, holding his free hand in the air, and walking towards the wicker-gate.

In his other hand, he held the two wrapped-up doorknobs.

'Bye!"

As he disappeared into the gentility of his wife's tea garden, he looked like one of the Seven Dwarfs, a very grumpy Grumpy, entering a grotto of make-believe.

"Turned out to be quite an acceptable don, did that one!" said Twaggin, turning away to resume their stroll down the main street. "I quite liked him."

"Yes! He surprised me!"

"But you said nothing to him about Sir Leslie's trousers," observed Twaggin.

"Would you?"

"No, I suppose not – in the circs! Newey might—!"

"—Exactly!"

Jonty explained that he could just imagine Newey reconciling himself to the doorknob fiasco, just – philosophically, he was always pushing doors marked 'pull', after all – but the associations that Newey would attach to a pair of trousers in that particular narrative might be rather more complex and somewhat harder to overcome. They were too near the knuckle, so to speak.

Jonty suspected that, well-intentioned though Newey might be in general, there was a characteristic point where his brand of undeliberate bastardy might topple into the deliberate variety, and that point was, at the moment, orbiting steadily around Sir Leslie's trousers.

Jonty recalled that Newey, during his entire three years of tutelage, had only once referred to a belief in procreation (in a purely herbivorous sense) and only then in the vaguest possible way; never once had he mentioned the notion of sex, let alone the word, not even by circumlocution or in connection with the breeding cycles of Deathwatch Beetles.

Considering he had mentioned everything else connected with them, a lot of significance had to be attached to THAT.

No; he'd been right to keep the trousers dark!

Redshins had been as good as his word.

He had contacted his reverend second cousin immediately he had reached his study, a moment or two after entering the wicker-gate, in fact.

At the other end of the telephone line, he could hear Newev giving his succulents a bad half-hour during the explanation; but in the end, the Dean had consented to try his best, and the successful outcome had been conveyed to Twaggin and Jonty in Hall that evening by the Dean himself – coldly.

"Like the dinner," Twaggin said afterwards.

The Owenses, the Dean maintained, were immensely relieved to recover their property, and Lady Owens had persuaded Sir Leslie to forget the whole thing – as "an unfortunate set of accidents" – for which they should be truly grateful.

The Dean could not help underlining it.

Twaggin and Jonty were constrained to agree with him.

They had said their penances, offered their thanks and given their goodbyes in a subdued mood; and it had been a very mortified Jonty who had had to explain to Twaggin that his chutzpah had failed him yet again, when faced with having to explain to the Dean how he had got a pair of Sir Leslie's trousers still hidden away.

Whatever the psychological barriers that Newey had put in his path, should he not have ignored them – and told him about the pants, anyway?

But he had known his cowardice would catch up with him one day.

With his arrival in Bletchley, that day had come.

He had been stuck with a pair of oversize pantaloons in a town he didn't like and with a plan he liked even less.

He couldn't follow his resolution to return them by post to Sir Leslie, could he? Sir Leslie would be much happier never realizing that he had lost his trousers, wouldn't he?

Absolutely!

That's why it had been such a brainwave to send them to the George Eliot specialist at Girton College.

Hence, emerging from the Post Office, he had erupted into his paean of self-praise.

They wouldn't fit her exactly, it was true: too small round the bust.

She would have to leave the top button undone.

But with the reasoned-out attitude she had to life and her Mrs Pankhurst stance on the relationship of the sexes in Victorian society, she would probably number a pair of braces among her most prized possessions.

If he found out she didn't, he'd buy her a pair for Christmas.

That would, at least, make them a practical present: he couldn't say fairer than that, could he?

Jonty felt it had all come out in the wash, after all.

What time was the next train to Birmingham?

He looked into the last few mouthfuls of his Bletchley beer and wondered if he had addressed the parcel correctly.

He'd got her name right, her College, and the fact that it was in Cambridge. The GPO would do the rest.

Eventually, a train for Birmingham pulled into the station.

Jonty boarded it, settled himself into an empty compartment in the First Class section and fell asleep, hoping that the Ticket Collector wouldn't bother to come round.

When he awoke, he was halfway to Brum and remembered he had never opened his father's letter. The doorknob fiasco had pushed it out of his mind. Where was it? Had he left it in – Yes! In the inside pocket of his jacket, nicely folded into his suitcase.

He took it out and settled back to read a longish letter, with a long PS and an even longer PPS.

Dear Son,

Hope things are going as well with you as they are with me! I daresay you'll be a Bachelor of Summat-or-Other by the time this reaches you. I guess congratulations are the Order of the Day!

All the O'Grady's here are as full of bullshit as ever. But I've worked out one or two systems these last three years in the Cuckoo Clock that are going to bring in the old B & B for Yours Truly for the rest of me Natural. (Beer & Bread, that is!) I've got a record in me little Black Book of all me winnings – that is, if they'd have allowed me the cash and allowed me the weekly flutter! So it's just a set of numbers. But figures don't lie. There they are and there they'll stay and they're lovely!

They're letting me out soon. They think I'm normal. That'll be the day! I was born with the name of the Favourite on my lips and that's how I'll go out. I said to the Doc, what's normal for you ain't normal for me, and what's the betting I'll have a nice little nest egg in a twelvemonth while you'll still be doing the rounds of all these loonies? Needless to say, he didn't take me up on it.

Anyway, son, look after yourself. I don't know where to find you, but you know where to find me. Be seeing you sometime!

Your loving dad,

Dad.

Jonty smiled as he finished the body of his father's letter. He sounded exactly the same as he always had. That, at least, was a comfort.

Whatever it was they thought they had cured, they hadn't managed to change the essential 'HIM'.

What on earth was in his long PS?… It seemed to be a description of another of his systems.

The gist of it was complex: it rested on the magic of words.

You took the name of any horse that held within it an abstract noun – provided the letters ran consecutively backwards or forwards, and spelt the noun without re-arrangement.

Had his father been reading the Cabbala just lately?

You then followed this nag up and backed it in every meeting.

You only met a problem if there was more than one horse that qualified for backing in the same race. Then, you simply chose the one you fancied.

His Dad swore he'd tested this theory out over a long time and it only remained now to back it up with the pennies.

He ended his PS with the words: "I shall then win another fortune."

Jonty read that sentence again, taking particular note of the word 'another'.

Had his father finally gone round the twist? It looked like it. Maybe the PPS would tell him?

When his son had finished reading the second postscript, Jonty was certain he had.

The old chap was claiming he had won thousands and thousands on a football pool – the Treble Chance – which the hospital authorities allowed everyone to fill in each week.

True, you only had to win it once and you could do it for as little as a shilling or so a week!

Had he? Or were his fantasies finally taking over from reality for him?

Jonty sighed; and thought sadly of his father's vivid descriptions of the progressive treatment he'd been receiving.

Jonty felt they sounded very like the regressive treatments that he had been receiving as tutorials from the Reverend Newey over the last three years, which would account for the similar reactions of Godley Senior and Godley Junior to the respective therapists, wouldn't it?

The inconsequentiality of both was striking; both were disguised by a kind of purposeful irrelevance, and by a vaguely religiose atmosphere: it sounded a good time for father and son to come together again, didn't it?

Yes, it did.

Jonty folded up the missive and put it in his pocket.

He then pulled down the blinds and went to sleep.

About the Author

R oy Holland was born in Birmingham. He went to Africa in 1966 to teach in the universities of the Boleswa countries. In 1971 he went to Greece for three years. He and his family lived on the island of Levkas for six months, the Gulf of Corinth for a similar period, and in Corfu for a little over two years. He wrote full-time until 1974, when he returned to the U.K. and worked on a research project until returning to Africa in 1977. Thereafter he lived in Southern Africa and worked in universities in Zimbabwe, Lebowa and Venda. He was Professor of English at the University of the North, the University of Venda, as well as Dean of the Faculty of Arts in the later 80's. He retired early to write full-time, and now lives in Ledbury, Herefordshire.

www.ingramcontent.com/pod-product-compliance
Lightning Source LLC
Chambersburg PA
CBHW031117030726

47496CB00002BA/579